Footprints
of a
Dancer

A Detective Elliot Mystery

Bob Avey

Deadly Niche Press
Denton, Texas

Published by Deadly Niche Press, and imprint of AWOC.COM
Publishing, P.O. Box 2819, Denton, TX 76202, USA. No part of
this publication may be reproduced, stored in a retrieval system,
or transmitted in any form or by any means, electronic,
mechanical, recording or otherwise, without the prior written
permission of the author.

Manufactured in the United States of America

ISBN: 978-1-62016-019-0

Visit Bob Avey's website www.bobavey.com

Dedication

For my wonderful mom, Ruby,
who has always been my biggest fan.

Acknowledgements

I'd like to thank my editors, Gretchen Craig, and Pamela Blunt for their hard work. I'd also like to thank my publisher, Deadly Niche Press, for making it all possible.

Chapter One

Seeing old friends isn't always a good thing.

Not many people run the trails along Riverside Drive after the sun goes down, one of the reasons Detective Kenny Elliot chose to do so, but another runner occupied the trail, and her silhouette bounced quickly toward him.

A sluggish wind blew across the Arkansas River, carrying an odor of decaying marine life, and suddenly a mood of darkness that had little to do with lack of sunlight engulfed Elliot's senses.

Elliot stepped off the pathway to avoid colliding with the runner, but in an unanticipated move, she came to a stop as well, and though she remained on the path she turned toward Elliot.

They stood only a few feet apart, and even in the small amount of light that filtered in from different sources, Elliot recognized her. She looked exactly as he remembered her. She'd often described herself as being half Native American and half Irish. She tossed her hair back, revealing her silver and turquoise earrings.

Elliot wiped perspiration from his forehead. She'd worn them the last time he'd seen her. When he broke the silence by forcing out one word, it came out as more of a question than a declaration. "Laura?"

With a sad look on her face, she seemed about to speak, but instead she turned away and resumed her run.

Elliot watched as she put distance between them. He was a cop, trained to know the difference between imagination and concrete detail, and yet, like a dream that fades upon awakening, he was already having trouble believing what he'd witnessed. He'd never been able to read Laura. As if she'd had some sort of defense up, everything about her was fuzzy. He was about to go after her when his phone went off. He didn't know the number, but he answered it anyway.

The caller sounded apprehensive, unsure he'd done the right thing. "Elliot? That you?"

The voice danced around Elliot's memory, but he couldn't place it. Happened all the time in his line of work. "Do I know you?"

"Sure you do. Come on, it's me, Gerald."

"Gerald?"

"You know, as in Stanley Gerald."

The name jolted Elliot back a few years. He glanced over his shoulder to see if the runner was still there, but she was not. "You've got to be kidding me?"

"I wish I were, but something's come up. I thought you should know about it."

A dull pain formed in Elliot's stomach. He stepped back onto the trail and began a steady walk back to his vehicle. "What is it?"

After a pause he said, "Do you remember Laura Bradford?"

Elliot's mouth went dry. It had been Laura Bradford he'd just seen on the running trail. He reached for the water bottle attached to his waist. Laura Bradford had disappeared during his and Gerald's senior year at Oklahoma State. Gerald had been a suspect. "What about her?"

As if reading Elliot's mind, Gerald said, "I didn't have anything to do with it. I was in love with her, Elliot. I always imagined we'd be together. And for all these years since, it's like she's been there all along, just beneath the surface, but now..."

Elliot pressed the phone against his ear. "What are you trying to say?"

"She's back. I've seen her."

Elliot took another swallow of water. He wondered what the odds were of seeing an old acquaintance you had thought dead, and getting a phone call from her boyfriend saying that he, too, had seen her. "Maybe it was just somebody who looked like her."

"You don't understand. I didn't just see someone similar, strolling along the sidewalk, or notice a familiar face in a crowd. She was in my car, Elliot. I glanced over and there she was, sitting beside me, staring at me with those dark eyes, like an answer to a prayer."

Elliot closed his eyes, trying to make sense of it all. He wondered if Gerald was pulling some type of sick prank. He didn't believe it, though. He'd questioned plenty of people in his time, developing a feel for whether or not they were being straight with him. Gerald was telling the truth, as he knew it. "What happened next?"

"I'm not sure. I mean, it's complicated."

Elliot reached his truck in the parking lot. It didn't seem wise to tell Gerald about his own encounter with Laura, not until he knew more about what was happening. "What do you mean you're not sure? What's going on, Gerald?"

"There's a lot you don't know. It's why I called. I mean, you're with the police, right? We need to talk."

Elliot started the truck. He wasn't sure how Gerald knew he was a cop, but his voice carried an underlying current of urgency he couldn't ignore. "What did you have in mind?"

"How about breakfast?"

He and Gerald and the ghost of Laura. The thought conjured up images of a strange dinner date at Eskimo Joe's, a bar and grill in Stillwater near the college, something Elliot had not consciously tried to forget, but had certainly shoved to the back of his mind. "Sure."

"Are you familiar with The Savoy?"

Elliot thought about the small restaurant on Sheridan Road. "I know where it is."

"I'll be sitting at the table in the southwest corner of the southern section. Ten o'clock, okay?"

"That'll be fine. And it's good to hear from you, Gerald. You caught me off guard, that's all."

"Off guard? You and me both, Elliot."

Chapter Two

Captain William Dombrowski leaned against the doorway to his office and watched Detective Elliot walk past, head down, something on his mind, the way he got when he worked a case that mattered to him. No, that wasn't putting it right. All of Elliot's cases mattered to him. But certain cases commanded his attention on a different level.

Elliot had more levels and layers than anyone Dombrowski had ever met. A hard guy to figure, keeping to himself for the most part. If you were looking for the life of the party in Elliot, you'd be looking in the wrong place, but if you were in the field and needed someone to watch your back, he was your man. You couldn't do better. Saying Elliot had a strong survival instinct was an understatement. What he possessed was a come-out-on-top, win-at-all-cost monitoring system that was humbling to say the least.

Dombrowski shook his head. The Zimmerman case came to mind. It'd been quintessential Elliot from the start. Dombrowski often wondered if anyone else could have solved it, but it always got him to thinking, wondering exactly how Elliot had pulled it off. He didn't like going down that road.

* * *

Elliot tried another search engine and another set of parameters related to Laura Bradford. He got a few hits, but nothing matched what he was looking for. Later, Dombrowski came out of his office and stopped at Elliot's cube. "What's up?" Dombrowski asked.

Elliot leaned back in his chair and swiveled around. He considered saying he'd received a strange phone call last night and he was looking for answers, trying to make sense of it, but it would come out sounding ridiculous. And Dombrowski hadn't asked him what he was doing, what he was working on. "Just trying to get some work done."

"That's what I wanted to talk to you about," Dombrowski said. "You seem preoccupied. Everything all right?"

Something was bothering Dombrowski, but he was tiptoeing around the issue. "I'm fine," Elliot said.

"How's your son doing?"

Dombrowski was making small talk. Something was definitely wrong. "He's doing well, playing football this year."

"I guess it was pretty tough on you," Dombrowski said, "finding out ..."

Elliot had just learned a few months ago he had a son, that he was a father. The captain didn't finish the sentence, but Elliot knew what he meant. A surprise of such magnitude wasn't easy to deal with. Carmen had kept it from him, but he didn't blame her. There was a lot more to it. They'd been separated in high school, both of them ending up thinking the other didn't care. A twist of fate and a murder investigation had brought them back in touch a few months ago. It was then that Carmen had told him. "Yeah," he said.

The captain gave Elliot a pat on the back. "We'll talk later."

Elliot noticed an email from Buddy Wheeler, an assistant coach at Oklahoma State who still kept in touch. He'd sent some humorous football related photos. Elliot replied to the email and logged off the computer. Dombrowski was acting strange. The last thing Elliot needed was a problem at work. He had enough to worry about already. As usual when he was under stress, he thought of Carmen, a source of comfort. He'd hoped they might patch things up, maybe even get back together, but it didn't look promising. He pushed back from his desk and stood. His trip down memory lane had faded his appetite, but he'd promised Gerald he'd be there. He left the office and headed for 61st and Sheridan.

Chapter Three

Inside the Savoy, an elderly gentleman at the nearest table lowered his newspaper and peered over the top, not a timid or covert gesture, but a subtle way of letting Elliot know he was a stranger.

Elliot made his way to the table in the southwest corner as he'd been told to do, but his day was starting off bad.

Gerald wasn't there. Elliot scanned the dining area, but saw no one who resembled his old friend.

Gerald had been an unusual sort, but being late was not his style, and a complete no-show was out of the question. Elliot pulled out a chair and sat at the table where he could observe the other patrons in the restaurant while still watching the front door. He suspected Gerald had chosen it for the same reason, which suggested he'd been here before.

Noticing Elliot's presence, a waitress picked up a menu and a set of silverware. She placed the items on the table and whipped out her order pad. She stared down at Elliot, her pencil hovering impatiently over the ticket, an over-experienced member of the staff, long past the point of caring.

Elliot ordered a piece of apple pie and a cup of coffee, and while the waitress wrote the order, he took the opportunity to slip in a question. "A place like this, you probably get a lot of regulars?"

She frowned.

"I'm looking for someone," Elliot continued. "And my guess is you see a lot of the same faces in here."

She lowered the pad, annoyed at the distraction. "The place's been here since 1975 and so have I."

"Do you know of anyone who sits at this table, goes by the name of Gerald?"

She shook her head.

"Real name's Stanley Reynolds."

"How do you get Gerald out of that?"

"It's his middle name."

She rolled her eyes. "Well, what does he look like?"

"I'm not sure. It's been awhile since I've seen him."

The waitress stuck the pencil in her hair. "Well, how do you think I'm going to tell you if he's been here?"

She whirled and scurried away.

Two cups of coffee and an hour later, Gerald still hadn't shown. He had led Elliot to believe the meeting was important to him.

Elliot pulled his phone and tried the number Gerald had left when he'd called, but there was no answer. He leaned back in the chair, letting the conversation he'd had earlier with Gerald run through his head. He didn't like where his thoughts were headed. People always think the worst. He was no different. He just couldn't shake the notion that Gerald had either been unable to make it, which meant something had kept him from it, or he'd gotten here and didn't like what he saw. Considering the clean, almost sterile-looking atmosphere of the restaurant, Elliot suspected it was the former. He wondered if Gerald would try and make contact again. He decided to take the initiative, find an address for Gerald, go there and check it out. It shouldn't take long. He had a few open cases, but he'd taken them to the point where there wasn't much to do but wait. Again, he studied the patrons in the restaurant.

The waitress didn't like it. She came over and handed Elliot the bill. He wasn't going to find anything here. He paid the waitress, left the restaurant, and headed to the office.

* * *

Elliot pushed back from his desk and stared at the notes he'd made. Gerald's last known address turned out to be in Stillwater. It appeared he'd stayed there after graduation, but the call Elliot received had come from here in Tulsa, more specifically a hotel just off 71st Street near Yale Avenue. The phone company had verified it. The hotel was near the Savoy restaurant, probably why Gerald had chosen it as a meeting place. If he'd been in town for a few days, he'd probably eaten there.

Elliot left the office and drove to the hotel. As he crossed the parking lot, his phone went off.

He checked the caller. Carmen Garcia's name and number ran across the screen.

Elliot had expected it to be Gerald, trying again to contact him, and the surprise caused him to lower the phone. He thought of Carmen, the way her dark eyes caught the light, her creamy skin reflected the sun. He longed to take her in his arms and never let go, and he wanted to tell her, but what came out when he finally brought the phone to his face was, "Carmen, what a pleasant surprise."

"Not so pleasant," she said.

Elliot gripped the phone. Bubble busted. "What's up?"

"It's Wayne. He was in a fight at school today."

"Is he all right?"

"He is not hurt, but it is not all right. I don't want him to be like... to exhibit that kind of behavior."

Elliot swallowed a lump in his throat. What Carmen had stopped short of saying was she didn't want Wayne to turn out like his father. Carmen still saw him as a pumped-up eighteen year old football player. He'd had quite a reputation in school. But a kid on his own has to learn to fend for himself. He'd gotten pretty good at it. When the bullies started to avoid him, so did everybody else. Admittedly, he'd done little to dissuade that kind of thinking. In fact, he'd ridden it into adulthood. It was easier being a cop when you had respect. Just like in school, you rough up a few bad guys and the word gets out. He wasn't such a tough guy, really. He just had trouble letting people know that. "Do you want me to have a talk with him?"

"I've arranged for a conference this afternoon. I think you should be there."

A smile made its way across Elliot's face. Some people might have been upset over such a thing, but he was happy to be included, proud to be a part of Wayne's life. "Sure," he said. "I assume it'll be in the principal's office." A place you should be quite familiar with, he imagined Carmen was thinking. "What time do I need to be there?"

Carmen gave him the information and disconnected.

Elliot shoved the phone into his pocket and stepped into the lobby. He walked over and laid his badge on the registration desk. "Detective Elliot with the Tulsa Police Department. I need to speak with Stanley Reynolds. I believe he's registered here."

Two people stood behind the counter, though neither of them acted as if they wanted to deal with the situation, but finally a young man who looked to be in his early twenties stepped forward. "I'm sorry, sir. What did you say the name was again?"

Elliot repeated the information.

The clerk began punching on a keyboard. Seconds later, he nodded, as if it all made sense now, everything in its place. "He's here all right. Is he dangerous?"

"I've known him to be cunning and devious, but not violent."

Again the understanding nod.

Elliot didn't have a warrant, and he didn't want to press the issue, so he figured he'd play it straight. "Could you ring his room, tell him I'm here in the lobby, and ask him if he's willing to speak with me?"

A thin smile formed on the clerk's face. "Sure. I can do that."

He picked up the phone, and seconds later began speaking into the mouthpiece. He turned to Elliot. "Someone's there, but I don't think it's who you're looking for."

Elliot grabbed the phone. "Hey, Gerald, what's up?"

"Gerald's not here."

Elliot closed his free hand into a fist to avoid wiping the perspiration that'd formed there against his pant leg. The voice seemed oddly familiar, but one thing was for certain. It didn't belong to Gerald.

"Who is this?"

"Has it been so long that you don't remember? Gerald and me, Terri, and you, at Eskimo Joe's?"

Elliot gripped the phone, thinking back to those days in Stillwater. Gerald had brought him into the group after Elliot had saved him from a beating. Gerald had managed to get the wrong kind of attention from a bunch of kids with tattoos and bad haircuts. Elliot had hurt one of them more than he should have, but he'd managed to convince them to leave Gerald alone.

Gerald had been a loyal friend from there on out. But there was much more to Stanley Gerald Reynolds III than being your typical college student. He was driven, like someone on a quest even he did not understand. He was drawn to the unusual, and he'd put together a loose-knit band of followers who shared his enthusiasm for the macabre; anything out of the ordinary and they were all over it. Elliot had thought he wouldn't fit in, but he began to look forward to the meetings, Thursday nights at Eskimo Joe's.

Everything changed when Laura showed up. Whether or not the evolution was for the worse, Elliot reserved judgment, simply because he wasn't sure. Laura awakened something in Gerald, ignited his drive and turned it into a passion, and together they led the group away from the mildly curious and put them on a collision course with the paranormal. No one said anything. They just let it happen. Word got around and the calls started to come.

Most of it was harmless—a bunch of scared sorority girls convinced they'd seen a ghost, or frat boys playing games—but not all of it. Laura never let on to the others, but she could tell what was real and what was not. So could Elliot. Laura knew that, too.

A chill ran through Elliot. If he'd been wearing a coat, he would've pulled it tighter. He was taking too long to answer, so once again he forced himself to say her name, "Laura?"

She didn't answer.

"Gerald might be in trouble," Elliot said. "If you know where he is, you need to tell me."

The phone was silent. Elliot didn't try again. It would do no good. And they would find the room empty. He knew that with a certainty he could not explain. His visions had gained clarity and strength since his encounter with Laura, but they were still, as always spotty and incomplete. Gerald would not be in the room, but other than that he had no idea of where he might be. The room might hold some clues. He turned away and started toward the elevator. He was halfway across the lobby when the hotel clerk intercepted him.

He'd come from behind the counter, and while he spoke he kept glancing around, as if someone might overhear what he had to say. "I'm guessing finding this Gerald guy is pretty important to you."

Elliot nodded. The kid wanted to help, a little secrecy, undercover work with the cops. He glanced at his nametag. "I appreciate your help, Phillip, but I don't want you to do anything that might get you into trouble."

The elevator opened and Elliot stepped inside, the clerk close behind.

"Ladonna," the clerk said. "One of the maids. I have a class with her son." He glanced at his watch and punched number three on the elevator console. "If I'm right, she should be somewhere in the vicinity."

The doors opened and they stepped into an empty hallway.

The clerk shook his head, a don't-worry gesture. "She keeps a pretty tight schedule. Wait here. I'll find her."

He strode down the hallway and rounded the corner. A few minutes later, a cart being pushed by the maid came into view. The clerk was right behind her. As they approached, they kept their voices down, the maid doing most of the talking.

Giving young Phillip a piece of her mind, Elliot thought. She appeared to be uncomfortable with the idea of letting a stranger into one of the hotel rooms. He stepped forward and introduced himself. "Don't be too hard on him. He was only trying to help."

The maid, a tough looking woman in her fifties, cocked her head in a quizzical manner. "Shouldn't you have a warrant for something like this?"

"Yes, ma'am. This is not yet an official case. I'm trying to intervene before it escalates. However, I understand and respect your position."

She jerked a thumb toward the room. "This guy you're looking for, he in some kind a trouble?"

Elliot thought about the phone conversation he had earlier in the lobby. *Gerald's not here.* "Yes, ma'am. I suspect he is."

The maid grumbled but resumed pushing the cart, stopping as she neared the door to Gerald's room. "I got to clean this thing sometime today. Now is as good a time as any." She knocked on the door, announced her presence a few times, and slid her card into the lock. "I guess there ain't no law says you can't glance into the room as you're walking past. Everyone else does."

Elliot nodded. "What do you usually do if you find anything unusual during your rounds?"

"Kind of depends on what it is."

"Say it's a gun or a knife."

She shrugged. "Anything looks like it ought to be reported to the police, I'd call the manager, let him handle it."

Elliot glanced at Phillip. "Would that be our young friend here?"

"God help us. I'm afraid so."

Elliot tried to hide his smile, but Phillip didn't seem to mind. He was smiling as well.

The maid propped the door open and went inside the room.

Stepping forward but staying in the hallway, Elliot studied the room.

The bed had been slept in. But no clothes hung in the closet, no shoes on the rack.

The hotel clerk stood beside Elliot, a confused look on his face. "Someone was in the room. We both talked to her on the phone." He glanced up and down the hallway. "Nobody came down the elevator. Where did she go?"

"She could've taken the stairs," Elliot said, "or got off on another floor."

"So she could still be here, in the hotel?"

Elliot shook his head. "My guess is she's long gone by now."

The look on the clerk's face was somewhere between worry and excitement. "Do you know who she was? I mean I can pretty much guess she's either the girlfriend or the wife of the dude you're looking for, but you got to admit this is kind of weird."

The maid had finished cleaning the room and Elliot stepped back to allow her access to the hallway. The kid didn't know how right he was, and it was best left that way. "It comes with the territory," he said, "being a cop."

The maid pushed the cart toward the next room, dropping a wadded piece of paper at Elliot's feet as she went past, making her way down the hallway.

Elliot bent over and retrieved the paper, unfolding it as he stood straight again. The maid didn't want Phillip to see her pass the note. She was trying to help, but she didn't want to get herself into trouble.

"What's that you got?" The clerk asked.

Elliot closed his hand around the paper. "It's nothing. Thanks for your help, kid. I'll be in touch if I need anything else."

Outside the hotel, Elliot sat in his car, studying the name written on the paper the maid had found in Gerald's room. The name was David Stephens, common enough by itself, but the prefix of *Professor* gave it distinction. It also dragged Elliot's thoughts back several years to a time when he'd walked into a counselor's office, a room full of heaviness and unhappy faces.

The events leading to the dissolution of Gerald's investigative group began with Angela Gardner, a student of anthropology.

At the head of the table in the counselor's office had been, of course, the counselor, but to his right was the one who'd ordered the meeting, a professor named Stephens, David Stephens to be exact, Angela's teacher.

Flipping the scrap of paper over, Elliot saw something had been scribbled there as well, a series of numbers and letters that read: W14SCheyenne. He didn't know what to make of it. He folded the paper and stuffed it in his pocket. The possibility that all of this could be nothing more than one of Gerald's practical jokes had not escaped him. Gerald was fond of playing them, or at least he had been. The finality of the notion disturbed Elliot.

But he'd have to think about Gerald later. Right now he had an appointment with Carmen and his son. He called Dombrowski, told him about the meeting at the school, and drove to the town of Porter where Carmen and Wayne lived.

Chapter Four

Carmen Garcia walked into the bathroom of the small house in Porter, Oklahoma, where she and her nine-year-old son Wayne lived and checked her makeup one more time. She saw her reflection in the mirror and considered the dress she'd chosen.

Was it conservative enough? She thought maybe it was. She turned toward the closet to have another look, but thought about what she was doing and stopped in the bedroom and checked her watch.

She did not like to be late, and yet here she was, acting ridiculous, agonizing over clothing choices like some schoolgirl. It was a meeting with Wayne's principal, not a party or a dinner date. But that wasn't the problem. She would see Kenny there, and though she wished she did not feel that way, the fact was she was looking forward to it.

Inside the school, Carmen tried to walk softly but her high heels clacked against the tiled hallway as she hurried along. She hoped some of the others would be late, too, but when she walked into Mr. Gaither's office everyone was seated and waiting for her. And there he was, Kenny Elliot, looking as cool and handsome as ever. He stood when she entered the room.

Mr. Gaither leaned his elbows against his desk and clasped his hands together. "Now that we're all here, why don't we get started?"

The beefy man with a florid face leaned forward. It was Paul Masterson, Blake Masterson's father.

"The way I see it, Wayne Garcia's the problem and there's only one way to fix it. The boy's a trouble maker and he ought to be suspended."

Kenny got up from his chair. Carmen reminded herself to remain calm. It was true she wanted Kenny to be there both for her benefit and for Wayne's sake, but she also worried about what he might do, the trouble he could cause. When she was young, he had frightened her, but it had been exciting to walk the schoolyard holding the arm of the boy everyone feared. But things were different now. She had grown up and she had responsibilities, like providing a good home and a proper environment for Wayne. She had wrestled with the idea of

2014 FORD F--250--550 GAS US

EC3J19G219AA

Oct 23. 2013 12:28

$255,529.68

6825
7215
14430
14040

31489.6

The American Institute
of Steel Construction

40.84   80
39.13

NAHB Research
          center

whether or not she should ask him to attend the meeting, and now she hoped he would not do anything to make things worse. She realized how little she knew about him now. Perhaps he had matured with age and changed, but she was not sure.

"Hold on a minute," Kenny said. "Before we go any further, I need to be brought up to speed. What exactly are we talking about here? What did Wayne do?"

"He jumped my boy. That's what he did. Hid behind a corner or something, I suspect, and caught him off guard, because he knew he wouldn't be able to take him otherwise."

Carmen smoothed her dress. She wished Mr. Masterson had kept quiet. And why was Mrs. Masterson just sitting there and not trying to corral her husband?

Kenny turned toward Mr. Masterson. "And you are?"

"Paul Masterson, Blake's father. And if you're who I think you are, you haven't done a very good job of raising that boy of yours. He's a nuisance and he needs to be disciplined. But I'm sure you won't do it. You're probably as big a coward as he is."

Carmen closed her eyes and shook her head, trying to will Paul Masterson to stop talking before he caused Kenny to lose control and ruin everything, which would confirm what the town already suspected: Wayne was his father's son, in every sense of the word. Carmen opened her eyes to confirm her fears had materialized.

Kenny now stood in front of Paul Masterson.

Masterson's face turned a deeper shade of red. "You better do something, Gaither, before I show this punk the road."

Mr. Gaither was also standing. "Now see here, gentlemen. Let's behave like adults. Don't make me call the police."

Mrs. Masterson still sat there, no expression showing on her face. Knowing she had to do something, Carmen rose from her chair. Always she hoped Kenny would change, that the gentler side of him, which at times she had to admit only seemed obvious to her, would prevail, but she was beginning to lose hope. "Kenny," she said, the words echoing through the small office with much more tone and volume than she had anticipated. "Please sit down."

Kenny turned toward her, his smile slow and confident as if everything in the world was right. Carmen smiled back. After all, it was Paul Masterson who was acting aggressive, not Kenny.

Carmen realized, though she was indeed worried about Kenny's behavior, that she loved him now more than ever, had never stopped loving him, and probably never would. She started to say something else, but Kenny shook his head.

Chapter Five

Elliot glanced around the room until his gaze came upon Carmen.

The expression on her face said she was again wondering what kind of man he really was.

"There's no need for concern," he said. "I just want to have a word in private."

He subtly yet forcefully urged Masterson from the room and pushed him against the wall in the hallway. "Let me introduce myself," he said. "Name's Elliot, and I don't like what you said about Wayne, or the way you said it. If you've got an explanation handy, now might be the time to let it out."

Masterson fidgeted and glanced toward the office. "I don't have to explain anything to you."

Elliot smiled. "I think I understand. Now's not the time or the place, is it? We can't raise our voices or do anything that might upset our friends here. But don't worry. I have a plan."

"I don't know what you're talking about."

Elliot tightened his grip. "Well, let me lay it out for you. With everyone being so agreeable, this meeting shouldn't take long. After it's over, we'll give it thirty minutes and meet at the ball field. I'm sure you know where it is. Without our audience, we should be able to settle this matter rather quickly."

"I'm not meeting you anywhere."

"Whatever you think. But if you're not there, I'll come looking for you."

"Hold on," Masterson said. "Let's be civil about this, go back inside, and have our meeting."

Elliot released his grip. He'd known all along Masterson would fold at the first hint of trouble.

Masterson straightened his clothes, gave Elliot a disgusted look, and turned and walked back into Gaither's office.

As soon as Elliot entered the office, Mr. Gaither sat down and folded his hands. "Ms. Garcia and Mrs. Masterson have decided to handle this at home. Since the incident happened off school grounds, I'm inclined to agree with them."

Elliot smiled and patted Masterson on the back. "Great," he said. "Paul and I have reached an agreement as well."

After a bit of small talk, the meeting was over, and Elliot walked Carmen to her car. Once there, she leaned against the car and looked up at him, her face unreadable.

He wanted to take her in his arms, but he pushed the notion from his mind. "Do you want me to talk to Wayne about this?"

She shook her head. "What advice would you give him? Use a two-by-four instead of your fists?"

"That's a cheap shot, Carmen, and you know it."

"Is it? You were about to cause a scene in there with the people we are supposed to be apologizing to."

"I don't think we owe them one."

"How can you say that, after what Wayne did to their child?"

"Considering no one has told me exactly what happened, I don't know what to think. In addition, I don't know what the other kid might have done, what his part in all of this was."

"It doesn't matter. Wayne should keep his behavior in check. I prayed he would not turn out like his father, always angry and provoked so easily. But my prayers go unanswered. He is just like you."

Elliot looked away. It hurt to hear Carmen talk that way, and he was inclined to leave it there and walk away, but instead he held his ground. "You don't remember me as well as you think. I wasn't angry, not really. And I was never easily provoked. Admittedly, it takes a while to calm down when I do get angry, but it takes quite a bit to get me there."

"Oh really? I guess it wasn't you in the school just now, scaring the wits from poor Mr. Masterson."

"Poor Mr. Masterson was out of line. And he was never in any danger. I was just trying to scare him. I know his type, plenty of money and a lot of influence, especially in a small town like this. It hasn't been that long since you and I went to school here, and I doubt things have changed much. If I hadn't stopped Masterson, he might have influenced Gaither to expel Wayne."

"And what do you think he will do now? You probably made things worse."

Elliot shook his head, trying not to smile. "He won't do anything."

Carmen looked away and the wind caught her hair, blowing it back and revealing the clean lines of her profile.

The moment caught Elliot with such power that he had to turn away. He wished they were married, raising Wayne together, and this was just one of those arguments couples have.

"This was a mistake," Carmen said. "I should not have asked you to come."

Elliot took a step toward Carmen, but stopped short of putting his hand on her shoulder. "I hope you don't mean that. I want to be part of Wayne's life." And a part of yours, he thought, but as with the touch, he stopped himself. "It means a lot to me."

She turned back, though she avoided direct eye contact.

Elliot smiled. Carmen had always been shy, not afraid to look at people, but rather, like with all beautiful women, she had learned to be careful with the amount of attention she gave men, especially with her eyes.

"I'm happy to hear that," she said. "But the trouble we have had in our lives, it all seems to…"

"Center around my propensity for violence?"

"That might be putting it too harshly."

Elliot smiled. "I know it's hard to tell, especially after what just happened, but I'm not like I used to be. I think about it all the time. And I was never as bad as everyone thought. You of all people should know that."

Carmen trembled and reached out, the first to break the no-touch barrier, and put her hand on Elliot's chest, though it was modest and quickly removed. "You're not bad. And I didn't mean to give you that impression." She shook her head. "I should be going."

Carmen unlocked her car and climbed in. Before leaving the parking lot, though, she rolled down the window and this time allowed her direct and lingering gaze to find Elliot's. "Maybe you could call me tomorrow and we can talk more about this."

Elliot smiled.

Chapter Six

Later that night after his meeting at the school with Carmen, Elliot sat in a recliner in the living room of his home in Broken Arrow, Oklahoma, sipping coffee and trying to decide if he should continue looking for Gerald, or simply wait for his old friend to contact him again. However, each time he leaned in the direction of the latter, a gut feeling pushed him away from it—Gerald was in trouble.

Laura Bradford, at least the one Elliot had known, had never officially enrolled at the university. Elliot had spent the afternoon and part of the night finding that out, though it hadn't surprised him. He'd never seen Laura in any of the classrooms or hallways or even on campus, unless she was with Gerald. Elliot thought about Terri Benson and he wondered how close Terri had been to Laura back when they all hung out together.

Elliot had always wondered if Laura's being in Stillwater involved more than scholastic endeavors, or even being Gerald's girlfriend. He'd suspected she had her own agenda. When she stopped coming around, he'd fallen back on that, figuring she'd found whatever it was she'd been after and with nothing else to keep her there, she'd gone back to wherever it was she'd come from. But what, exactly, she'd been after, he wasn't sure. He'd learned at an early age that he was more intuitive than most people, but his uncanny guessing-game talents had their limits.

Elliot kept going back to Angela Gardner, the anthropology student. It had been shortly after Gerald's encounter with Angela and her teacher, Professor David Stephens, that Laura had disappeared. After that, Elliot would see Gerald and Terri now and then, but the meetings at Joe's began to taper off, never going further than casual conversation, until they just quit meeting altogether.

Elliot retrieved the scrap of paper that had been found in Gerald's hotel room, focusing this time not on the name of Professor David Stephens, but rather on the previously unintelligible series of numbers and letters on the reverse. Gerald had a habit of scribbling things down in a hurry and he'd often run everything together, his own brand of short hand.

In light of this, Elliot saw the message as it should be, and *W14SCheyenne* became West 14th Street and South Cheyenne Avenue. It was an address, or at least an intersection.

Elliot glanced at his watch. 11:30 p.m. He laced up his shoes and grabbed a jacket from the closet. In the hallway, he considered the weapon that hung there.

He put on the shoulder holster and slid his jacket over it as he left the house. Inside the garage, he thought about the pickup, a better choice on such a night, but he'd recently acquired a Harley, one of those spur of the moment things he had to admit feeling a little silly about.

He straddled the bike and hit the garage door opener. When the garage door closed behind him, he fired up the Harley and motored out of the neighborhood.

The road unfolded in front of the handlebars, and while Elliot twisted the grip of the Harley, he wondered about the sanity of his actions, driving around this part of town at this time of night, but as soon as he crested the hill that overlooked the address Gerald had scrawled onto the paper, he knew this whole thing was a bad idea.

Elliot slowed the bike and brought it to a stop, hoping that the darkness and the vibration of the bike had caused a visual distortion, and he had not seen who he thought he'd seen in the mirror.

But there she was, Laura Bradford, standing not more than three feet behind him, those haunting black eyes that he'd never been able to completely eradicate from his mind staring right at him.

He tore his concentration from the mirror and twisted around.

She wasn't there.

Elliot wanted to blame his failing visual acuity on lack of sleep and poor eating habits, but he knew better. There was another avenue to explore. His believing that Laura was a vision didn't necessarily make it true. Each time he'd seen her, it had been dark, and had occurred in areas where deception was possible. She could have simply stepped off the trail and disappeared into the darkness. Even now, she could have darted behind a tree or a building. He thought back to a time when his mother had passed in her sleep and he was with her, in the house, by himself but not alone, and it was a feeling like that which now crawled across his senses.

A scream, like a wounded animal might make, cut through the air.

Elliot scanned an area about two hundred yards ahead where he thought the sound had come from.

The shadowy forms of homeless people who had gathered around a campfire near the lawn of an old apartment building were now scattering in several directions, disappearing into the streets and alleyways nearby.

Elliot tightened his grip on the handlebars of the Harley. The homeless did not relish being observed in daylight, but during the night they were not a timid bunch, especially on what they considered their own turf, but the scream had frightened them.

Elliot put the bike in gear and started toward the scene, but by the time he arrived the only thing remaining was the campfire.

Elliot leaned the bike against the stand and started toward the house, an old mansion that had been converted into an apartment building. One of the logs had fallen to the side of the campfire, though it was still partially in the fire and burning on one end.

Constantly surveying the area, he crouched slightly and when he had the torch in hand he straightened and resumed his journey, slowly climbing the stairs leading to the front entrance. The doors and windows had been boarded up. The place was empty.

Still using the torch for light, Elliot descended the stairs and walked across a grassy area leading behind the building.

The backdoor was secured as well, but when Elliot stepped away from the door, he saw another possibility.

A set of concrete stairs led into the earth, barely visible by the faint light of a distant streetlamp.

It was the entrance to the basement. Elliot pushed aside his wild ideas of what might be hiding in the dark space beneath the house and started down the steps, the light from the torch tossing the darkness around in haphazard shapes.

A door blocked the entrance, but it was old and decayed, and even if it had been locked it would not have offered much resistance.

Elliot shoved it open and stepped into the room.

The smell of damp earth and organic substances that had gone bad filled the air. Footprints spotted the muddy floor of the basement, meandering toward the back wall, stopping at the base of a set of wooden stairs.

Elliot raised the torch.

The wooden stairs went from the floor of the basement to an open doorway leading into the house. The light dimmed further as the torch died down to nothing more than glowing embers.

Elliot let the torch fall to the damp floor where he knew it could do no harm and retrieved the flashlight he kept in the breast pocket of his jacket. Stopping at the base of the stairs, he directed the light upward, toward the opening.

It was as if someone had gone into the basement to retrieve a jar of canned fruit, intending to quickly return to the kitchen.

Elliot lowered the beam and quickly directed it about the room, checking each corner and shadowy place where he thought someone might hide.

He slowly climbed onto the bottom stair and bounced his weight against it, testing the integrity of the structure. The stairs were solid, but Elliot remained cautious, taking his time, letting each step prove itself before proceeding to the next. When he reached the top, he eased through the doorway and entered the first floor.

Tall wooden cabinets with glass-fronted doors covered two walls, and remnants of linoleum patched the countertops. Wooden planks stretched across the floor. What had once been a grand estate was now little more than the material it had been constructed from.

Standing in the darkness sent a chill up his spine. Elliot thought of leaving. Again, he had to focus on why he was there. He had to find Gerald's connection to the empty house, if indeed there was one.

Elliot left the kitchen, moving slowly through what had been the dining area, and when he reached the empty expanse of the great room, the beam of the flashlight revealed something much more than shadowy distortions. He walked slowly around the object, a scaled-down version of a step pyramid, studying it from all angles.

The structure, a type of altar, like some mad stone mason's private creation, rose at least seven feet from the center of the floor. The coppery scent of fresh blood filled the air. It had run down the sides of the altar to form pools on the floor.

Elliot steadied himself and stepped onto the pyramid, and when he had climbed a few steps he raised the flashlight so that the beam fell across the top of the structure.

The victim lay sprawled across the altar, his back arched, his arms lying at his sides. He had aged, of course, and put on weight, even grown facial hair, but Elliot immediately recognized him as he stared into the dimly lit face, the death mask of Stanley Gerald Reynolds III.

Elliot braced himself against the stonework and ran the light across Gerald's corpse.

An eight or nine inch gash ran horizontally across his abdomen, just below the rib cage. Blood still oozed from the wound. An image of Gerald laughing at one of his own jokes ran through Elliot's thoughts, and his eyes moistened.

As Elliot fought to regain composure, to understand what was happening, he again thought of Angela Gardner, and along with her image something she'd said formed in his mind: *Sacrifice is made to give sustenance to the gods.*

A familiar sound from outside tugged at Elliot's conscience, but in his current sate of confusion it took him a moment to identify its source.

Someone was trying to start the Harley.

Elliot stumbled across the room to the foyer. When he reached the front door, he placed his face against it and stared through the cracks in the boards that covered it.

His pulse quickened. Someone was out there.

Elliot scrambled through the house, maneuvered the muddy floor of the basement, climbed the cement steps and stumbled into the backyard. Gaining his footing, he ran to the front of the property.

Elliot bolted across the yard toward the ragged man struggling to push the Harley into the street.

It moved easier once he got it into neutral. It might have been a few years, and maybe some type of pain-soothing substance was hindering his performance, but the thief had clearly been around bikes before. He wouldn't have gotten this far otherwise.

Like a linebacker who had the angle on his opponent, Elliot caught the man and dragged him to the ground. The weight of the Harley pinned the guy's legs to the asphalt, and even in his medicated state he screamed from the pain.

Elliot hoisted the bike upright and dragged the old guy to a softer, grassy area between the sidewalk and the street.

He smelled of sweat and fermented fruit. Wrinkles lined his face. The age of those with hard lives can be deceiving, but he had to be in his seventies. "Who the hell are you?" Elliot asked.

"Did you just do what I think you did?"

"What are you talking about?"

"You lifted the bike up off of me like it was nothing. The Harley's got to be close to seven hundred pounds."

Elliot shook his head. He hadn't exactly picked it up, just put it back on its wheels, using the width of the frame as leverage. "Why were you trying to steal it?"

"You got it wrong, man. I wasn't going to steal it."

"Oh, I get it. You were just going to push it down to the car wash and shine it up for me."

He pulled a twenty from his pocket and showed it to Elliot. "Dude gave it to me. Said he'd give me another, when I done the job."

"What dude?"

"The one who hangs around the old apartment house."

A vision of Gerald, lying inside the house with his stomach cut open ran through Elliot's head. He grabbed the ragged man by the lapels of his jacket "Tell me where he is. I need to talk to him."

"I don't know anything, man. To tell you the truth, I thought you was the dude until I got a better look at you."

Elliot released his grip. "Since you're bright enough to know I'm not the same guy, why don't you tell me what he does look like?"

He opened his jacket, exposing the booze he'd tucked away. "Do you mind?"

"All right, if it'll help you talk. But not too much."

He unscrewed the lid and turned the bottle up. Afterward he replaced the cap. "He looks a little like you, the way you dress I mean. He's older, though, grey hair and all."

"Do you know where I can find him?"

"No. But I see him around the old place every once in a while. I just figured he owned it or something, maybe going to fix it up, rent it out or something."

Elliot had interrogated a thousand drunks. Looked like this one was telling the truth. He helped him to his feet. "Are you hurt? I can take you to the hospital, if you want."

"I just want to be left alone. I'll be all right."

Elliot reached for his wallet. "I'm going back inside, take care of some business. You said the man promised you another twenty. I'm making it up to you, but if you want to live to spend it, leave the bike alone."

"You don't have to worry. I don't want no trouble with you."

Elliot drove the Harley back onto the yard in front of the building. After shutting it off, he said. "You used to ride, didn't you?"

"What makes you say that?"

"Just the way you handled it, like you knew what you were doing."

The old guy's eyes seemed to cloud over as he shook his head. "It was a long time ago, another lifetime, I guess."

"You could get it back, if you wanted to bad enough."

"I think about it sometimes. But I don't know how."

"Cut back on the booze," Elliot said, "in small increments. Instead of two bottles a day, drink one and three quarters, pour the rest out. Next, go to one and a half, like that until you get it under control. It won't be easy, but you can do it, if you put your mind to it."

"Maybe I will," he said, "but let me ask you something? The sound that brought you down here, you ever hear anything like it before?"

Elliot thought about the animal-like screaming he'd heard earlier. He shook his head.

"I wouldn't go back inside the place if I was you. It's where the sound always comes from, and why I did what the man asked, taking your bike and all. You understand what I'm saying?"

Elliot continued toward the house. "Use your fear as an incentive to get off the street."

"All right. But you got to listen to me. Things been going on down here."

"Like what?"

He took a drink, wiped his mouth, and said, "Something straight out of hell, I reckon. And I know what you're thinking. He gets all juiced up, he wouldn't know a scream from a country song, but you'd be wrong. I been around this old world for a long time, know a little about people dying. I know a death scream when I hear one. He cuts their hearts out. That's what they say. You'd do well to get back on your motor and get on out of here."

"I found somebody inside all right," Elliot said, "murdered, cut with a knife. You know anything about that?"

Fright shot across the old guy's face. "No, sir. Dude told me to hide the bike in the bushes. I don't anything about no murder. Honest to God."

Elliot turned away and retraced his steps across the lawn and through the basement. He had his phone out when he reached the parlor, intending to call the department and report what he'd found, but what he sensed caused him to rethink his options.

The expanse of dilapidated oak flooring stretched across the room, but something had changed. The altar was still in the middle of the living room, but no sacrifice was atop it, and no blood pooled on the floor.

Elliot shined the light around the room, wondering if someone had come while he was gone and removed the evidence, but as quickly as the idea formed, he dismissed it. He might have been gone long enough for someone to have hidden the body, but not to have cleaned up the mess. Although he could see from this angle and distance that the altar was empty, he again climbed the side of it to be sure.

Gerald was gone and so was the blood.

Elliot returned to the kitchen where his attention was drawn to the door leading to the basement. No trail of blood showed on the floor where someone might have dragged the body. The basement door was still open.

Elliot moved the door to the closed position.

A padlock hanging from the back of the door banged against the wood. Attached to the door frame was the corresponding hasp.

Elliot slid the hasp in place and replaced the lock, though he did not secure it. He had no desire to be trapped in such a place. However, with the door partially secured, no one could enter through the basement unless they knocked the door down, and anyone trying to get out would be slowed down considerably. It just might give him the opportunity to catch them, whoever that might be.

Elliot went back through the house to the foyer where a set of stairs led to the second floor. The only place he hadn't been. He shined the light up the stairway, pressed his back against the wall, and began climbing, looking ahead, but glancing back occasionally to make sure no one came up behind him. The nerves on the back of his neck kept tingling.

At the top of the stairs, Elliot directed the beam around the dark chasm, but the light began to dim. The batteries were going dead.

His hands began to shake. He wanted to search the rest of the building, but the feeling of being vulnerable, exposed to whatever presence was behind this overwhelmed him. The absurdity of the situation, his being inside an abandoned house in the middle of the night, struck him. He thought about seeing Laura on the running trails at the River Park and later in the mirror of the Harley. An image of Gerald lying in sacrifice atop the altar exploded through his head. Had any of it been real? Sure, he was a little more intuitive than most people were comfortable with, but nothing like this had ever happened. Again the thought of insanity played around the corners of his mind.

Calling the police no longer seemed like a viable option. What would he tell them? What would he show them?

The light flickered again.

Elliot shook the flashlight. If it failed, he would be left in near total darkness.

He started back down the stairs, hearing nothing other than the sounds of his own movement and seeing only what the dim light revealed, but he was not alone. He knew that now with certainty.

As he passed through the living room, he checked to see if the body had reappeared, but it had not. The altar was still empty.

By the time he reached the kitchen, the flashlight had weakened further, its output reduced to a faint glow, but when he shined it on the basement door, it offered enough light to confirm his fears.

Someone had snapped the padlock shut. He was locked in.

Chapter Seven

Elliot reached beneath his jacket, pulled the Glock, and held the weapon within inches of the door.

From somewhere nearby, one of the boards that made up the oak flooring creaked.

Elliot wondered if it was the settling of the old structure, or if someone had walked across the floor.

Fingers gripped his shoulder.

Nightmarish images ran through his imagination. He spun around, his finger on the trigger, and barely stopped himself from blowing the head off the Harley thief.

Elliot lowered the weapon. "I could have killed you. What the hell are you doing?"

The old man took a few steps back. "I couldn't bring myself to go off and leave you here. Come on, I'll show you another way out."

"Why is the door locked? Was it you?"

"You don't want to be hanging around this place at night. Besides, the man you're looking for, he's gone. I saw him out back a few minutes ago."

Elliot holstered the Glock and gestured for him to lead the way.

He took Elliot to the foyer. Just south of the front door, several boards covered a window. He shoved them aside. After crawling through, he held the boards in place, waiting for Elliot.

Elliot squeezed through the opening and stepped onto the front porch. Once outside, he said, "It's a creepy old house, but I guess it beats sleeping in the rain."

He shook his head. "Nobody sleeps here, won't even come near it. Can't say as I blame them, can you?"

He asked the question as if he understood what Elliot had been through during the night. Elliot turned away and repositioned the boards over the window.

When he turned back, he saw the old guy walking away. It was eerie how the homeless slipped in and out of the night.

Elliot straddled the Harley. Whether his hallucinations of Gerald and Laura had been elements of the past, premonitions of the future, or simply the product of an overworked imagination, he wasn't sure. But one thing was certain. Ghosts didn't put locks on doors.

A disturbance, like trashcans being knocked over, came from the back of the house.

Elliot fired up the bike and sped behind the abandoned house. In the alley, he positioned the bike and swept the beam of the headlight across the area like a searchlight.

Something streaked across the yard and disappeared into the shadows.

Elliot tried to follow the prowler or whatever it was with the light, but it moved too fast, and as it blended into the darkness, he wondered if it was an animal or a man that had lowered himself to the ground to run on all fours.

From somewhere in the distance, a car engine started.

Elliot swung around.

A vehicle parked alongside the street about thirty yards west of the house pulled onto the roadway and sped past, going east.

Elliot twisted the grip of the Harley and rocketed forward, nearly losing the bike as he sped onto the street. Recalling what the salesman had told him—If you don't respect the bike, it won't respect you—he eased off the throttle and regained control.

Several automobiles were on the roadway. One of them had to be the car he'd seen near the old house.

Without slowing down, a green Honda turned east on 11th, its tires squealing.

Elliot turned after it.

The driver of the Honda increased his speed, weaving around the other cars.

Elliot had made the right decision. Of course the driver had no way of knowing he was a cop. He couldn't blame him for trying to evade some crazy motorcyclist on his tail.

The driver of the Honda slammed on the brakes and the car came to an abrupt stop.

Elliot imagined the Harley hitting the back bumper of the car, his body flying like a wilted mannequin through the air. He leaned to the left, just missing the vehicle, then redistributed his weight back to vertical as he rocketed past the Honda. Regaining his composure, he slowed the bike and did a half circle in the middle of the street.

The Honda squealed its tires and lurched toward him.

Elliot twisted the throttle, a head on collision waiting to happen, but as he gained momentum he again harnessed the power of gravity to alter the bike's course. He'd found the respect the salesman had told him about. The Harley was incredibly responsive, almost an extension of his own body. The smell of burning rubber filled Elliot's senses as he slid past the Honda, avoiding the crash by inches.

Once again, Elliot turned the bike around.

The Honda had kept going and was now turning north onto Peoria Avenue.

Elliot continued the pursuit, increasing his speed until he reached the intersection of 11th and Peoria.

The driver pulled off the road, jumped out of the Honda and darted across Peoria toward Oaklawn Cemetery. When he saw Elliot idling at the corner, he glanced across the street at the Honda, spun around, scaled the fence surrounding the cemetery, and dropped to the other side.

Elliot maneuvered the bike onto the sidewalk. He didn't exactly fear cemeteries, but he never visited them without reason, and he'd certainly never entertained the idea of walking the narrow streets of the dead during the black of night. But he had to. And he was somewhat familiar with the place. He'd been to a funeral here. He dismounted, then climbed the fence and stepped onto the damp, spongy soil of the cemetery. He pulled his service weapon and scanned the area.

Shadowy outlines of tombstones and silhouettes of scraggly trees dotted the dark landscape. The Honda driver could be hiding and waiting for him to follow, or he could have lingered near the fence.

The muffled sound of a twig snapping against the soft earth came from Elliot's left. He swung toward the sound, his imagination hosting visions of undead creatures crawling up from the graves and surrounding him.

A shadowy form emerged from the darkness and disappeared behind a mausoleum.

Elliot squeezed the handle of the Glock, but did not fire. His nemesis was not armed. Otherwise, he could easily have taken the advantage, but he'd chosen to run instead. He could be trying to draw Elliot deeper into the cemetery, away from the street where a passerby might not hear a shot, if fired, or ascertain its approximate point of origin. Elliot gathered his nerves and started toward the mausoleum. When he reached the small building, he put his back to the wall and edged around the structure, making two complete revolutions in this fashion before stopping near the entrance to the burial chamber.

The act seemed both ridiculous and terrifying as Elliot grasped the cold metal handle and checked the entrance to the mausoleum.

The door rattled, but it was secured.

A small prayer of thanks crossed Elliot's lips, though his relief was short lived.

From somewhere in the distance, footsteps padded against the soft ground.

Elliot stumbled toward one of the blacktopped roads that meandered through the cemetery and when he reached the hard surface he ran toward the fence where he'd first seen the suspect climb over. He braced himself against the fence and stared through it, looking across Peoria Avenue.

The Honda was still there.

Staying close to the fence, Elliot visually searched the cemetery grounds.

He did not see anyone, but he now recognized this part of the cemetery.

He walked a few paces north, and even before he reached the grave marker he knew what he would find there. The name on the headstone read Sergeant David Conley.

Conley had never been Elliot's partner, though they had once worked together. Conley's role had been closer to a wise old uncle who always seemed to be there when needed. The chain of events leading to Sergeant Conley's death blossomed in Elliot's mind. Conley had taken a bullet intended for Elliot.

Elliot touched the cold stone of the marker. "Hey, old buddy," he said, "sure could use some good old Conley advice right now. I've been meaning to come and see you. Never got the chance to tell you how sorry I am, things turning out the way they did."

Elliot had no more than uttered the words when he again heard footsteps.

About ten degrees to his left, someone dressed in dark clothing emerged from the darkness and advanced toward him.

Elliot swung around, aiming the Glock.

Even in the dim light from the streetlamps along Peoria Avenue, he recognized the young man. He wore gothic clothing, and his black hair hung to his shoulders. Shane Conley, David's son.

Elliot lowered the weapon. "I don't know who I expected to find out here, but it sure wasn't you. Kind of late to be strolling around the city of the dead, wouldn't you say?"

"Look who's talking."

"I'm a police officer. I'm supposed to do stuff like this. What's your excuse?"

Shane Conley reached beneath his coat.

Elliot tensed, but the kid only pulled out a pack of cigarettes.

Shane lit up and blew out smoke as he tucked the pack inside his coat. "I work here, Detective Elliot, a sort of night watchman. By the way, I heard what you said. Dad would've appreciated it. He always liked you, said you were special."

Elliot felt guilty for thinking it, but a security guard at a place like this seemed a befitting occupation for the kid, the way he dressed and all. But Shane was only fifteen, too young to snag such a job. "He was a good man, your father."

Shane remained quiet, continuing to draw on the cigarette. He cleared his throat and said, "Yeah. I really miss him. More than I thought I would."

"I do have a reason for being here," Elliot said. "I was in the middle of a pursuit. The guy bailed out and ran through the cemetery. You didn't happen to see anyone, did you?"

Shane contemplated his answer. "No. But this place will do that to you, give you a case of the jitters, make you see things. It takes some getting used to."

"I can imagine. But I was chasing the guy, saw him climb the fence. I suspect he came here to hide. Lots of places to do that in a cemetery at night."

"You might be surprised. I can help you look for him, if you want."

Elliot shook his head. "He's probably gone by now. Do you see the Honda parked across the street?"

"Yeah, what about it?"

"Is it yours?"

He shook his head. At the mention of the car, he'd tensed up.

"Do you know who it belongs to?"

Shane's eyes darted back and forth. "Can't say I do."

Shane wasn't being completely honest, but Elliot couldn't fathom what the kid's involvement with Gerald might be, if indeed there was any. And somehow, standing over the grave of Sergeant Conley, it didn't feel right, interrogating his son. "Thanks for your help," he said.

By the time Elliot had gotten over the fence and drove back onto Peoria Avenue, the Honda was gone. Had Conley's son driven it? And did he actually work at Oaklawn? It would be easy enough to check.

Elliot didn't relish the thought of going to bed without knowing what had happened to his old friend, but fatigue made him sluggish and he couldn't trust his reasoning. He found the highway and drove toward home in Broken Arrow.

Elliot stared at the road ahead of him, feeling as heavy and as slow of wit as a stone statue. He needed rest, but he also needed some answers. He couldn't get the old house out of his mind. Even though he'd found no tangible evidence to support his suspicions, he suspected something was going on there, and whatever it was it had something to do with Stanley Gerald Reynolds III. Elliot still wasn't sure about what he'd seen there, or if it was all in his head. Someone had to own the old building. He would find out, and go from there.

Chapter Eight

Later, in his home, Elliot collapsed onto the bed. He was used to late hours and losing sleep over unusual cases, but what had transpired in the last few hours was so far beyond ordinary that even now he found it difficult to wrap his mind around it.

Just before he drifted off to sleep, he noticed the message light on the phone blinking.

He reached over and punched the play button.

"Call me when you get home, Kenny. Don't worry about the time."

It was Carmen.

Elliot checked his watch. It showed 2:30 a.m.

Carmen had said to call, but a cop's definition of late doesn't necessarily agree with anyone else's. On the other hand, had he detected an underlying current of concern in Carmen's voice?

He grabbed the phone and punched in the number. Even with that, however, he began to feel intrusive, and when the second ring had finished he thought of disconnecting, though he let it ring one more time.

"Kenny?"

She had answered, and her voice was not harsh or annoyed, but soft.

"Yeah," Elliot said. "Sorry about the time. Is everything all right?"

"Don't be sorry. You spend too much time worrying about what others think."

"Not everyone. Just a chosen few."

She exhaled heavily, a sort of laugh. "You're probably wondering why I called."

Maybe Carmen had just come out of a restful sleep and had yet to put up her defenses, but she seemed relaxed and friendly. "The thought crossed my mind."

"I want to ask you something."

Hope for the future of their relationship formed in Elliot's thoughts, and he reminded himself it probably meant nothing. "Sure."

"Wayne and I talked about it, and we want to go to a movie tomorrow, and we'd like for you to come along."

Elliot glanced at the glass of water on the nightstand. He wondered if he'd come home and found the message light blinking, or if he'd dropped onto the sofa instead, where he now slept, dreaming. "Sure," he said. "I'd love to."

Sensing she was about to hang up, Elliot attempted to keep the connection going a little longer. "Carmen?"

Elliot wondered if he should save it for another time, or drop it altogether, but he could not hold back. He needed Carmen's stability, her logic. "Do you remember when I told you about seeing Mom, after she passed away?"

"I remember. You were worried I might think you were crazy."

"A concern that's still very much alive. And it's happened again."

"Your mother?"

Disjointed scenes from earlier in the night played through Elliot's mind. "No. But it was just as real, and even more unsettling."

"Would you like to tell me about it?"

Elliot wondered, and not for the first time, if he should leave this thing alone, but, even as the doubts crossed his mind, the words came out. "I saw a couple of old friends from college."

"That doesn't sound so bad."

"Let's not forget about Mom."

"You mean...?"

"I don't know what to believe. Things are happening that I don't understand."

"You work long hours in a tough job, and even when you're not, you're thinking about it. Maybe your mind is looking for a way to release the pressure."

"I'm not crazy, Carmen. At least I don't think so."

"I didn't say you were. It's not the same thing. Have you considered seeing a doctor?"

Thoughts of an old girlfriend, Molly Preston, danced through Elliot's head. He and Molly had had a similar conversation, and Elliot had let his guard down. Molly had been a friend, not a doctor, but she'd betrayed his trust just the same. "I tried that once. It didn't work out so well."

"Maybe you should stop fighting it and just let it happen. My Aunt Maria spoke of such things. She said it was a gift."

Elliot's stomach tightened. Carmen had never indicated she actually believed him, when it came to such matters. "And what do you think?"

"I believe you are simply tired and overworked."

"I like that scenario. Let's go with it."

"You are much too easy."

Elliot felt his face stretch into a smile. "Yeah. And I know you're tired as well. I'll let you get back to sleep. Thanks for listening."

Elliot disconnected with the words *I love you* hanging in the air but going unspoken. Later, as he drifted off to sleep he thought he saw the shadow of someone walk past his bed, but when he sat up and checked, no one was there. Maybe Carmen was right. He was working too hard. He plopped back to the bed and rolled over to sleep. He'd seen enough for one day.

Chapter Nine

Wayne Garcia realized he'd fallen asleep when the clock clicked over to 4:00 A.M. and woke him. It was just his rotten luck. Now he was all groggy and the plans he'd put so much time into seemed far fetched and unreal, like some sort of dream.

He almost drifted off again, so he forced himself to sit up. Getting out of bed, he rubbed his eyes and started across the floor. His mom had been up forever last night, talking to someone on the phone, Mr. Elliot most likely. A few months ago, his mom had told him Mr. Elliot was his dad, but he didn't understand any of it. Anyway the house was quiet now.

Wayne tiptoed down the hallway and stopped just outside his mom's room.

He heard no sounds.

He went back to his room and took the suitcase from the top shelf of his closet and placed it on the bed.

Again he wondered if he should go through with it. It wasn't going to be easy. His mom was good to him. But that was exactly the reason he had to do it. Mr. Elliot was a pretty cool guy and all, with all those football records and stuff, but he could be kind of scary, too. He seemed nice enough, but what if was just acting that way, so his mom would start liking him again? She said he used to be her boyfriend. Besides, some people around town didn't like Mr. Elliot very much. You mention his name, and they look at you kind of funny. Mr. Elliot was pretty big, too. A guy like that could be a real problem if he decided to get mean.

Wayne packed the suitcase and closed it. Mr. Elliot couldn't be his dad, because his real dad had left home only a few months ago, and it'd been because of him, on account of his getting into trouble all the time. And now he'd gone and done it again, nearly getting kicked out of school this time. He shook his head. He figured his mom was just trying to make things better, but he didn't want her to marry some big cop from Tulsa just because she thought he needed a dad. He had a dad. And he was going to Arkansas and bring him back home. He'd given this a lot of thought and he knew what he had to do. His dad had gone to Arkansas because that's where his family was. Wayne would go there and find him and tell him how sorry he was and ask him to come back home. The quicker he got this over with, the easier it would be. He went out the back door, closing it as quietly as he could.

As Wayne stepped into the street, he began to wish he'd put on a warmer coat, but he wouldn't dare go back in. He might not have the courage to leave twice in the same night. Jimmy Snider said he could hang out in his garage for a spell, until he decided what to do. Jimmy said it'd be a good place to hide because his parents never looked in there on account of it was so full of junk and all, and they were afraid if they opened the doors it'd all come spilling out.

Wayne clutched the suitcase with both hands and started toward Jimmy's house. His mom would definitely be mad when she found out he was gone, but everything would be all right, once he brought his dad home again.

Chapter Ten

The morning had crawled over the horizon as if uncertain it should bring such a day to light.

A similar case of apprehension tugged at Elliot's senses as images from the night before danced inside his head. It turned out the property at 14th and Cheyenne was owned by the city. That didn't help much. Somehow he didn't think the City of Tulsa was murdering people in the living room of an abandoned house.

Elliot knocked on Dombrowski's door.

Without looking up, Dombrowski motioned for Elliot to come in and take a seat. "What's on your mind, kid?"

The expression on the captain's face was intense. Not the mood Elliot had hoped for. "Something's come up. I need some time off."

The captain studied Elliot's face. "Not a problem. Like I told you before, you need a few hours, maybe a day, just let me know."

"It's a complicated issue. I'm not sure how much time I need."

Dombrowski pushed aside some papers and leaned forward, his elbows supporting him against the desktop. "What's going on, Elliot?"

Elliot pulled out one of the chairs in front of Dombrowski's desk and lowered himself into it. Dombrowski was all right, but he would never understand the complexity of the situation. "A few years ago, when I was in school, a friend of mine got into a jam. He settled it, or so he'd thought. Now it's come back to haunt him. He's asked for my help. I intend to give it to him."

Wrinkles creased Dombrowski's forehead. "What kind of trouble are we talking about?"

Once again, several possible answers ran through Elliot's head. "His girlfriend disappeared back when we were in college. They never found her. He was a suspect but no charges were filed. I know the guy. He's a little weird, but he's no killer."

"Can you take care of it after hours?"

"Not really, sir. It wouldn't be fair to the department. Until I get this thing taken care of, my mind wouldn't be on the job."

Dombrowski frowned. "You're hard to figure, Elliot. A few months ago, I couldn't run you out of here. Now you're asking to take off for an undetermined amount of time."

"I'm sorry, Bill. It's something I have to do."

Dombrowski lowered his gaze to the work he had on his desk. "All right, Elliot. Take care of your business, but don't make me wait too long."

Elliot thought about trying to explain further but decided against it. He turned and walked out. Before leaving, he stopped at his desk and called the Department of Motor Vehicles. The answer he got wasn't what he wanted to hear, though it wasn't completely unexpected. The Honda he'd followed from the old house turned out to be registered to Susan Conley. The fact resurrected the question of Shane Conley's involvement. He'd have to drive over to Susan's house and have a talk with her.

Elliot found David Conley's name in his address book and was about to connect, but it occurred to him calling ahead might not be a good idea, at least from a cop's point of view, which like it or not was the role he intended to play. He tucked the phone away and walked out of the office.

A few minutes later, Elliot parked at the curbside in front of Conley's house and climbed out of the truck. Even though he suspected his current state of mind was embellishing his senses, he felt out of balance, like he'd made a wrong turn in a strange city. As he walked toward the house, images of Sergeant Conley filled his head. He remembered the day Conley had taken a bullet. It wouldn't have happened if Elliot hadn't asked for help on the case.

Susan answered on the second knock. She had a drink in her hand, her expression reflecting a mixture of surprise and anger. "Well, well, well, look who's come to visit."

Elliot wondered if she had been expecting him, or if she was just drunk. "We need to talk, Susan. May I come in?"

Susan turned and walked into the house, leaving Elliot standing at the door.

Elliot stepped inside, closing the door behind him.

The furniture showed no dust, the floor no debris, nothing out of place. A photo of his friend David, dressed in military attire, hung over the fireplace.

Elliot tried to think of something to say, but nothing came to mind.

Susan picked up a bottle from a bureau against the west wall and refreshed her drink. Elliot found his nerve and prepared to explain the nature of his visit, but before he could, Susan cut in.

"My husband was a likable and friendly guy, but he chose his true friends carefully. He counted you as one of them. He respected you, and I respected him. You don't owe me anything, Mr. Elliot, but I will ask one favor of you. I want you to walk out the door you came in and don't come back."

Elliot suspected Susan understood, on some level, how hard it was for him to be there. This was the first time he'd come since Conley's death. He'd tried dozens of times, but kept losing his nerve. He felt responsible for Conley getting killed. Now, he sincerely wished he didn't have to do what he'd come for. "I stopped by for a reason," he said. "It's Shane. I need to speak with him."

Susan Conley tried to maintain her facade of defiance, but her trembling hands betrayed her. "What has my illustrious son gotten himself into this time?"

"It could be nothing. I saw him last night parked near a house I'd staked out. I just need to know what he was doing there."

She shook her head. "He never tells me anything, where he's going or what he's up to."

Elliot felt bad for Susan. Losing her husband and the father of her children had been tough on her. "I'm sorry, but it is important."

"I haven't seen him since last night. I don't know where he is. I just don't know."

"Try not to worry, Susan. I'm sure he's fine. But he shouldn't be driving by himself at fifteen. I'll let myself out. If you see Shane, tell him he's not in trouble. I just need to talk with him about a few things."

Elliot reached out to Susan Conley, not only to comfort her, but to lessen his own pain as well.

She recoiled, pulled away from his touch.

Elliot turned away. He could only imagine how she felt, and he held no animosity toward her. She blamed him for her husband's death. And she had good reason. He left her standing there and walked out.

As Elliot stepped around someone sitting on the concrete steps leading from the porch, he realized it was Shane's younger sister, Megan. He'd made it down the steps and onto the sidewalk when she spoke.

"You're dad's friend, aren't you?"

"That's right," Elliot said.

"What are you doing here?"

It was a direct question, and as was often the case with young people, even a kid entering her teens, there was no pretense involved. "I came to see your brother."

Megan cocked her head and closed one eye, as if partially blinded by the sun. "Why would you want to do that?"

"I have my reasons. Maybe you could help me out with a few things."

She shrugged. "Like what?"

"Do you know if Shane works at Oak Lawn Cemetery?"

"Are you kidding? Shane doesn't have a job. I don't think he even understands the concept."

"He was driving your mother's car last night. Do you know anything about that?"

"He isn't supposed to, but he does it anyway."

"Thanks. Do you know where I can find him?"

She shook her head. "What do you want with him, anyway?"

"He might have some information I need. Could you do me a favor?"

She smiled with her eyes. "Sure."

"If you see Shane, tell him I need to talk to him."

Megan waved to someone on the sidewalk, a guy in his late twenties, possibly even early thirties.

He waved back. "Hey, good looking, when are you going out with me?"

She crossed her legs and smiled. "Come back later and we'll talk about it."

Elliot started to walk away, but Conley's daughter was screaming for guidance. He owed his old friend for a lot of things. It was time he paid a little back. "You should be more careful about who you associate with."

She frowned, her whole face changing. "What's it to you, anyway?"

"He looks like bad news. You should find someone closer to your own age."

"I'm a big girl. I can handle it."

"You don't understand. The world is full of crazy people. You might not know who you're dealing with until it's too late."

"You sound like my dad."

Elliot handed her one of his business cards. "Do me one more favor, okay? If you ever need to talk, about anything at any time, give me a call."

She took the card and folded her hand around it. "I'll think about it."

"Just remember what I said."

Elliot walked to his truck. As he pulled onto the street, he saw Megan waving goodbye.

He returned the gesture. He hoped he had gotten through to her. David Conley had been one of the finest men he'd ever known and it hurt to think about his children in trouble, turning out bad. He considered waiting around the neighborhood until Shane returned, but if Shane was involved and he suspected Elliot was on to him, he would probably run. A question had been banging around in Elliot's head ever since he'd made the connection between Shane and the Honda: What did the unruly son of David Conley have to do with Stanley Gerald Reynolds III?

Elliot needed to know more about why Gerald had come to Tulsa, and why he'd called to talk about Laura Bradford. His gut feeling was he'd find some answers in Stillwater.

Chapter Eleven

A little over an hour after leaving Tulsa, Elliot stood on the sidewalk in a neighborhood of Stillwater. He checked the address, turned onto a cobblestone pathway leading to the house, and rang the bell.

Seconds later, a lady with short, blonde hair opened the door.

Elliot reached for his badge but realized his error and belayed the action. Not only was he on his own, he was out of his jurisdiction as well. He had not expected to find anyone other than Gerald. He'd even hoped his old friend might actually be there.

The lady's expression reflected annoyance. "Can I help you with something?"

"I'm looking for Gerald," Elliot said. "I was hoping to catch him at home."

Surprise showed on her face. "Sorry, hon. He's not here."

Elliot pulled a business card and handed it to the lady. He wondered if she was Gerald's wife. "Do you know where I might find him? It's important."

"What do you want with him, anyway?"

Realizing she might have the answer in her hand, the lady studied the card Elliot had given her. "Is Stan in some sort of trouble?"

"What makes you say that?"

She held the card out and shook it for emphasis. "Says here you're a cop."

"But I'm not here as a cop, just a concerned friend."

The lady placed her hands on her hips. "And why should you be concerned?"

"He called a few days ago, said he had something to discuss with me, but he never showed. I haven't heard from him since."

"Sounds like Stan," she said. "If lack of communication is the only reason you're worried, you must not know him very well."

A man appeared behind the lady. It wasn't Gerald.

"This guy bothering you, Cheryl?"

The lady glanced at Elliot and said, "He's just a friend, helps us out around the house, does the lawn and stuff."

Elliot studied him through the doorway. "Does lawn-boy know where Gerald is?"

"Hey, like the lady said, he's not here. So why don't you get out of here before I step outside and help you along?"

Elliot tensed, but forced himself to relax. "If this is a bad time, I could come back when it's more convenient for you."

"Just give me a minute," the lady said. She pushed lawn-boy aside and closed the door.

Seconds later, the garage door opened, and a late model Mercedes backed out and drove away. It was lawn-boy.

When the lady returned, she said, "Why don't you come on in?"

Elliot followed the lady to a dining area situated near a bay window. The light coming through showed a dirty tiled floor.

She sat at the table and gestured for Elliot to do the same. "All right, Detective, what's this all about?"

Elliot chose the chair directly across the table from the lady. "What's your relationship with Stanley Reynolds?"

A puzzled look crossed her face. "I had the impression you'd already done your homework. My name's Cheryl. I'm Stan's wife."

Elliot leaned back in the chair. Cheryl Reynolds was awfully calm, considering her husband was missing. "I hadn't heard from, Gerald, or Stan, since college. He said he was in trouble. Do you know anything about that?"

"He's been acting a little strange lately, but he never said anything about trouble."

Elliot's nerves were tingling, like something was about to happen. He halfway expected lawn-boy to come running into the room, carrying a shotgun. "When was the last time you saw your husband, Mrs. Reynolds?"

She looked away, staring at something outside the window. "It's been a few days. Look, I'm not going to pretend everything is okay. You've probably already figured it out anyway. Stan and I are having problems. We've been having problems for months, but recently it's gotten worse."

"Any idea why?"

"He's been getting phone calls. He said she was an old friend. I think he said her name was Laura. I suspect they're having an affair."

"Laura Bradford?"

"Yes, I believe you're right. Do you know her?"

Elliot thought about seeing Laura on the running path, the voice on the phone at the hotel. "She and Gerald used to hang out together in college."

"Were they lovers?"

She was in my car. I turned around and she was there. "I don't know. It's possible."

Cheryl Reynolds' expression more resembled resignation than defeat. "I'm not trying to do your job for you, Detective. But the way I see it, it's pretty simple. You find this girl, Laura, and that's where you'll find Stan."

Elliot saw no indication of children with the marriage; no photos on the furniture, no memorabilia on the walls. "Does Stan have an office or a study in the house?"

"Why do ask?"

"Maybe he left something behind," Elliot said. "Any kind of clue at all would be helpful."

Mrs. Reynolds pursed her lips. "Stan's pretty protective of his little domain. He asked me not to let anyone in there. In fact, he asked me to leave it alone as well, said he'd keep it clean and for me not to worry about it."

"And did you?"

"Did I what?"

"Leave the office alone?"

Cheryl Reynolds got out of her chair and walked across the room and down a hallway.

Elliot followed.

Near the end of the hallway, she retrieved a key from the top of the door frame, unlocked the door and pushed it open.

An eerie, bluish light glowed from the screen of a computer, but other than that, the room was empty.

Elliot glanced at Mrs. Reynolds.

"Stan always liked the room neat and uncluttered, but nothing like this. I have no idea what he did with all the stuff."

"What about the computer?" Elliot asked.

"I've tried. Everything's password protected."

Elliot noticed a document lying in the printer tray, and he picked it up and examined it.

The printout depicted a photograph of the Spiro Mounds area, an ancient, Native American ceremonial center. The caption across the top read: Caddo Fundamentals—Spiro and the Arkansas Basin.

Elliot's stomach tightened. Laura had claimed to be Native American, and more to the point, she had said she was Caddo. He showed the printout to Mrs. Reynolds. "Does this mean anything to you?"

She shrugged. "Stan was always fascinated with such things, Native American Culture and all."

Another question formed in Elliot's mind. "Have you checked with Stan's employer?"

"I doubt it would do any good. He got himself fired a few weeks ago."

Elliot placed the printout back in the tray where he'd found it. Gerald's life had recently changed, and the turn had taken him to the point of losing his job and wrecking his marriage. Was Laura to blame, or was the failing marriage the cause and not the effect? Cheryl Reynolds' actions didn't fit those of a jilted wife. Elliot suspected the source of her irritation was more complicated than marital problems.

"Could you give me the name of the company where your husband used to work?"

A guarded expression came across her face. "I already told you he won't be there."

Elliot pulled his notepad. He was on to something. Cheryl Reynolds had become a little more defensive. "Someone from the company might be able to help."

"Gerald and I did love each other at one time," she said, "but people change. And then old girlfriends show up."

Chapter Twelve

The door to the side entrance of the garage rattled.

Wayne Garcia dove behind a cardboard box, snagging his shirt on something near the old workbench. He shouldn't have messed around and knocked over the toolbox. Someone must have heard the noise. Jimmy said nobody would bother him there, but someone was definitely trying to make a liar out of Jimmy.

The bottom of the door dragged noisily across the cement floor, as it had when Jimmy had let Wayne in, and let the sunlight in.

Wayne held his breath. Whoever it was had come into the garage. He did his best not to move, not to make a sound, but he was sure the thumping of his heart would give him away.

"Is anyone there? I have a phone. I'll call the police if I have to."

Wayne relaxed a little. It was Jimmy's mom. He thought about giving himself up. But what if she'd already called the police? Worse yet, what if she had a gun? His scaring the wits out of her by standing and announcing his presence could get him shot.

"Jimmy, is that you? If you're in here ditching school I'll make you wish you hadn't. And you'll have your father to deal with, too."

Wayne shook his head. He was getting Jimmy into deep trouble.

It was quiet for a moment, then the light went out and the door closed.

Wayne waited a few minutes and dared a peek over the box.

Jimmy's mom was gone. Probably to call someone, maybe even the police. He couldn't put Jimmy in any more danger. He had to get out of there. He stepped away from the protection of the box, out into the open.

The word *Christmas* was scribbled across the box he'd hidden behind.

His mom loved Christmas, and the thought caused him to worry about her, and what his running away might do. His vision blurred, but he was doing the right thing. He crept across the garage floor and went to the side entrance Jimmy's mom had used. It wasn't the only way out but it was his only option. He'd been there when Jimmy had opened the overhead doors at the front and they'd made plenty of noise.

Near the door, a hooded sweatshirt hung from a clothes rack.

Wayne pulled it down and wiggled into it. He guessed Jimmy had outgrown it, but it fit him well enough. Jimmy couldn't help it. He liked to eat, that's all.

Wayne zipped the jacket and pulled the hood over his head, edged to the door, opened it a bit, and peeked through.

Jimmy's house sat about fifty feet away from the garage. Jimmy's dad had built the garage later and he'd wanted it there for some reason.

Wayne took a deep breath and readied himself. He didn't know if Jimmy's mom would see him or not when he left the garage, but he couldn't think of anything else to do. And the longer he waited, the worse things could get. He laid his shoulder against the door and shoved it open. He didn't bother closing it again. He ran for the weeds behind the garage where he hit the ground and rolled beneath the barbed wire fence that separated Jimmy's yard from old man Langford's property.

Wayne lay still in the weeds, watching Jimmy's house.

Nothing seemed to be happening. He had to find Jimmy. He belly crawled through the weeds for a spell to get some distance, and when he'd gone far enough he rolled back under the fence. He headed for the school. He wasn't sure what he would do when he got there, but he'd think of something.

Wayne made his way along the street, and a few minutes later he was near the school.

Most of the kids were outside.

Wayne checked his phone for the time. Sure enough he'd caught some luck and arrived during lunch break.

An idea of what to do next came to him. He'd go inside the school building. With all of the commotion, he probably wouldn't be noticed and he'd make his way to Jimmy's locker, maybe even find him there. If not, he'd leave a note. He started toward the building, but halfway across the playground, someone tugged at his shirt.

"Wayne, is that you?"

Wayne turned around to see Patricia Cook, standing only inches away. She was cute, real cute, though they'd never really hit it off. He took a step back. "Hey, Patricia."

She grinned. "What are *you* doing here?"

"I go to school here, just like you do."

"Not today you don't."

"What do you mean?"

"Everybody's talking about it."

Wayne pulled the hood tighter around his face. "I don't get it. Why's my missing a day of school such a big deal?"

"Don't know. Why are you dressed like that?"

Wayne glanced around. "I'm not supposed to be here, remember?"

She giggled. "Well, if you're trying to skip school, this isn't exactly the place to do it. Besides, you look like a gangster."

"Funny. Anyway, I need to talk to Jimmy."

"Wouldn't you rather hang out with me?"

Wayne's face grew warm. "Well, sure, but I'm kind of busy right now."

He stared at the ground. He was blowing this big time. "What I mean is this is real important."

Wayne turned and resumed his walk toward the school.

"Wait," Patricia said. "What if you don't find him?"

"I'll leave a note in his locker."

"It's not a good idea."

"Why not?"

Patricia put her hands on her hips. "You're already in trouble. They catch you inside and you're in deep. Let me do it for you."

Wayne glanced across the schoolyard. Patricia was right. It would be safer to let her do it. "All right. Do you have a pen and some paper? I'll write one up."

"You've got to be kidding me? You came here just to leave someone a note, and you didn't bring anything to do it with?"

"I didn't really plan any of this. It's just sort of happening."

She shook her head. "I'll take care of it. But you need to get out of here. We're starting to draw attention."

Wayne glanced around. Some kids were talking and pointing in his direction. He nodded. "See you around."

"Wait. What do you want me to tell Jimmy?"

"Tell him to meet me at the ball field."

She shook her head. "Not a good idea. Under the bleachers at the high school would be better."

"Okay. And thanks, Patricia. I mean it."

She smiled, but didn't say anything.

Wayne knew he should be leaving, but instead he looked into Patricia eyes. He'd heard being hungry could do strange things to a person, and he guessed he must be starving. The thought of never seeing Patricia again went through his head and he leaned close and kissed her on the cheek.

She pushed him away. "Go."

Wayne glanced at the school. A small crowd had gathered and now a teacher was coming onto the playground.

Wayne turned away and started walking. He heard Patricia tell him to be careful. He quickened his pace, and when he reached the fire station he broke into a run.

They were on to him. It wouldn't be safe to meet Jimmy at the ball field or the bleachers. He ran back to old man Langford's and once he was again on his belly in the weeds he pulled his phone and called Jimmy. He only let it ring a couple times because he knew Jimmy wouldn't answer. But he'd call back.

A few seconds later, Jimmy came through.

"Wayne, what's up?"

"There's been a change of plans. I can't stay in your garage."

"You wised up and decided to go back home?"

"Not exactly. It was your mom. She almost caught me."

"Of all the rotten luck. Are you sure she didn't see you?"

"I don't think so. But she knew somebody was there. She might have called the police."

"Aw man. Don't tell me."

"It's okay. I'm all right. But I have to get out of here. I know what I need to do now."

"Go home and forget about it, right?"

Wayne truly wished he could do that. "I can't."

"Why not?"

"I have to talk to my dad."

"So call him on your phone."

"It won't work as well. I need to be there, so I can see his face when I ask him what I done wrong."

"Aw, Wayne. You didn't do nothing."

"Well somebody must've, else he wouldn't be gone."

"Why do I get the feeling you're getting ready to do something really stupid?"

"I have to, Jimmy. Don't you understand?"

"So how are you going to get there? And how will you find him if you do?"

"I found one of his letters on mom's desk, and it had an address on it."

Footsteps clicked against the road near Langford's fence.

"I got to go, Jimmy. I'll call you later."

Wayne turned off the phone and stuck it in his pocket. Whoever was out there started talking. He couldn't be sure, but he thought one of them might be Chief Stanton.

Chapter Thirteen

Elliot wore the hard hat the receptionist gave him and walked through a large bay door leading to the work area, a massive metal building behind the office. The address Cheryl Reynolds had given him was for a manufacturing plant on the east side of town.

An average sized man wearing a clean uniform and a hardhat waved to Elliot and started across the concrete floor of the plant. A few feet in front of Elliot, he stopped and said, "How can I help you, sir?"

A noisy forklift scooted past and exited through the bay door, disappearing into the yard.

Elliot couldn't imagine Gerald working in such an environment. "I'm looking for someone, a former employee of yours, a guy named Stanley Reynolds."

He shifted his weight from one foot to the other. "Melba Jean said you were asking about him. What do you want to know?"

"I need to talk to him, thought maybe you might know where he is, if he got a new job or not."

"Does he owe you money or something?"

"It's a little more complicated. What happened here? Why did he lose his job?"

He glanced over his shoulder and when he turned back, he spoke in a hushed tone. "Look, mister. I don't know who you are, or why you're here, but I've been told to keep my mouth shut. Besides, the boss man's coming this way. I'd be careful how I used the name Stanley Reynolds around him."

The other man drew near, his face reflecting a mixed bag of emotions. It was lawn-boy, the guy Elliot had encountered at Gerald's house.

"Interesting coincidence," Elliot said, "seeing you here."

The first man Elliot had spoken with tried to make an exit, but lawn-boy stopped him. "Get back here, Ben. I might need a witness." To Elliot he said, "What the hell are you doing here?"

"People don't usually answer rhetorical questions."

Lawn-boy whipped out a phone and punched some numbers, but when he spoke, his words were directed at Elliot. "You've got about five minutes to get off this property."

"And if I don't?"

As if on cue, several security guards appeared. "Then I'll have you escorted from the premises."

Elliot glanced at the one called Ben. "Pretty strong reaction to a few questions, wouldn't you say?"

He didn't answer.

"It looks to me like your boss has something to hide," Elliot continued.

Lawn-boy made a gesture and the security detail stepped closer.

Elliot raised his hands, signaling no conflict, and pushed past the guards. He strode across the concrete floor and exited through the bay door.

Elliot drove away from the plant. He couldn't figure Gerald working in such a place, especially with lawn-boy for a boss.

Later, as Elliot drove along the streets of Stillwater, he found a burger joint and pulled in. As he walked across the parking lot, a car pulled beside him and the window rolled down.

It was Ben from the plant. "You got a few minutes?"

"Sure," Elliot said. "Come on in. I'll buy you lunch."

After they were seated, the man extended his hand across the table. "Name's Ben, Benjamin Leeds." He took a bite of burger and washed it down with some soda. "Sorry about the way I acted at the plant. I think you understand, though. If Bogner knew I was here talking to you, I'd have more to worry about than losing my job. Five years, I'm out of there, but right now I need the money. Anyway, what Bogner did to Stanley Reynolds wasn't right. I don't want you to think I'm part of it."

"Some honest answers might help."

Benjamin Leeds turned away, his eyes focusing on something outside the glass wall of the restaurant. When he turned back, he said, "I've been at the plant for thirty-five years. Things were pretty good until Darrel took over, nothing like his old man. Nobody likes the jerk, but more to the point of your question, he's been messing around with Stanley Reynolds' wife. Everyone knew about it, except for Stan. If he did, he certainly didn't show it."

"Does Bogner have a habit of fooling around?"

"You got it right, and then some."

Elliot took a drink of soda. He wanted to believe this was nothing more than marital problems, but he suspected there was much more to it. "Did Stan deserve to be let go?"

"Not really. He didn't set the world on fire or anything, but he did his job well enough."

"How long had he been there?"

"Six or seven months at least."

"Sounds like he moved around a lot."

Ben shrugged. "That's the way it is with general labor."

Once again, the notion of Gerald working in a manufacturing environment struck Elliot as odd. He'd been good with words, not tools. "What else can you tell me about him?"

"Not much. He was a quiet sort, kept to himself mostly."

Elliot glanced at the table. Ben's description of Gerald didn't sound like the bright, energetic journalism student he'd known in school. "How about friends, relatives, hangouts, hobbies, that sort of thing?"

"This is starting to sound serious. I thought you were just a friend who wanted to talk to Stan, but maybe there's more to it than that, like maybe he's really..."

"Missing?"

"What's going on here, Mr. Elliot?"

"I was hoping you could tell me."

"I've told you pretty much all I know about it."

Neither the face of Benjamin Leeds nor his mannerisms gave any indication of deception. "Thanks for your help," Elliot said. He gathered his trash and started for the exit.

Mr. Leeds followed. "I do remember something. It might not mean anything, but..."

Elliot kept walking. "I'm listening."

"It's about Stan's car. He always kept it clean, but the last few days before he got canned, it was full of stuff, not messy, but like maybe he'd been living out of it or something."

Elliot threw the trash into the container. He'd wondered about Gerald's transportation, if he'd driven his own car to Tulsa, or if he'd hired a rental. "What kind of car was it?"

"A 1989 Cadillac DeVille, sort of beige-colored, not restored or anything, but it ran good, real smooth. Cars are a hobby of mine."

Elliot pushed through the restaurant door and stepped outside. Cheryl Reynolds had not mentioned her husband had been living out of his car. However, she had made a point about his getting phone calls from an old girlfriend. "How did Stan feel about the relationship? Did he ever stray outside the marriage, or express an interest to?"

Ben shook his head. "Not that I know of, unless you count Terri Hill out at the plant. She and Stan had lunch together occasionally, but it didn't look like anything romantic, just friends I'd say."

The name caught Elliot's attention. Gerald had known Terri Benson before Laura had come along, and they continued to hang out together after Laura had disappeared.

Ben Leeds looked as if he'd swallowed something bitter. "I'm starting to get a real bad feeling about this."

"That makes two of us," Elliot said. "Do you know of anything, other than the affair, that caused Stan to get on the wrong side of Bogner?"

The look on Ben's face said he hadn't intended to get himself in this deep. "They had an argument right in the middle of the shop floor a few days ago. I assumed it was about the affair, but I don't know for sure."

Elliot considered confronting Bogner about it, but decided the time wasn't right. "This friend Stan had lunch with, her maiden name wouldn't happen to be Benson, would it?"

"I don't know, Mr. Elliot. But she hasn't been to work in a couple days. She called in sick."

Elliot remembered Terri Benson leaning toward the eccentric side of life. "Any idea of how I could get in touch with her?"

Chapter Fourteen

Terri Benson stood along the wall beside a set of pool tables, watching a guy with tattoos covering his arms lean over to make a shot. It was a bar just outside of town called Harry's. Benjamin Leeds had told Elliot he might find Terri there. She had the same hair style, the same gothic clothing, the same pale, unearthly complexion as when Elliot had last seen her.

Elliot walked over to the pool tables. "Hello, Terri."

Terri Benson snatched a long neck from a nearby table and took a sip.

Elliot wondered if she might smash the bottle against the side of his head.

Instead she held her arms open, signaling for a hug.

The tattooed man took note of this. He'd stopped playing the game and stood like a soldier, the cue stick a rifle at his side.

Elliot gave Terri a quick hug then stepped back. "It's good to see you," he said. "You're looking well."

Terri touched the tattooed guy's shoulder and smiled. "It's just another old friend from college that I never expected to see again."

To Elliot, she said, "Do you two always travel in pairs?"

Elliot scanned the bar for familiar faces, wondering if someone had followed him in. "I was hoping you might know where Gerald is."

Taking a cigarette from a pack on the table, Terri lit up. She blew out smoke and said, "No one calls him Gerald anymore."

"I've been to his house and the plant where he worked. Things aren't right. What's going on?"

"You're the ghost from Christmas past. You tell me."

Elliot stared across the table, wondering if Terri was drunk, or just too far gone to care. "I spoke with Ben Leeds earlier. He said you haven't been to work in a few days."

Mr. Tattoo watched with interest.

"It's Laura," Terri said. "She's come back. Gerald never could keep his mind straight when she was around. Need I say more?"

"Plenty more, Terri. I need to know where he is."

Terri finished her beer and signaled for another. "Gerald and I had a good thing going back in school before she showed up. He slept at my place more than he did his own."

Terri stopped talking while the waitress sat the beer on the table. Afterward she leaned close and lowered her voice. "Those were the best days of my life. It's been crap ever since."

Elliot glanced at the table. "Doesn't it strike you as odd that Laura would be here? Or have you forgotten she disappeared?"

"All I know is she keeps getting in the way."

Elliot's stomach tightened. He hadn't realized there was more than friendship between Terri and Gerald. But he knew how it felt to love someone you couldn't have.

"I never thought I'd put my hopes on something negative happening to someone, but with Gerald's marriage being in trouble, I thought we might finally get our chance. He never said as much, but we'd been having lunch quite a bit, and there was something he wanted to tell me, but he couldn't bring himself to do it. I could see it in his eyes."

A song began to play on the jukebox, some country number Elliot had never heard before. It'd been quiet in the bar before, and though the music wasn't loud it was enough to muffle their conversation.

Terri lit another cigarette. "He told me he'd moved out and he was sleeping in his car. He even said where he was going to park that night. I thought it was an invite. I sat around the house, wondering what to do until I figured it had to be fate or something. I slipped out and went over there, you know, to give him some company, maybe even some comfort. It sure didn't turn out the way I thought it would."

"What happened?"

Terri's eyes glistened with moisture. "He'd chosen a good spot all right. It was plenty dark and all, but I stumbled around until I found the car. Hell, I'm standing there knocking on the window, like some giddy fool, until my eyes finally adapted and I saw what was happening. She was wrapped around Gerald like a teenager on her first date."

"It could have been anyone. You said it was dark."

"It was Laura all right. I'd know her face anywhere. But it was the way she looked at me that almost stopped my heart. It wasn't like she was mad at my being there, or even gloating over the victory, but a pitiful look, like she was in pain or something. It scared the hell out of me. I ran back to my car and drove home fast as I could."

Elliot's phone went off, but he was so engrossed in Terri's story it took him a moment to realize it. The ID showed it was Carmen. "I need to take this," he said, "but don't leave. We have more to talk about."

He brought the phone to his ear. "Carmen, what's up?"

"I called earlier, but you didn't answer."

Elliot squeezed the phone. It wasn't like Carmen to get upset over trivial things like a dropped call. "Sorry. I guess I didn't hear it."

"Where are you?"

"I'm in Stillwater."

"What are you...? Never mind."

The juke box started again. It seemed louder now. To make things worse, Terri Benson began to laugh. Elliot cupped the phone, but it was too late.

"Are you with someone?"

Elliot watched Terri kiss her tattooed boyfriend. "It's a client. I'm on a case."

"Your occupation always makes itself known. I'm sorry I bothered you."

The phone went dead.

Elliot tried calling her back, but there was no answer.

"I'm worried about Gerald, too," Terri said. "And you've got cop written all over you, so I know something's up. Find him for me, Kenny. Bring him home."

Elliot stuffed the phone into his pocket. "What you thought you saw with Gerald and Laura in the car, when did it happen?"

"Late Sunday night."

Elliot looked at Terri. Gerald had called Monday morning. "What do you know about Darrel Bogner?"

She shrugged. "He owns the plant where I work."

"What about the fight he and Gerald had?"

"I wasn't there when it happened. Gerald didn't want to talk about it, so I didn't push it."

"What did he talk about?"

Terri took a drag on her cigarette. "He'd been going on about artifacts and things, you know, like he used to, talking about his grandfather's estate, and what he did or didn't get from it."

Elliot thought about the printout of Spiro Mounds he'd seen in Gerald's office. "Something in his life recently changed, dragged him into his past. Do you have any idea what it might have been?"

Terri wiped her eyes with a napkin, smearing the dark circles of makeup. "I think his old lady might have sold part of his collection or something."

Elliot stared across the table at Terri. She'd finally said something that made sense. "Did Gerald tell you that?"

She nodded. "It has something to do with Laura. She sends a shiver up my spine, Kenny. She always did."

Elliot pushed away from the table and handed Terri one of his business cards. "I'll sort this thing out," he said. "Anytime you want to talk, just call."

He walked out of the bar but his confidence didn't match the promise he'd made. Again he tried calling Carmen, but again she didn't answer. She hadn't said anything was wrong, but... He needed to get back to Tulsa, check on her if he couldn't reach her on the phone. He also needed to look for Gerald's Cadillac. If he'd been living out of the car, he would have driven it when he went to Tulsa.

Chapter Fifteen

Back in Tulsa, Elliot arrived at the intersection at 14ᵗʰ and Cheyenne where the abandoned house had been. He checked the street signs to make sure he was in the right location, even though he already knew he was.

The old house was not there. A couple of bull dozers lumbered across the landscape, pushing a pile of rubble into a hole where the basement had been.

Elliot parked across the street and flagged down one of the workers.

The worker operating the dozer shut down the machine and leaned over, a questioning expression coming across his face.

"What happened?" Elliot asked.

"The old place caught fire. It was in shambles anyway. I think it was some wino trying to keep warm. It happens."

With a blank stare, the worker fired up the dozer and resumed his task.

Whatever evidence there might have been was now buried beneath several feet of dirt. Elliot turned away and started toward his truck, but as he reached the edge of the property, something reflecting the light of the sun caught his attention.

He leaned over and scooped up the object.

Even before Elliot opened the palm of his hand, he knew what it was. He'd recognized the jewelry, and as he stared at the earring, crafted of silver and turquoise with a tiny dream catcher dangling from the metal, his stomach churned. Laura Bradford had been wearing the earrings when he'd seen her on the running trails at the River Park.

Elliot stuffed the earring into his pocket and crossed the street. Seconds later, he pulled away from the curb and went south on Cheyenne Avenue. He planned to search the area in increasingly widening circles until he'd satisfied himself that Gerald's Cadillac was either there, or it wasn't.

As it turned out, it didn't take long. Halfway up the block on Carson, Elliot found an old, beige Cadillac parked along the curbside. Elliot pulled in behind the car. How many beige, 1989 Cadillac Devilles could there be? He slipped out of the truck and walked around the vehicle, but as he reached for the driver's side door, someone challenged him.

"Mind if I ask what you're doing?"

An elderly gentleman stood in the yard near where the Cadillac was parked.

He'd probably seen Elliot poking around, and had come outside to see what was going on. "Do you know who owns this car?" Elliot asked.

He rubbed his chin, the expression on his face going from concern to oh-I-might-as-well. "No, sir, I can't say as I do. A man pulled up about 10:30 in the morning yesterday and got out and walked away. The car's been there since."

Elliot went to the rear of the vehicle, pulled his notepad and jotted down the number on the license plate. "What did this guy look like?"

"Oh, average height, a little pudgy around the middle, short reddish hair. He had one of them little beards, a go-tee I think they call it."

Elliot went to his truck and pulled a Slim Jim from behind the seat. The nosy neighbor had just described Gerald, at least as Elliot had seen him on the altar.

The neighbor pointed to the tool. "What are you planning on doing there?"

Elliot started to explain the situation but decided the concept would be lost on the old guy. "I'm a private investigator," he said. "I realize how this must look, but I'm working on a case. It's rather touchy at this point, so I can't give you the details."

On the passenger side of the vehicle, Elliot worked the notched end of the tool between the glass and the rubber, just above the lock. He fished it up and down until the notch snagged onto the control arm, and with an upward pull the lock disengaged. He removed the tool and opened the door.

Elliot laid the Slim Jim on the asphalt and climbed into the Cadillac, sliding into the passenger seat.

The vehicle smelled of polish and well-worn leather. Other than a couple of blankets and a pillow stacked neatly in a corner of the backseat, the interior of the car was clean.

Elliot searched the glove compartment and found some repair bills, a few pens and pencils, and a tire gauge. The other storage areas, a console between the seats and pouches on the backside of the front seats, yielded a flashlight and few recent issues of *American Archaeology*. Elliot lowered the sun visors and found nothing, but as he leaned over to look under the seats, he found a sheet of paper.

Elliot retrieved the paper and examined it.

It was another photocopy, this one depicting a knife, its carved handle worked into a figurine from which protruded a blade constructed of a shiny rock-like substance.

From the curbside, the neighbor watched, his expression reflecting a mixture of interest, and trepidation. "What you got there?"

Elliot flipped the page over. Written on the backside was the address of the old house at 14th and Cheyenne.

Elliot climbed out of the Cadillac and relocked the door.

The old man followed Elliot to his truck. "What are you going to do?"

"I've told you all I can. Don't worry about the car. I'll send someone for it."

Elliot climbed into the truck and closed the door. He suspected the artifact shown on the photocopy had been what Gerald was after, and the reason he'd come to Tulsa and ultimately to the old house at 14th and Cheyenne. Elliot thought about the earring he'd found there. The ancient knife had something to do with Laura Bradford as well.

Chapter Sixteen

Wayne Garcia heard a rumbling sound behind him.

He stepped completely off the pavement and stood in the grass alongside the highway, watching the eighteen-wheeler go past.

About fifty feet up the road, the truck came to a stop.

Wayne glanced around looking for a route he could take in case he needed to make a run for it. Something was up. He'd asked his dad once about trucks making that sound. He'd called it Jake Braking. It meant the driver needed to stop in a hurry. Wayne figured he was the reason the driver had done that. Wayne thought about the teenager who'd picked him up earlier outside of Coweta. He'd seemed pretty cool, and Wayne didn't think he would've told anybody about him, but he couldn't be sure. Then again, even if he had, the truck driver probably wouldn't know about it yet.

The passenger door popped open and a man with a square face leaned out of the cab and waved. "Hey, kid. You need a ride?"

Wayne stood alongside the highway, watching as cars sped past. His mom had made it clear about avoiding strangers, but Arkansas was a long way from here, and if he was ever going to get there, he'd need a ride. Besides, it was starting to rain, and the driver seemed nice enough. He pulled the hood of the sweatshirt over his head and started toward the truck. One of the cars that'd gone past was a highway patrol. He'd seen the markings. He didn't think the trooper had noticed him, but he didn't want to take any chances.

The door on the other side of the truck slammed and a few seconds later, the driver came around the front of the truck. He reached up and opened the door on the passenger side. "Let's get you out of the rain," he said.

Wayne looked up at the truck. He couldn't remember being this close to one before. It was huge. He put his foot on a step and climbed up, scooting into a large seat on the passenger side of the cab. It smelled kind of oily.

After getting back into the truck, the driver asked, "What are you doing out here all by yourself?"

Answers ran through Wayne's head, but none of them seemed right, so he settled for at least part of the truth. "I'm going to see my dad."

The man gunned the truck and pulled back onto the road. He drove for a few seconds then said, "Where does your dad live?"

Wayne thought through what he would say, but again he came up empty. "Arkansas."

"Whereabouts in Arkansas?"

"Siloam Springs."

"Is that where you live?"

Wayne thought about his answer. The driver could have heard by now that someone from Porter was missing, and he might turn him in if he said the wrong thing. Maybe the truth wasn't the best way to go after all. "No, sir. I live in ... Muskogee."

"There's a lot of road between Muskogee and Siloam. You weren't planning on walking were you?"

"I guess so. Kind of a dumb idea, huh?"

The driver smiled "You could say that. But it's not a problem. I just happen to be going there myself."

The man opened a console beside his seat and pulled something from it. He tossed it to Wayne.

Wayne caught the object and turned it over in his hands. It was a sandwich in a plastic bag.

"Thought you might be hungry."

"Yes, sir. I should have thought to bring something."

The man pulled out a can of soda and handed it to Wayne. "Name's Jim," he said. "What do they call you?"

Wayne almost blurted it out. He'd have to be more careful. "It's Mike... Mike Roberts."

The driver didn't say anything.

Wayne wondered if he believed his story, or if he was just playing along.

Finally he spoke again. "Tell me something, Mike Roberts. Do you have people back in Muskogee who might be wondering where you are?"

Wayne didn't like where this was going. It could be just his imagination, but the man's voice seemed different now, a little less friendly. And he kept looking at him, taking his eyes off the road a little too often.

Wayne checked the passenger door, looking for a handle or a button that might open it. He took his phone from his pocket and pretended to check for messages. "Nothing yet, but thanks for reminding me. If I don't call in every so often, they will start to worry."

"I see. And who might be worrying about you?"

"You know, my mom and dad."

"I thought you said your dad was in Arkansas."

Wayne checked the road signs: Highway 69, and they were heading north. He'd been this way before. "That's true, but it don't stop him from calling me. He wants to see me. He asked me to come." A bunch of lies, but Wayne wasn't about to let the driver know he was fibbing.

The truck driver shook his head. "I don't know, son. I don't think either of your parents would want you hitchhiking across the state. Why don't you tell me the truth? You're a runaway, aren't you?"

Chapter Seventeen

The nosy neighbor who'd told Elliot about the Cadillac stood in his yard watching.

Elliot studied the strange image depicted on the photocopy he'd found in Gerald's car, and as rain began to splatter the windshield of the truck, an old tune played on the radio: *Burning Down the House*; Talking Heads. One of Gerald's favorites.

Elliot placed the photocopy on the seat and retrieved the earring he'd found near the remains of the old house.

The interior of the truck turned cold as the earring dangled from Elliot's fingers, the tiny dream catcher attached to it twirling.

Elliot remembered a myth he'd heard about dream catchers—they would catch the evil dreams and spirits, letting only the good ones through—and as he closed his hand around the jewelry it grew warm against the flesh of his palm.

He stowed the earring in the glove compartment of the truck, waved to the neighbor, and pulled away from the curb, hoping his jumbled senses would guide him in the right direction. He had a few suspects, but none of them seemed right. Logic landed on the side of Gerald's wife, Cheryl, and her boyfriend, Darrel Bogner. However, there was no getting around Laura Bradford being somehow in with the mix. The list also included Shane Conley, Terri Benson, Angela Gardner, and, not to be forgotten, Professor David Stephens.

Elliot kept driving, making the turns necessary to get to Highway 64, working mostly on intuition, which was telling him to check out the artifact.

Elliot headed west to Gilcrease Road, exited and drove north until he reached the museum the road was named after.

Inside, he approached the information desk where an elderly gentleman looked up and smiled. "Welcome to Gilcrease. Could I direct you to a certain area, or answer any questions?"

"I need to speak to someone," Elliot said, "who could help me identify a Native American artifact."

"Artifacts you say? I suspect that'd be Doctor Cramer. Have an appointment, do you?"

"No appointment. I just dropped by."

The museum worker rubbed his chin. "Doctor Cramer doesn't usually have folks just dropping by. Who should I say is calling?"

"The name is Elliot."

"Elliot, is it? Well, let me see what I can do."

"I'd appreciate it."

Not long after speaking with the guy at reception, Elliot sat in the office of Doctor Cramer, who seemed interested though quite nervous about the nature of the visit. Finally he folded his hands and leaned forward. "Are you a collector, Mr. Elliot?"

"No, sir, I just need some information."

Doctor Cramer studied the photocopy Elliot had given him. "I see. However, if you do have some items like this, I'd be most interested in taking a look at them."

The movement of someone in the hallway outside the office caught Elliot's attention. He turned to see a couple of security guards standing beside the doorway, and it occurred to him where this was going.

"I'm afraid I've given you the wrong impression," he said. "I'm a detective with the Tulsa Police Department, though I'm working independently on this case. I was attempting to get the information off record for a number of reasons. I apologize if I misled you."

Doctor Cramer frowned. "What exactly do Native American artifacts and museum curators have to do with your case, Detective Elliot?"

Elliot indicated the image displayed on the photocopy. "This artifact might be connected to someone's disappearance. In order to determine the validity of such an assumption, I need to know exactly what it is and what it represents."

Doctor Cramer nodded and the security guards disappeared. "Sorry for the misunderstanding," he said, "but a bit of prior interest in this item had us on alert. A gentleman called just yesterday asking about the artifact you have depicted there on the page. He wanted to know if we had anything like it, or if someone had approached the museum attempting to sell such things."

"How did you know the caller was inquiring about this specific artifact?"

"The gentleman described it rather well, Detective. And the item in question belongs to a class of artifacts in which I have a good deal of knowledge."

"Could you be a little more specific?"

"My expertise is in Mesoamerican culture. You might know it better as Incan, Mayan, or Aztec. What you have there is a depiction of a *tecpatl*, an Aztec ceremonial knife."

Elliot remembered the printouts of the mounds he'd seen in Gerald's office. "Could something like this have come from the Spiro Mounds area?"

Doctor Cramer shook his head. "The settlement near Spiro was an important trading center during its time, with materials coming in from places as far away as the Gulf Coast, which would put it in the range of the Aztec Empire. But it's unlikely contact took place. In addition, such a knife would have sacred religious meaning to its people and, therefore, not something they would trade."

Elliot leaned back in his chair. A curious look had come over Doctor Cramer's face when he'd asked about the mounds. "Tell me something, Doctor Cramer. How can you be so sure the knife is Aztec?"

"It's the handle. It's carved into a figurine of Tezcatlipoca, an Aztec God."

Elliot examined the carving. "You said the knife was ceremonial. What type of ceremony are we talking about?"

"It would have been used in religious activities, Detective, at times involving ritual human sacrifice."

A sensation of heat crawled through Elliot's stomach as he recalled the words of the homeless man he'd apprehended at the old house. *He cuts their hearts out. That's what they say.* "And how exactly was this carried out?"

"In different ways, depending upon the god the sacrifice was being offered to, but typically the knife was used to make a large enough incision in the abdomen to allow the priest to reach up beneath the ribcage and remove the victim's heart."

A vision of Gerald lying atop the altar invaded Elliot's senses. "You mentioned someone calling yesterday, inquiring about the knife. Did you happen to get the name?"

Doctor Cramer opened his desk and pulled a leather-bound organizer from the drawer. "He gave the name Bradford, L. Bradford."

Elliot swallowed a lump in his throat. "Are you sure it was a man who called?"

"Yes, quite. I talked with him myself."

Elliot leaned back in his chair. It must have been Gerald who'd called, and he used Laura's name because he knew Elliot would follow up on it if something went wrong. "Did Mr. Bradford leave any contact information?"

Doctor Cramer shook his head. "He declined. However, I retrieved the number from our phone records."

Doctor Cramer scribbled the number onto a piece of paper then pushed the note across the desk. "The call came in yesterday at 9:45 AM. Is it possible the person you're looking for is a dealer or a collector of Mesoamerican artifacts?"

"He definitely had an interest in such things," Elliot said, "especially items from the Spiro Mounds area."

"And yet, he called inquiring specifically about an Aztec sacrificial knife."

"What are you getting at?"

Doctor Cramer smiled. "The ethnic identity of the people who inhabited the Spiro area is a debatable subject. The popular theories of ancestry include the Caddo, Kitsai, Wichita, and Tunica. But there was another group of people known as the Tula and some anthropologists believe they are the true ancestors of the Spiro inhabitants. There is debatable evidence supporting the theory of the Tula originally coming from Central America, ancestors of the Aztec."

"Earlier you said it was unlikely such an artifact came from the mound area. Are you now telling me it's not out of the question?"

"Rumors of the existence of such an artifact, one that would indicate ties between North American and Mesoamerican cultures, have been circulating around the anthropological and archaeological communities for years. What I'm saying is should such an artifact actually exist...well, I think you can understand the significance of it. If by some twist of fate this particular ceremonial knife should come into your possession, I would be extremely grateful, as curator of the museum, of course, if you would notify me immediately."

Elliot retrieved one of his business cards and gave it to the museum curator. "Of course," he said. "I trust you will do the same if you again hear from Mr. Bradford, or anyone else inquiring about the knife."

Doctor Cramer's face went blank. "You have my word. However, I must caution you. Most people in the business consider this to be somewhat akin to Bigfoot or the Loch Ness Monster. I have my reputation to consider. I ask for your discretion in the matter, to whatever degree possible."

"Not a problem," Elliot said. "It's a delicate issue on my end as well. Let me ask you something else. The suspect seems to be focused on this particular knife. What's the significance of the figurine you pointed out, the carved handle?"

Doctor Cramer rubbed his chin. "Mesoamerican religions were intricate, vastly more complex than most modern-day scholars realize. However, to compact it for time's sake, Tezcatlipoca was originally the sun god, but during a battle, for some sort of supremacy I guess, he was defeated by his brother, Quetzalcoatl. After that, Tezcatlipoca became a shadow god, a god of the night and other things dark and mystical. During another showdown, the brother gods both assumed human form. Tezcatlipoca possessed one of his own priests, mutated him into a beast, half jaguar and half human, and started a wave of human sacrifice. Quetzalcoatl again defeated his brother. However, Tezcatlipoca vowed to return one day and destroy the world."

Elliot shook his head. "That god sounds like a nasty piece of work."

Elliot left the museum. As he drove out of the area, he called Dombrowski to set up a meeting.

Later, through the windshield of the truck, Elliot watched the pavement of the downtown library parking lot turn wet as rain began to fall. Dombrowski sat beside him in the passenger seat of the truck. With a few exceptions, that being the ghostly visitors, Elliot had told him everything, ending with his visit to the museum.

Dombrowski's complexion now matched the dreariness of the cloud cover. "Having you around sure makes life interesting," he said. "Whether or not that's a good thing, I can't say."

"I take comfort in the fact you're still undecided."

"Funny. Anyway I appreciate you're being worried about your friend. I hope he turns up safe and sound."

"It'll end up being homicide," Elliot said.

"You're that certain?"

"Yes, sir. I'd like to find a way to make it official, but either way I intend to see it through."

Domrowski shook his head. "Why are you even telling me this? You know I go by the book, can't do anything until I get enough evidence."

"It just seemed like the right thing to do."

"You're a hard person to understand, Elliot."

"I know."

"Come back to work and let me give you come cases to keep you busy. If it's like you say it is, something will turn up."

"I can't just put this aside and wait. It's something I have to do."

"You know I can't give you my blessing to go poking around on your own. Let me ask you something. If I pulled some strings and got the basement of the old house dug up, would we find anything?"

"I don't know. The fire was intentionally set. If anything's left, it'll be mixed with dirt and rubble. It could go either way."

Dombrowski climbed out of the truck. "I got to think this over. I'll get back to you."

Dombrowski turned and walked away, but it wasn't the captain's departure that had Elliot's attention, but a presence, as if someone else had climbed into the cab of the truck. The name *Angelina* formed in Elliot's thoughts. Angela Gardner's friends had called her that. Angela had been Gerald's last client before the group broke up. She'd also been a student of Professor David Stephens.

Elliot gripped the steering wheel, something physical, for reassurance. He started the truck and dropped it into gear.

Chapter Eighteen

The brick house on Wheeling Avenue belonged to George and Emma Gardner, Angela Gardner's parents. Elliot had found the address with minimal research. Most of the students who attended the State's universities were from Oklahoma, and the bulk of the State's population clustered around two cities, Oklahoma City and Tulsa. Elliot stood at the door as the same dark Infinity that had pulled into the neighborhood behind him crept slowly past, as if the driver was in the market for real estate and was interested in the property. When the car finally disappeared around the corner, Elliot turned back and rang the doorbell.

An elderly gentleman wearing brown slacks and a button up sweater answered, a questioning look forming in his eyes.

"I'm sorry to bother you," Elliot said. "The name's Elliot. Angela and I were friends in college, and since I was in the neighborhood, I thought I'd stop by and say hello."

The man's face wasn't hard to read. Elliot's mentioning his daughter did not please him. "You're wasting your time, son. Angela doesn't live here anymore."

A voice from inside the house, asked, "Who is it, George?"

"Some guy who says he knows Angelina."

A lady rushed to the door. "Well for heaven's sake, George, don't just leave him standing there. Ask him in."

"We don't know who he is. Maybe he's one of them."

"Nonsense. Maybe he can help."

Even though the lady had verbally disagreed with her husband, she seemed to share his distrust. Standing together, she and George looked as if they might be actors, chosen to portray the perfect grandparents in a movie script.

"You don't know that, Emma. We don't know if anyone can help."

"Well, we won't know until we ask, will we?"

Emma Gardner took her attention from her husband and placed it on Elliot. Some of the friendliness had left her face. "What did you say your name was again?"

"Elliot, ma'am. Kenny Elliot."

"Well, you seem like a nice young man. Tell me, how exactly did you come to know Angela?"

"Our paths crossed a few years ago at school in Stillwater."

George cocked his head at a slight angle. "Paths crossed, now what exactly does that mean?"

"We knew each other, but not well, ran in different circles, so to speak."

"Well I guess that explains it. If you really knew Angela, you wouldn't have come here looking for her."

Emma stepped forward, her face a mixture of hope and sorrow. "Do you know where our daughter is, Mr. Elliot? If you have any information, any at all, please tell us."

Elliot lowered his gaze to the floor, wondering what kind of damage he'd caused. Some sort of problem had obviously torn the family apart, and his being there created hope for George and Emma Gardner, however misplaced it might be. "No," he said. "I was hoping you could tell me."

The old couple glanced at each other before turning their attention to Elliot. It was Emma who spoke. "You're with the police, aren't you, Mr. Elliot?"

Unsure of how to answer, Elliot remained silent.

A sad grin formed on Emma's face. "I used to teach sixth grade," she said. "And it was always the good little boys who couldn't lie very well. I guess big ones can't either."

Elliot smiled. Emma was right. When called to task, he had to tell the truth. "I am a detective with the Tulsa Police Department," he said, "but I'm here in an unofficial capacity."

"I'm not sure what that means," George said, "but your being here must certainly mean something. You see, Angela got herself mixed up with some crazy religion there in Stillwater, some kind of voodoo or something."

"Now, George, we don't know that's what it was."

"Well we know it wasn't good, don't we?"

George Gardner paused, then said, "Emma and I didn't like what she was up to, so we talked to her about it."

"What happened?"

"It didn't go well. Some teacher she'd met at school was the reason, filling her head with nonsense. She said she was in love with him." George shook his head. "We haven't seen her since. She hasn't called or anything. We don't know where she is, or even if she's..."

George glanced at his wife.

Emma took her husband's hand and said, "Something's happened, hasn't it, Mr. Elliot? Otherwise, you wouldn't be here."

"A friend is missing," Elliot said, "a mutual acquaintance of mine and Angela's. I had hoped she might be able to help."

George Gardner's face grew stern. "You said you knew Angela, and you had some of the same friends. So I have to ask you something, Mr. Elliot. Did you have anything to do with Angela getting mixed up in that hoodoo crap?"

Elliot thought about the word *hoodoo*. Both Dombrowski and Captain Lundsford had used it when questioning him. "No, sir, I did not."

"You know more than you're saying, though, don't you?"

It was Emma, the school teacher, who asked the question.

"Otherwise, you wouldn't have taken the trouble to find us. Whoever you're looking for, or whatever it is you're up to, it has something to do with Angela. We want to know what it is, and we want to know now."

Elliot looked past the couple and into the house. George and Emma Gardner had been through a lot of pain, and they were right about Angela being influenced by people who wanted to coerce her into their way of thinking. Gerald had tried to help, but it had turned out badly. "I'm sorry. I wish I knew more. You mentioned Angela had been romantically involved. Do you know who she was seeing?"

"She never really told us," Emma said, "but she let it slip once that someone named David was trying to protect her."

Elliot wondered if *David* could have been Professor David Stephens. "What, exactly, was he trying to protect her from?"

Again, the elderly couple exchanged glances. "She said it was a spirit, Mr. Elliot, the ghost of an Indian girl. I'm well aware of how that sounds, but we want Angela to come home. Nothing else matters now."

Emma wiped her eyes. "She had a name for... well, whoever was bothering her. She called her Laura."

An image of Laura Bradford silently running past him in the park formed in Elliot's mind. Angela had been involved with some form of alternative religion. If she was in town, or even if she had been, Elliot might be able to get some information from some of the local occult shops.

Chapter Nineteen

Wayne Garcia sat forward on the seat and studied the scenery that flew by the windows of the truck. They had turned off onto another road. Wayne's stomach tightened and he wished he hadn't eaten the sandwich. Maybe the driver had changed his mind and was now heading back to Oklahoma, or to the nearest police station. Another possibility, one Wayne had tried not to think about, came to mind. The driver acted strange, even for an adult, and he asked a lot of weird questions.

The driver glanced at Wayne. "Everything all right?"

Wayne quickly looked away, back toward the window. His mom had warned him about such things. How could he have been so stupid? He took a breath to calm himself "Are we in Arkansas yet?"

The driver kept his eyes on the road. "After I drop the load, I'm heading back to Tulsa. Why don't you come with me, and forget about this running away stuff?"

Wayne shook his head. Why was the driver so interested in his plans, anyway? "I need to see my dad, talk things over."

"What makes you think he wants to talk to you?"

Wayne frowned. "Why wouldn't he?"

"Well son, whether it was a good one or not I suspect your old man had a reason for running off to Arkansas and leaving you and your mom behind. I'll bet he'll be right surprised to see you standing on his doorstep, too. If I was you, I'd go back to your mama and just leave it alone."

"You said you'd take me there."

"I just don't want to see you get hurt, finding out your old man don't want you."

"He does so want me. You don't know anything about it."

"Well, I wish that was true, but it isn't. That doesn't mean nobody likes you, though. Take me for instance. I like you just fine. I think you're a great kid. Too bad I'm not your dad, huh?"

Wayne didn't answer the question. He didn't know if he should feel sorry for the guy, or be scared of him. Scared was probably safer. "Maybe you're right. Could we stop pretty soon, though? I have to go real bad."

"I don't think there are any good places around here."

Wayne stared through the window, not sure of what to do or say next. When he saw a sign beside the highway that said there was a service station at the next exit, he looked at the driver. "Hey, mister, how about we pull in here?"

The driver shot past the exit. "Just dirty restrooms that don't work most of the time. Anyway, there's one in the back. You can crawl up into the sleeper and get some rest afterward."

Wayne quickly looked away. He knew what the driver was talking about. Behind the cab of the truck was an area with a bed and stuff. No way was he going back there. But an idea occurred to him. If he was in the back, the driver couldn't see him. Maybe he could call home. His mom would be plenty mad, but she'd know what to do. "Okay," he said, "how do I get back there?"

The driver grinned. "Just push through the curtain."

Chapter Twenty

After leaving George and Emma Gardner's house, Elliot checked out the occult shops he knew about. There weren't many, and he hadn't had much luck, but there was one more, a rundown place just off 11th Street. Elliot pushed open the door and stepped inside.

The shop was nearly empty, the shelves timidly exhibiting candles, incense burners and a few odd items.

Elliot walked to the counter. "Anybody here?"

A young man came from a backroom, pushing through a doorway curtained with alternating strips of leather and beads. The boy was physically handicapped by choice, his pants being too big for him, causing him to constantly occupy one of his hands to hold them up. "Something I can do for you?" He asked.

"I'm looking for someone," Elliot said. "She might be a customer of yours."

"So?"

"So I'd like to talk to her."

"What's stopping you?"

"The term *looking for someone* implies you don't know where they are, slick. I was hoping you might be able to help me out."

"We don't give out information about our customers."

As the young man spoke, his free hand slid beneath the counter.

Elliot stepped forward and caught the boy's arm. He wasn't taking a chance on the kid going for a weapon.

The beaded curtain moved again and a man holding a shotgun came into the room.

Elliot shoved the boy against the wall and pulled his badge. "Detective Elliot with the Tulsa Police Department. Lower your weapon and place it on the floor in front of you."

The shop owner glanced toward the boy.

The kid's pants had slid down around his knees. He gave a vigorous nod.

The shop owner leaned over and laid the shotgun on the floor.

"Step away from the weapon." Elliot said. "And, you, get away from the wall and join him. I want you both together."

The kid pulled his pants up and shuffled across the floor. When he reached the area where the other guy was, he stopped, his gaze searching Elliot's face, as if looking for further instruction.

Keeping his attention on the pair, Elliot scooped the shotgun from the floor. Behind the counter, he found what the kid was going for: A .38 Smith & Wesson. He put the weapons on the counter. "You have quite an arsenal for a bunch of candles. What gives?"

The shop keeper's hair stretched back into a ponytail; a trimmed beard adorned his face. He clicked his heels together and gave a slight nod, like some English butler might do. "Let me apologize for our actions. The name's Randle Harper, the proprietor of this shop. I'm afraid we've become a bit cautious. A few days ago, a man came into the store and started waving a gun around. Scared the wits out of us." He nodded toward the boy. "My companion, Roger."

Elliot tucked the badge into his pocket. "In a place like this, if you give the people what they want, they probably come back, a lot of the same customers."

Neither of the men said anything.

"I'm looking for someone," Elliot said. Working on memory, he gave the best description he could. "She's in her twenties, curly blonde hair, five foot four, hundred and twenty pounds. Goes by Angela, Angel, or Angelina, last name Gardner."

Harper's expression showed that either the name or the description had registered.

"I have reason to believe this person has information that could lead to an arrest in a murder investigation."

Randle Harper raised his eyebrows but remained silent.

Elliot walked over and stuffed a business card into the shop keeper's shirt pocket. "If anything comes to mind," he said, "give me a call. It's important."

Elliot turned and walked out of the store. He'd driven about a mile when his phone rang. It turned out to be the kid from the shop.

"I know the girl you're talking about," he said.

"I'm listening."

"Don't be too hard on Randle. He's had a bad life, lots of crazy things going down all the time. Anyway, this Angela chick used to be a regular, but I haven't seen her in a while."

"How long is a while?"

"It's been a couple of months, at least."

Angela could've moved on, but Elliot didn't think so. She'd grown up in Tulsa, and she'd come back after college, staying long enough to have been seen a few months earlier. "Do you know where I can find her?"

"I don't know where she lives or anything, but I asked around about her, you know, just curious why she stopped coming around."

"And?"

"Word is she took up with one of them massage parlors. Never figured her for that sort, but hey, I guess you never know."

"Do you know which parlor she works for?"

"No. I mean I didn't really ask. Sorry."

"That's all right," Elliot said. The kid was big on apologies, probably shoved around most his life. "You did good, son. Thanks for your help."

Elliot disconnected and made a right turn. He had a pretty good idea of where to start. He made a few calls, pretending to be a customer, looking for a certain girl. The third person he talked with knew about Angela. A few minutes later, he walked into the Crescent Moon, a place that offered more than a rubdown, if you knew how to ask for it.

The place smelled of perfume, and soft music played in the background. A well-dressed Asian lady sitting behind the counter nodded and smiled. "Something I can do for you?"

"I hope so," Elliot said. He gave her the spiel.

"Why you want this girl? We have others."

"All right," Elliot said. "I'll level with you. I used to know Angela. We went to school together. Her parents haven't seen her for quite some time. They asked me to help."

"I am sorry. She is gone now, and doesn't work here."

"Do you know where I can find her? It would mean a great deal to her parents."

The lady spoke loudly, using her native tongue. Seconds later, two more Asian people came into the room, a man and a younger woman. A cacophony of the same language erupted among the trio.

Finally the younger woman turned toward Elliot and said, "My mother is right. You do not look like someone who would be friends with Angela Gardner."

"It's been a few years since I've seen her."

"I cannot comment on the past, only the present, in which the person you seek has many problems."

"What kind of problems are we talking about?"

"Under more ordinary circumstances, drugs and alcohol would be a sufficient answer to your question. However, when such things are a result and not the cause, one must look deeper to know the nature of the imbalance."

"I understand your hesitancy to get involved," Elliot said, "but this is a matter of great importance. Do you know where I can find her?"

"No. We were forced to let her go. She was disturbing the customers."

"And when did this happen?"

The more mature Asian lady came to the counter. "Three days ago. She not here. You go. You go now."

Elliot understood their motive. Having a stranger around asking questions wasn't good for business. "Thanks for your help," he said. After that he walked away.

Outside in the truck, Elliot made a note to have vice check the place out. However, as he pulled onto the roadway, an idea that he should check the local hospitals came to mind.

On the way, he called Carmen, but again got her answering service. He left a message, asking her to call.

Seconds later his phone lit up. It was Carmen.

"Hey," Elliot said, "I'm glad you called. Look, I'm sorry about the situation earlier, but I'm on a case."

Fear laced Carmen's voice. "It's Wayne. He didn't show up for school this morning, and he hasn't come home. I don't know where he is. I don't know what to do."

A car horn sounded. Elliot had swerved into the next lane. He slowed the truck, pulled off 11th Street, and parked against the curb. He fought to get the air back into his lungs. "Where are you?"

"At City Hall, in Chief Stanton's office."

"You did the right thing," Elliot said. "I'll be there as soon as I can."

"I know where Wayne was trying to go," Carmen said. "His friend, Jimmy Snider, got to feeling bad about it and told me. He meant to visit his... his stepfather. I called Anthony. He hasn't seen him. He didn't make it, Kenny. I don't know where he is."

Elliot gripped the steering wheel of the truck. "Does he have his phone with him?"

"Yes, I think so, but he does not answer."

"Do you have tracking enabled?"

"I did not think it was necessary."

"That's all right. The phone's probably GPS equipped. Even if it isn't, the provider should be able to narrow down its position based on the towers it's closest to."

"I do not know how to do any of that."

"Chief Stanton's probably already on it, but if he isn't, ask him to get started. I'll see what I can do. I'll call you right back."

"The divorce hasn't been easy for him," she said. "He's been quiet about it, holding too much inside. I thought he was doing better. I should have paid more attention."

Elliot struggled to fend off the hundreds of *what if* situations threatening to paralyze his concentration. He did not want to show a lack of confidence. Carmen had enough to worry about. "I'll find him, Carmen. I'll need Davenport's address."

Carmen tried to keep her voice flat and monotone, but emotion still leaked through.

After receiving the information Elliot disconnected. Anthony Davenport lived in Siloam Springs, Arkansas, just off of Highway 412.

Carmen said Wayne wasn't answering his phone, but Elliot tried it, just to be sure.

"Who's there?"

Recognition of the hushed voice went through Elliot like an electrical current. It was Wayne. A roaring sound filled the background. An answer of *your father* formed in Elliot's thoughts, though he did not speak the words. "It's Mr. Elliot." That was what Wayne called him, the name he knew him by.

"Oh, man, am I glad it's you."

A dull pain started in Elliot's stomach and spread through him. He recalled holding the boy close after he'd found him hiding in the closet a few months ago, terrified by an attacker who'd taken his mother hostage. He'd suffered too much pain in his young life. "Are you all right?"

"Sort of."

"What does that mean, Wayne?"

"I did something really stupid. I was on the road and this truck driver picked me up. I'm inside his truck."

Cold beads of perspiration formed on Elliot's forehead. An old memory of finding his mother cold and stiff in her bed snaked through his mind. A similar empty and lost feeling had formed in his stomach. "Is he there? Does he know you're talking to me?"

"No. I'm in the back. It's kind of like an RV, only hooked to the truck. I don't think he can hear me back here. At least I hope not."

The air seemed to seep out of the cab of Elliot's pickup. "Has he done anything to you, hurt you in anyway?"

"No, but he's kind of weird. I don't like the way he looks at me."

Elliot started the pickup and pulled onto the roadway. "Have you asked the driver to pull over and let you out?"

"Yeah. I told him I had to go to the bathroom, but he wouldn't stop. There's a bathroom back here, though, so maybe he isn't crazy. I just don't know."

Elliot turned onto Highway 44 and headed east. "You're doing fine. Do you know where you are, or where the truck is going?"

"Not really. I told him I wanted to go to Arkansas, but I don't know if that's what he's doing."

"Is there a window or something you can look through?"

"There's one by the dining table, and a door, too, but I don't know if it'll open or not."

"Can you get to the window without drawing the driver's attention?"

"I don't know. There's a curtain hanging across the entrance to the truck, so maybe he won't see me."

"All right," Elliot said. "Here's what I want you to do. Act casual, but move over to the window, nice and easy like you're just looking around."

Seconds later, Wayne said, "Okay, I made it. Now what?"

"Look through the window and tell me what you see."

"Just the side of the road and a bunch of trees and stuff."

"How about signs that tell you what road you're on, or what city you're near?"

"I don't see any now, but earlier I did, when I asked the driver to stop."

Elliot passed several other cars on the highway, going faster than he should. "You're doing fine. Do you remember if a town or a city was listed?"

"Nah, just a blue sign showing there was a travel stop."

"How about an exit number?"

"A what?"

"The roads leading off the highway are usually numbered. It would've been on the sign that advertised the travel stop."

"I don't remember seeing any numbers."

"That's okay. Tell me what the land looks like. Are there a lot of hills, or is it mostly flat?"

"Wait a minute," Wayne said. "I can see a house now."

"Can you tell me what it looks like?"

"It's a white one, and kind of old. Now we're slowing down."

Elliot's throat tightened. Thoughts of what to do next scrambled through his head. "All right, Wayne. If the truck stops, try the door you told me about. It might be locked. If you can get it open, get out of there. Run as fast as you can. Don't let the man catch you. I know you can do it."

"Yes, sir, but I don't think he means to stop. Nope, he's turning. We're getting off this road and going onto another one."

"Tell me what you see."

"Cars, trucks and gas pumps. He's stopping all right. I'm going to do what you said."

The phone went dead.

Elliot stared through the windshield of the truck and tried to clear his mind except for thoughts of Wayne, and just let it happen, a process he wasn't accustomed to. He'd always tried to fight it. He pressed the accelerator pedal to the floor. Maybe it was nothing more than memories triggered by Wayne's description of what he'd seen through the window of the truck sleeper, but images that had been forming in his mind solidified. He knew Wayne's location. It seemed fantastic, but the last couple of days had been filled with instances blurring the boundaries of credible thought. Fifteen minutes later, a time span in which Elliot was all too aware that much could happen, he turned onto Highway 69, just south of Chouteau, Oklahoma, then wheeled into the travel stop located just past the exit.

Elliot skidded to a stop beside the tractor trailer rig. It was the only one with an oversized sleeper. He jumped out of the pickup and started toward the rig.

Wayne came around the front of the rig, a tall but slender man flanking him, his hand on Wayne's shoulder.

Elliot quickened his pace, an approach that would put him on the right side of the man, away from Wayne. He'd already chosen his strategy. A body shot would put him down, and from there Elliot would destroy him.

Wayne broke free and ran toward Elliot. "I had it all wrong, Mr. Elliot. Jim wasn't trying to hurt me."

Elliot stroked Wayne's head then fell to one knee and pulled him close, taking in the scent of his hair and the feel of his heartbeat. "Are you all right? You don't have to be afraid now. Tell me the truth."

"I'm okay, honest."

Elliot turned his attention to the trucker and rose to his feet. "I don't know what kind of game you're playing here, but you need to start explaining yourself, and you need to do it fast."

The trucker took a step back. "Now hold on, mister. I was just trying to teach the boy a lesson. I ran away myself when I was about his age. Really messed up my life. When I saw the boy walking along the highway, I knew something wasn't right, so I picked him up. We got to talking and I realized I'd pegged the problem on the head. Like I said, I was a kid once. If I'd started preaching to him, it wouldn't have done any good. I figured I'd drive him around, give him time to think about it. Later, I'd drop him off with the cops, or have him call his folks or something. I admit it sounds crazy, now that I hear myself saying it, but it's the honest to God truth."

Elliot studied the man's face then looked at Wayne.

He nodded his agreement.

Elliot tried to look stern, but he couldn't pull it off. He was too happy to see the boy. "Why didn't you call and tell me everything was all right?"

Wayne shrugged. "When the truck stopped, I did what you said. I got the side door open and ran for it." He pulled the remains of his phone from his pocket. "I dropped it and it busted on the concrete."

"You could have used the phone inside the store, or borrowed the driver's."

Wayne looked at the ground, a flash of red coming across his face. "Mom programmed my numbers a long time ago. Without the phone, I couldn't remember any of them."

Elliot pulled his phone and clicked on Carmen's number. As soon as she answered, he said, "I found Wayne. I'm bringing him home."

He handed the phone to Wayne then returned his attention to the driver. "I hope you realize something like this could end your career and ruin your life."

The driver nodded. "I can be real stupid at times."

"You might not want my advice, but don't do anything like this again."

"You got my word on that."

"Heaven forbid there should be a next time," Elliot said, "but if there is, call the authorities."

"Yes, sir. I'll do that, for sure."

Wayne was still talking on the phone.

Elliot helped the boy into the pickup. After getting inside, he pulled onto highway 69 and headed south toward Porter.

Wayne stopped talking and handed the phone back, his head drooped, ready for another lecture.

A menagerie of words and phrases tumbled inside of Elliot's head, but what came out was, "I love you, Wayne."

Wayne shot a glance at Elliot then fixed his gaze on the floorboard.

Fumbling for his footing, Elliot continued with, "You scared your mother. She's going to be pretty upset for a few days."

Wayne looked up, his eyes flicking back and forth. "It seemed to make sense at the time. But all I did was make things worse."

Elliot thought about trying to explain the divorce—It's not your fault, people change and grow apart—but he figured he'd bungle it, so he settled for, "Don't be so hard on yourself."

"Thanks, but it was a dumb thing to do. I know that now."

A few hundred feet ahead, a black, horse-drawn buggy left the safety of a side road, its Amish driver coaxing the horse into a fast trot across the highway.

Elliot wondered what it might be like, living inside such a subculture, and if their clinging to the past and simple ways effectively insulated them from the problems of the world. In some ways, he suspected, it might, but like any society they were bound to have their share of insanity. "Let's just say you're extremely lucky it turned out the way it did."

"Mom's gonna kill me."

"Most likely," Elliot said. A smile turned the corners of his mouth. "I'd try to smooth things out for you, soften the blow, but I'm not exactly in good graces with your mother either."

"You got it all wrong," Wayne said, "She likes you a lot. She never says as much, but I can tell. She wants you to be my...."

Wayne stopped short of finishing the sentence.

A few seconds later, Elliot said, "You're a good boy, Wayne."

"I'm glad somebody thinks so."

"Don't be so hard on yourself. Yes, your mother is upset with you, but only because she loves you. Anyway, I'm proud of you."

He looked up, his eyes reflecting the question before he spoke it. "For running away?"

"No, not for that, but for the reason you did it. And just for being you."

Wayne shook his head. "I'm not sure I understand, but thanks. And I got it all wrong. I was so scared back there in that sleeper. I've done some dumb things before, but I really iced the cake this time."

"The next time you get some wild idea," Elliot said, "give me a call before you do anything. I have a lot of experience with the consequences of doing dumb things."

Wrinkles formed briefly across Wayne's forehead. After thinking it over, he smiled. "Thanks for coming to get me. How did you know where I was, anyway?"

Elliot tightened his grip on the steering wheel. "Just lucky, I guess."

Chapter Twenty-One

After taking Wayne home and visiting with Carmen, Elliot resumed the investigation. His suspicion turned out to be right. He found Angela Gardner in a semi-private room at St. Francis, an IV feeding clear liquid into her arm. Even though her eyes were half closed and her movements sluggish, she appeared cognizant.

Elliot approached the bed and asked Angela what she'd undoubtedly already been asked several times. "How are you feeling?"

"I'm not sure," she said.

"You probably don't remember me, but the name's Kenny Elliot. We met briefly in college."

A puzzled expression crossed her face. "I do know you. You were the one in the truck at the library. I saw you, but you couldn't see me. At least that's the way it seemed. I'd thought it was a dream."

Perspiration formed on Elliot's hands and he wiped them against his pant legs. He could rule out insanity now. Angela had just confirmed that she, at least in some form, had been inside his truck when he'd sensed her presence.

The doctor came into the room. She brushed past Elliot and smiled at Angela. "How are we doing today?"

Angela didn't answer.

The doctor took some readings. Later, she motioned for Elliot to follow her into the hallway. Stopping a few feet outside the room she said, "I'm Doctor Shaffer. Are you related to the patient?"

"No. Name's Elliot. I'm a friend of the family."

A quizzical expression formed on the doctor's face. "I called you out here because you seemed to be communicating with the patient."

"Is that a problem?"

"Not at all, but she hasn't talked to anyone since she got here, except for you."

Elliot rubbed his temples. "We met a few years ago, but it was brief and informal. I guess a bit of recognition was all she needed. If you don't mind my asking, how did she get here, to the hospital I mean?"

Doctor Shaffer raised one eyebrow. "What exactly are you doing here, Mr. Elliot?"

"Angela and her parents had a falling out a few years ago. They haven't seen her in a while, and they asked me to find her. Looks like I did."

The doctor stuffed something into her pocket. "She walked in and passed out in our waiting room. We almost lost her."

"What's wrong with her?"

"She had high levels of Valium and Chlorpromazine in her system."

Elliot ran the name through his memory but nothing came up. "I'm not familiar with the last one. Could you explain?"

"Certainly, but I'd like to know who I'm talking with. Are you a police officer?"

Elliot leaned against the wall. Why did everyone seem to know he was a cop? Had his association with the business changed his appearance, or did his actions give him away? He showed his badge. "I'm a detective with the Tulsa Police Department. But I'm here unofficially. It's a private matter."

Again Doctor Shaffer analyzed Elliot. "Chlorpromazine is a drug used to treat the symptoms of schizophrenia."

"Are you saying Angela is schizophrenic?"

The doctor shook her head. "We don't know. She didn't have any identification, and no additional medication or a prescription with her. We've been calling the local psychiatrists, but no one's claimed her as a patient. I've scheduled a neurological. Doctor Van Zandt, one of our resident psychiatrists, said he'd visit with her tonight."

Elliot watched a nurse roll someone past. The wheels of the gurney squeaked against the tiled floor. Schizophrenic behavior might explain a few things. "Her name is Angela Gardner."

The doctor jotted the information down. "Could you help us get in touch with a family member, or a relative?"

Elliot recalled the conversation he'd had with George and Emma Gardner. They'd be delighted he had found their daughter. "Her parents live here in town. It won't be a problem."

Doctor Shaffer smiled. "Now let's see if you can get the patient to talk again."

Elliot walked into Angela's room, the doctor following close behind.

Angela's eyelids fluttered open. "Are you an angel?" She asked, directing the question toward Elliot.

"We met in college," Elliot said. "Your memory is just a little foggy. It'll come back to you."

"Why are you here? What do you want with me?"

Elliot glanced at the wrinkled sheets of Angela's bed. He didn't wish to cause her any more stress, but she needed to know. "I met with your parents earlier today. They want to see you. They want you to come home, Angela."

Angela said nothing, but her arm slid from beneath the covers and when she found Elliot's hand her cold fingers wrapped around it. "If you think I should."

The doctor put a hand on Elliot's shoulder and nodded.

Elliot pulled his notepad and jotted down the address and phone number for Mr. and Mrs. Gardner. He tore off the page and handed it to Doctor Shaffer.

"I appreciate your help, Detective."

"No problem."

"Angela," Doctor Shaffer asked, "Are you under the care of a doctor?"

"Am I going to die?"

"I'd say you have a good chance of walking out of here soon. You need to take it easy on the Valium, though, and whatever else you've been taking. You might not be so lucky next time."

Angela seemed to ignore the doctor, but again spoke to Elliot. "What did you say your name was again?"

"Detective Kenny Elliot."

"You're a cop?"

"I'm here as a friend, but I would like to ask you some questions."

"All right, but if it's about college, I don't remember much about those days."

"Do you remember meeting me?"

"My roommate, Amy, got us involved with the spiritualism stuff. It was okay at first, but it turned ugly and dark."

"What about Professor David Stephens?"

A smile found its way across her face. "How is David?"

"He's not with the school anymore. Do you know where I can find him?"

"He was so nice. It didn't work out, though."

Elliot glanced at Doctor Shaffer. "What did you mean when you said it got dark and ugly?"

"They talk to me, try to make me do things."

"Who talks to you, Angela?"

She put a finger to her lips and shook her head.

Elliot rubbed his temples. From what little he knew about paranoid schizophrenia, Angela certainly seemed to be exhibiting the symptoms. And, if she'd had the affliction a few years, it would explain her behavior on campus back then as well.

Again Angela reached out and grasped Elliot's hand. "When I saw you earlier today, I wasn't dreaming, Kenny. I was dead. I know because I've experienced it before, with the voices, more than a lack of light, even an opposition to it. Do you have relatives, Kenny?"

"Sure," Elliot said, though a real family was something he'd never had. "Why do you ask?"

"When I was young, I stayed with my Aunt Kathryn one summer. I don't know why, but she found a church and she asked me to go with her. It was my only experience with church. I think it might have been that way for her as well. Anyway, we went every Sunday, until I went back home. Whenever the darkness came, I would think about Aunt Kathy, and the church. I don't want it to take me. Can someone like me be saved?"

Elliot squeezed Angela's hand, and though he wondered how he might explain what he barely understood, the words came out easily. "Yes. Of course you can."

"There's a lot missing, chunks of time that I can't remember. I don't know what all I've done, but I think it has something to do with your friend, the one with the dark eyes and black hair."

Elliot tore his gaze from Angela and visually swept the room.

There was no one except for Doctor Shaffer, who had stayed in the room but had remained silent.

He released Angela's hand and went to the door.

The hallway was busy with people, but none who fit the description of the person Angela was talking about.

She was referring to Laura. Elliot went back to Angela's bedside. "I don't see anyone. When was she here?"

"Just seconds ago."

Elliot strolled to the window and stared at the cars below.

A grey colored Infinity, one similar to the car he'd seen cruising past George and Emma Gardner's house, glided across the parking lot and pulled onto the roadway.

Chapter Twenty-Two

Elliot flipped on the lamp beside the bed, and though he saw no one, the notion lingered, unwilling to be dispelled by mere visual verification.

Someone had been in the room, hovering over the bed, just inches from his face.

After leaving Angela at the hospital, Elliot had driven home with the intention of grabbing a shower and a quick nap. Carmen had planned on an evening together, but a glance at the clock showed he'd slept through the night. It was 6:00 AM.

Something clanked against the house, followed by footsteps thudding across the backyard.

Elliot scrambled from the bed and struggled into a pair of pants. He grabbed the .38, a secondary weapon he kept in the drawer of the nightstand, and stepped quickly from the bedroom. When he reached the breakfast area behind the kitchen, he unlatched the patio door and stepped outside.

The footsteps continued on the west side of the house.

The prowler was on the run and moving fast. Elliot followed the sound, but when he reached the area, the gate swung open and banged against the fence.

A black silhouette ran through it and across the front yard.

By the time Elliot reached the driveway, the distinctive sound of an automobile pulling away from the curb sent a shiver up his spine. It was the roar of the Infinity.

Elliot turned and ran toward his pickup, digging into his pockets for the keys, reprimanding himself for leaving them in the house. But the truck wasn't going to be the way he caught the intruder.

As if it had been crippled from overuse, the truck leaned lower on one side.

Elliot ran his hand across the fender of the truck, a curious understanding playing around the edges of his consciousness. Someone had let the air out of the tires, and he had a pretty good idea who it was. Angela indicated someone fitting Laura's description had been in her room. He'd watched someone leave the parking lot of the hospital, driving the grey Infiniti. Even more curious, Elliot connected the incident to a story Terri Benson had told him. She'd once followed Gerald to find out where he'd been going at night. He'd driven to a small house located a few miles from the university, where he met with his new love. If Laura Bradford had indeed been resurrected, he would find her at the small house in Stillwater.

A few minutes later, Elliot fired up the Harley and drove out of the neighborhood. He took Highway 169 to 412 and headed west.

Chapter Twenty-Three

Terri Benson had remembered the incident in detail. Not only had she given Elliot the address, but directions as well. Elliot had caught her at the trailer court, where she lived with Mr. Tattoo.

The old sandstone structure Terri had described occupied a piece of ground among a clump of maple trees.

Elliot shut off the bike and leaned it against the kickstand. In the front yard of the nearest house, a man sat on an overturned bucket, working on a black 1959 Chevrolet, a bumper jack holding up the driver's side wheel.

Hoping to get some information, Elliot strolled over to the neighbor. The name on the mailbox read Walter Shelby.

He stopped working and looked up. "Something I can do for you, son?"

"I hope so," Elliot said. "Do you know who owns the property next door?"

The man, who wore striped bib overalls, glanced at the old house. "Why do you want to know?"

"I'm looking for a friend who used to live there."

He shook his head. "That old place has been empty for a long time, son."

"She was a Native American girl," Elliot said, "about eighteen or nineteen at the time."

He put a four-way lug wrench on the last nut, spun it loose and dropped the nut into a hubcap. After that, he removed the wheel.

"Her name was Laura Bradford."

He rolled another tire and rim around, lined up the holes, and lifted it into place. Using the four-way, he secured the wheel with the lug nuts.

"It's important," Elliot said. "Do you remember her?"

A nervous look slid across the man's face. "I couldn't tell you one way or the other about the name, but I know who you're talking about." He stood and pulled a shop towel from his back pocket and wiped his hands. "I used to see her out there in the backyard at night. She'd light a fire and move around like she was dancing or something." He stuffed the rag back into his pocket.

"Would you mind if I had a look around?"

"Permission isn't mine to give. Don't know who owns it either. But I can tell you this. Several people stopped and looked around over there after your girlfriend left. None of them stayed for more than five or ten minutes. After awhile, they just stopped coming."

He gathered his tools and started toward his garage. "I got curious about it once. Now, I'm a God fearing man, son. But there's something not right about the place. You can feel it when you walk through the door."

"Thanks," Elliot said. He turned and walked toward the abandoned property. When he reached the front entrance, a once white-painted door with three rectangular windows, he thought about Mr. Shelby's warning. He shook his head and shoved open the door, stepping inside the house where Laura Bradford had lived.

Standing in the hollow of the living room, Elliot had the unsettling notion that the air from outside remained there because its counterpart had become different, inhospitable. Even the light trickling in through the open doorway seemed reluctant in its intrusion. Wide planks of oak flooring stretched the length of the house, while intricate crown moldings, also carved from oak defined the ceiling. Arched doorways separated the dining area from the living room and the kitchen. No beer cans littered the area, no graffiti decorated the walls, and no makeshift sleeping-quarters crowded the corners.

If Elliot hadn't known better, he might've thought the prior occupants had stuffed their belongings into the back of a truck late last night and left to avoid past due rent.

Barely visible, prints of mud showed someone had come part way into the house only to stop and turn back.

Elliot suspected the footprints were those of Walter Shelby. Fighting an urge to follow Shelby's lead, he walked deeper into the living room until a doorway along the north wall caught his attention.

The passageway led Elliot into another room where the window shades had been drawn.

Elliot found his flashlight and switched it on.

The light fell across more blank walls and empty flooring.

The next area was a bathroom with two doors connecting it to both bedrooms. Wallpaper with a pattern of pink and blue flowers decorated the walls, and a medicine cabinet with a mirrored door clung to the wall above the sink.

When Elliot opened the medicine cabinet, although no toiletries sat upon the glass shelves, the aroma of bath powder filled the air. The odor did not diminish as Elliot left the area but became stronger, strengthened even with a hint of perfume.

Elliot stepped into the back bedroom and the light fell across something.

Having moved the beam in a wide sweep, Elliot jerked the light back to the corner.

A small writing desk caught the light and reflected it back.

Using the flashlight, Elliot applied upward pressure to a corner of the desk, lifting the writing surface.

The action revealed a storage area beneath the lid.

He pushed the top higher, causing the sliding hinge to lock into place. Repositioning the light, he shined it into the storage tray.

An issue of the *Stillwater News Press*, the local newspaper, lay folded in the desk. The date indicated it had been printed eight years ago, approximately three weeks before Laura showed up on campus.

Elliot picked up the paper and scanned an article that had been sectioned off, bracketed by the black markings of an ink pen.

The article talked about a band of people, drifters who'd started a commune near Stillwater, only to abandon the place. It wasn't detailed, nothing much more than a side note, but someone, probably Laura, had found it significant. It struck a note with Elliot as well, reminding him of what was happening in Tulsa.

Even though the room had become noticeably colder, a bead of sweat fell from Elliot's forehead and dropped onto the yellowed newsprint. He remembered hearing about it. Some of the students had joked, others had worried, but beneath it all had been a suspicion of the events being underplayed.

From the bottom of the desk tray yet another newspaper glared at him.

Placing the Stillwater paper on the floor, Elliot took the next paper and brought it close.

Originating a few days after the vintage *News Press* issue, *The Daily O'Collegian*, a university press, covered the same story.

Elliot's throat went dry. The college piece had been written by his old friend, Stanley Gerald Reynolds III. He'd put a more sinister spin on the story, pointing out that the drifters had left under curious circumstances, leaving behind pets, clothing, even food in ice chests.

The thought that the newspapers could be evidence and should be left alone had not escaped Elliot, but a lingering question took precedence. Had Laura been fascinated by the unusual events of the case, or was it the coverage itself publicity for her own acts that had intrigued her?

Elliot found his notepad and copied the dates and issue numbers of the papers. He also recorded the name of the investigating officer. He returned the papers to the desk and walked into the dining room.

In the darkened area defined by archways, a sound faint and yet unnerving whispered from the kitchen.

Elliot mentally reprimanded himself for letting his guard down. He had his back to an unsearched area. He drew the Glock and whirled around.

No immediate danger presented itself, no intruders hiding in the corners, no armed suspects, and yet all was not ordinary. As if they were attempting to emphasize that there was nothing else to see, the drawers and cabinets of the kitchen hung open.

Elliot entered the room, wondering if the anomaly before him had been caused by vandals, although Walter Shelby said no one had been inside the house for any appreciable amount of time since Laura Bradford had left. He strolled across the kitchen and peered through the window of the backdoor.

Past the screened porch, near the northwest corner of the property, a massive oak grew, and beneath it a pile of rocks shaped like a pyramid protruded from the weeds.

Elliot decided he would check it later. He turned and walked back through the dining area to the living room. As he neared the front entrance, the atmosphere seemed to thicken, even to the point of resistance, as if each step maneuvered through the slush of dreams.

The dream-like quality escalated when he found the front door closed. He'd intentionally left it open.

Elliot wrapped his fingers around the glass doorknob and twisted, but it did not turn. He stowed the flashlight and used both hands, but the door, as if it had not been used in years and was frozen in place, would not move.

Leaning against the door, Elliot struggled for breath. The idea of Laura luring him here to die permeated his thoughts. He strode through the house to the kitchen exit. Once there, he grabbed the knob and twisted.

With ease, the latch released and the door swung open.

Elliot scrambled across the threshold and onto the back porch where the outside air fell over him like water. He pushed open the screened door and stepped into the backyard.

Barely visible beneath the weeds, the remnants of a trail led toward the curious stack of stones near the old oak tree.

Weaving through the tall grass, Elliot followed the pathway until he reached the pile of rock.

Up close, the pyramid more resembled a pile of debris constructed of old bricks and broken pieces of cinderblock. A metal band, approximately one foot tall, encircled the mound.

Elliot recalled Walter Shelby's story about seeing Laura dancing around a campfire. The rocks covered what had once been a fire pit.

From what had been a near motionless atmosphere, wind swirled through the yard. Several limbs broke from the tree and crashed to the ground, and, in a near simultaneous action, a crow flapped to a landing atop the stack of rocks. When the bird landed, the wind stopped. The crow showed no fear, but lingered briefly before jumping to the ground near the base of the fire pit. As if to gain a better visual angle, the crow cocked its head, glancing at Elliot and back to the rock again.

Elliot followed the bird's line of sight, the unusual antics of the crow having drawn his attention.

Something out of place protruded from the haphazard stack of rock.

He leaned down and examined the object.

Confirming his suspicions, a fragment of bone extended from the debris, and a glint of something shiny sparkled through the cracks.

The crow again took flight, its pumping wings spread like black-gloved hands.

Over-riding his logic, Elliot shoved the rocks aside until he reached the bottom of the pit, uncovering what was hidden there.

In the disrupted rock of the fire pit, the skeletal remains of a human lay in scattered disarray, including the hand, which held a silver and turquoise piece of jewelry, an earring with a tiny dream catcher attached.

A chill crawled up Elliot's back. The earring was like those Laura had worn as she'd run past Elliot on the trails of the River Park, and identical to the one he'd pulled from the dirt at the ruins of the old apartment building where Gerald had disappeared.

Cawing again reverberated through the air. The strange bird had returned. From atop the oak tree, with its head cocked in a quizzical manner, through its bottomless black eyes, the bird seemed to ask of Elliot what he intended to do about all of this.

Chapter Twenty-Four

The officer identified himself as Detective William Ryan. He had been the investigating officer for the disappearances depicted in the old newspapers. The detective surveyed the premises, an apprehensive attitude underlying his actions. "First off, I want to know why you just happened to be here at the old house?"

Elliot recognized Ryan. He'd also been the police detective who'd questioned him and his friends after Laura disappeared. He gave Ryan the story, or at least enough of it to explain, then gestured for the detective to follow him to the back of the property. As he made his way through the weeds, Elliot glanced over to see Walter Shelby watching from his front yard. When he reached the fire pit, Elliot showed Ryan the skeletal remains and pointed out the earring.

Ryan squatted and examined the remains, his expression reflecting a mixture of surprise and fear. "Curious," he said, "that you would stumble on to this, and know right where to look. Are you always so intuitive?"

Elliot scanned the oak tree, but the crow was gone. Most people didn't think to ask about his intuition. "I saw something glistening through the rocks. It turned out to be the earring."

"Tell me again why you were here in the first place."

"I came looking for Laura Bradford. I didn't really expect to find her, especially not like this."

"How do you know it's Ms. Bradford? You seem awfully sure of yourself."

"It's the earring," Elliot said. "She wore them the last time I saw her."

"You have a pretty good memory. What was it, eight or nine years ago? Yeah, I remember you. I had my doubts about you even then."

Elliot turned and started toward the house. "There's something else you need to see."

Elliot led Ryan into the house, and when they reached the desk in the back bedroom, he showed the detective the newspapers.

Ryan scanned both papers, his jaw tightening.

"When you came on campus to investigate Laura's disappearance," Elliot said, "your demeanor indicated you thought it was a waste of time. But someone from your department heard about some strange things happening on campus and thought it might be related. You should have stuck with it. It seems they were right."

A smirk crawled across Ryan's face. "As I recall, you kids were pretty guarded about your answers. I thought you were just being protective of your spooky antics. Maybe I was wrong."

"The dean scared us, threatened us with expulsion. Told us to drop it and let the school handle it."

"Are you telling me the dean was involved?"

Elliot shook his head. "He was just trying to do his job."

Some of the color drained from Ryan's face as he tapped the newspaper in his hand. "It's time you leveled with me."

"I'm trying to," Elliot said. "Laura Bradford was rapidly becoming my prime suspect. Looks like she's cleared herself."

Ryan jerked a thumb toward the backyard. "But what happened here? Who did this?"

"There must have been a connection between what was happening on campus and the disappearance of those drifters. Laura got too close to the truth and it got her killed."

"And what about Stanley Reynolds?" Ryan asked. "Is he another missing person, or are you saying he's the killer?"

He cuts their hearts out. That's what they say.

"I don't know," Elliot said. "I haven't covered enough ground, but when the case goes official, I'd like to count on your cooperation."

Detective Ryan frowned. "Well, let's see. Out of your little group of ghost hunters, who by your own admission had something to do with all of this, one is dead, one is missing, and one is in the hospital. And then there's you. What happens in Tulsa is your problem, Detective. But this is my town, my case."

Elliot started to reply but changed his mind. He turned and walked away, leaving Ryan alone in the house. When he reached the drive, he straddled the Harley, pulled his phone and called Dombrowski.

"Elliot. I'm glad it's you. The car you called in about, the old Cadillac."

Elliot studied the patrol car in the drive. The captain's voice sounded tired. "Yeah, what about it?"

"It was gone when the wrecker got there. The old guy whose house it was parked in front of said someone came along right after you left and drove off in it."

"Did the witness get a description?"

"Not really. Say, you don't suppose it could've been your old school buddy, the one who's missing?"

Elliot had known Dombrowski's thinking would eventually come around to that.

"When are you coming back to work?"

"I don't know, Bill. This might take some time."

A city vehicle pulled into the drive behind Elliot, while another parked alongside the roadway. "Have you excavated the old house site?"

"No, you haven't given me enough to justify it."

"I'm working on it. Anyway, I just found the missing girlfriend. She's dead, been that way for a while. What's more, she disappeared around the same time a group of drifters went missing from the Stillwater area. There are a lot of similarities."

"Similarities to what?"

Elliot watched Detective Ryan come from the backyard and hurry to his car. He had a spooked look on his face. "Their social status, the way they disappeared."

"That doesn't tell me much."

"The killer is targeting homeless people with little to no family connections."

"Your friend was dating a homeless person?"

"Laura wasn't homeless. It's what she knew that got her killed. Gerald knew something about it, too. I don't know why he waited until now to start looking into it, but he must have believed the same thing was happening in Tulsa."

"You're not making sense, Elliot."

"The murders aren't being reported."

"What murders? The only evidence you've found belongs to your old buddy's girlfriend. That doesn't look good for him, does it? And why wouldn't the murders, if there were any, be reported?"

"Because of who the victims were. Some of the other street people might talk among themselves, wondering what happened to so and so, but their curiosity wouldn't be stirred much. They're a transient subculture, and they'd figure their buddy had simply moved on."

"But sooner or later somebody would run across something."

"Maybe, unless the killer is disposing of the bodies and there's nothing left to find."

"How do you know all of this, Elliot?"

"I've asked a few questions here and there."

"I hope you're not making a nuisance of yourself with the local authorities."

"I wouldn't dream of it. Hey, I got to go. I'll get back with you."

Elliot disconnected, then crawled off the bike and walked over to Detective Ryan's car and tapped on the window. When Ryan rolled it down, Elliot handed him a business card. "Sorry to drag all of this up for you. If there's anything I can do to help, give me a call."

"Just remember what I said."

"Not a problem. Could I bother you with one more suggestion?"

After a brief period of silence, Ryan said, "What is it?"

"If you want to get to the bottom of this, you should find Professor David Stephens and bring him in for questioning."

Ryan's jaw twitched, his lips drew tight. "I'll take it under consideration."

"Why does this case make you so defensive, Ryan? Or are you always this hard to get along with?"

"Go home, Detective Elliot. Don't make me tell you again."

Elliot turned and walked away. Ryan was going to be a problem, but he couldn't leave town, not just yet.

Chapter Twenty-Five

Elliot fired up the Harley and drove out of the neighborhood, leaving Ryan and his team to deal with what he'd found behind the old house. The investigation had taken a turn. He had no doubt the remains belonged to Laura. Terri Benson had said Laura had lived in the house, and Walter Shelby, who lived next door, had confirmed it. In addition, Shelby had often seen Laura in the backyard near the fire pit. All of that added to the distinctive earrings made it pretty clear. The question was: Why had her ghost come back to stir all of this up again?

Elliot twisted the grip of the Harley, and as the bike's speed increased he wondered what Dombrowski might do in such a situation.

The captain would act like a cop and go after the prime suspects, which should be Gerald's wife, Cheryl, and her boyfriend, Darrel Bogner. But these were not ordinary circumstances, and Dombrowski would agree with Detective Ryan and tell him to get back home and stop poking around in someone else's backyard.

That was not a plan of action Elliot could live with. He considered dropping by the manufacturing plant Bogner owned, but instead he followed another route. He drove to Harry's Place, the bar where he'd talked with Terri Benson. It turned out to be a good decision. Bogner's Mercedes was parked on the south side of the building.

Elliot slowed the Harley and pulled off the road, coming to a stop on the gravel lot beside another bike. He climbed off and made it halfway across the lot before someone grabbed his left arm.

The hand belonged to a tall, lean fellow with long hair. "That's my spot you're taking."

Elliot twisted free of the man's grip. "I'll only be a minute."

A grin turned the corners of the man's mouth. "I told you to move the bike. In fact, I don't even want you around here. So crawl back on your ride and get the hell on down the road."

Elliot didn't have time to waste on some washed-out biker. He opened his jacket and showed the biker his shoulder holster. "I got business here."

The biker's grin did not fade, but he held both hands up, like he was being robbed. "All right. I'm feeling generous anyway. Go ahead on... do your thing."

Elliot closed his jacket and walked into the bar. He found Bogner leaning against a standup table, flirting with some women who were trying to shoot pool.

"You're just who I was looking for," Elliot said. "We didn't finish our conversation about Stanley Reynolds."

Bogner frowned. "I got nothing to say to you." He leaned over to one of the pool-playing ladies. "If I kick this idiot's ass, will you give me a kiss?"

The lady giggled.

Bogner slammed his beer down on the table and came forward.

The move surprised Elliot. Bogner came at him from a slight angle, not something a rookie would do. But Bogner carried a false sense of security. He'd been to a few dances, might've even made it to the floor a few times, but, like most novices, if the music got complicated he'd quickly lose the beat. Elliot faked right with his head but took a step to his left.

The movement caught Bogner off guard, and his right-cross bulleted through the air, missing its mark. His surprised face hung over his left shoulder like a target.

Elliot planted a straight right halfway between lawn-boy's forehead and his nose.

Bogner let out a wail and stumbled backward, reinforcing his lack of experience by covering his busted nose with both hands, leaving his body exposed and unprotected.

Elliot had been right about Bogner. He was no newcomer to trouble, but, being a big guy, he'd relied on the advantage, leaving his fighting skills at a rudimentary level. Elliot lowered his hands. Even though he'd taken an immediate dislike to Darrel Bogner, he didn't have the heart to continue. It was just too easy. Instead, he pinned him against the wall. "Welcome to Saturday night, lawn-boy. Now, do we talk, or should I ask the band to strike up another tune?"

"What do you want from me?"

"The truth, lover boy."

"No big deal. I'm not going to lie to you. So I've been doing the bad thing with your friend's wife. You want me to stay away from her? You got it. Problem solved, right?"

"It's a little late, don't you think?"

"What are you saying?"

Elliot shoved him harder against the wall. "A fling wasn't enough for you. You wanted it all. So you killed Reynolds to get him out of the way."

Bogner's complexion became a mixture of white and pink splotches. "You got it all wrong. I didn't kill nobody. Why do you want to go and say something like that?"

"Oh, I don't know. Maybe it's because you were sleeping with his wife. You were seen fighting with him. You fired him from his job."

"I didn't do it. I swear to God."

"It's all pointing in your direction, slick."

"I know how it looks, but I let Stan go because he deserved it. To be honest, I think the guy must have snapped or something."

"What makes you say that?"

"He'd been acting all crazy, you know, not doing his job, and all the talk about curses and stuff. What's a guy supposed to think?"

"Don't toy with me, Bogner."

"Okay, okay. I'll level with you. Cheryl asked me about it once."

Elliot loosened his grip. "Are you telling me Cheryl Reynolds asked you to kill her husband?"

"That's not what I'm saying. She asked me about it, that's all. I told her it was stupid. It's all about some dumb prenuptial thing. I don't know the details. She didn't want no divorce, said it wasn't a viable option."

"You better be playing it straight, Bogner. That kind of testimony could put somebody away."

"I didn't kill anybody. That's all I'm trying to tell you."

"Maybe she got somebody else to do it."

A mixture of worry and doubt showed on Bogner's face. "I don't think so. I told her it was a dumb idea. She's just blowing smoke anyway. That's what I think."

Elliot felt a tap on his shoulder.

"Hey, brother, need any help?"

It was the biker.

"Thanks, but the situation is under control."

"You might want to reconsider," the biker said. He pointed toward the door.

Two uniformed officers had come into the bar.

"Just keep your head down," the biker said, "and follow me."

At the moment, complying with the biker seemed to be Elliot's best plan of action. He shrugged and walked behind the stranger, keeping his gaze fixed on the floor as he passed the officers.

Outside the club, the biker climbed onto his own Harley, fired it up and headed south.

Elliot didn't know if it was out of curiosity, wondering who the biker was and why he'd helped, or just a gut feeling the guy knew something about Gerald, but he followed him, staying close on his tail.

A few miles later, the biker pulled off the road onto a concrete parking area in front of a large metal building, a garage or storage unit.

As soon as Elliot pulled into the lot, the biker drove around the building, the sound of his engine coming to a stop seconds later.

Elliot pulled the Glock and checked it for readiness. He slid the weapon back into its holster and coaxed the Harley along the same path his strange new acquaintance had followed.

He found the biker sitting on his ride, lighting a cigarette. He held out the package of smokes, a gesture of sharing.

Elliot shook his head. He understood why the biker had chosen the spot. Due to the positioning of the building and natural growth of trees, nothing behind the garage was visible from the road. Several old engine blocks and a few bike frames made up a small junk pile.

"Thanks for the help," Elliot said. "But why did you do it?"

The biker shrugged. "You pack a wicked right hand. Never seen old Bogner back down so easy."

"His kind usually do when put to the test."

The biker grinned. "Did you have a beef with Bogner, or do you just go around looking for trouble?"

Elliot wasn't sure why he was compelled to level with the biker, but he pulled his badge.

The biker leaned forward and studied the credentials. "A homicide detective? If you're a cop, why did you run back there?"

"I'm a little out of my jurisdiction."

"I didn't know you guys took your turf so seriously."

"It kind of depends on the situation."

"What kind of situation are we talking about?"

Elliot shook his head. "It's your turn to play the identity game."

The biker took a drag on his cigarette. "People call me Jake."

"Is that your name?"

He smiled. "Why wouldn't it be?"

"You tell me. You seem to know Bogner pretty well. What's your connection?"

"I see him at Harry's now and then."

"He a friend of yours?"

"Not exactly."

Elliot studied the terrain while the sound of a passing vehicle filtered through the air. The biker didn't seem to be lying, but he wasn't playing it completely straight either. "Why did you help me out back there?"

"I was under the impression I was honoring the code, helping out a fellow man of the road. Guess I was wrong though."

Elliot smiled. "So what happens now?"

"Hey, anyone who rides a Harley can't be all bad. You might want to stick around a few minutes, though. They're probably looking for you out there."

"Maybe," Elliot said, "but I don't think Bogner told them anything."

"Why wouldn't he?"

"He had a run in with a man named Stanley Reynolds, a guy I'm looking for. While I'm on the subject, does the name Reynolds mean anything to you?"

"Can't say it does."

Elliot repositioned himself on the seat of the Harley. "Are you sure? I thought, with your being friends with Bogner and all, you might know something about his conflict with Mr. Reynolds."

A somber expression came over the biker's face. "I wish I could help, but I can't. Anyway, I'm heading back to the bar. You can tag along if you want."

"I'm not sure I like the plan. Do you have more information to share?"

Jake shrugged. "Keeping beneath the radar seems to work for me. You might give it a try."

"I think I'll pass on the bar."

"Can't say as I blame you," Jake said. When he leaned forward, a silver chain spilled from his shirt. Swinging from it, attached by a silver and turquoise bracket, was an arrowhead.

Elliot glanced at the jewelry. It wasn't unusual in Oklahoma for people to wear such things, but the blend of silver and turquoise piqued Elliot's curiosity. "I once knew a girl who was interested in jewelry like that."

Jake held the arrowhead between his thumb and forefinger, rubbing the artifact. In addition, three silver and turquoise rings decorated his hand. "I'd love to stick around and chat with you, but I really need to be going."

"Her name was Bradford. Laura Bradford. Maybe you knew her?"

"Doesn't ring a bell," Jake said. He kicked the Harley to life and revved it a couple times. After bringing it back to an idle, he added, "Try to stay out of trouble."

Jake twisted the throttle and the Harley lumbered toward the pathway leading back to the road.

Elliot fired up his own ride and did the same, the rear tire of the bike grabbing for traction against the rock and grass as he neared the drive. Jake, the biker, had him puzzled. He wanted to like him, but at the same time, he didn't trust him.

Chapter Twenty-Six

At Eskimo Joe's, a bar and grill in Stillwater, Elliot sat in the area created by an arched section of tinted glass attached to the side of the old rock building on Elm Street. It was where he and his friends used to meet, and he figured Terri Benson would look for him there.

A few minutes later, she showed up, dressed in her usual gothic attire. She tried to smile as she sat, but her pain showed through.

"Thanks for coming," Elliot said. "I ordered you a cheeseburger, like you asked."

She wiggled out of her jacket and hung it on the chair beside her. "Thanks, I'm starved."

Terri's demeanor was different than when Elliot had spoken with her at the bar. An aura of sadness still hung around her, but she seemed sharp and alert, more like the girl he remembered.

"What's up?" she asked.

"I want to ask you about someone I ran into at Harry's, a tall, biker, goes by the name of Jake."

"Yeah, I've seen him there a couple of times."

"What's his story?"

"I don't know really. He's kind of new, hasn't been around for long."

It was pretty much what Elliot had expected. If Jake had been just another bad boy from Stillwater, Terri would've known him, or at least about him.

"Why do you ask? Does he know something about Gerald?"

"I'm not sure. I had a run in with him earlier. Something about him doesn't seem right, but I can't figure out what it is."

"This is where Gerald and I used to eat," Terri said. A look somewhere between hope and despair crossed her face, as she glanced around the room, and when her gaze once again found Elliot's, her eyes glistened. "I can't be here if Laura shows up, especially if Gerald's with her. I'm not strong enough. I wish I could make you understand."

Elliot reached across the table and squeezed Terri's hand. "I can promise you that's not going to happen."

Terri's expression reflected puzzlement, and a current of doubt showed through as well. "What are you trying to tell me?"

"I had a look around the old house outside of town, the one you told me about."

"She's still there, isn't she? You found her."

Elliot averted his eyes and looked at the table. Terri asked the question as if she thought the answer could actually be yes. "She's dead, Terri. Laura Bradford is dead."

"No. You're wrong about that. She was in the car with Gerald."

"You said it was dark. It was someone else."

She shook her head. "I know what I saw."

Elliot took the silver and turquoise earring from his pocket and placed it on the table. He didn't tell Terri he'd found it at the abandoned house site in Tulsa, or that her eyes were not failing her because he and Gerald had also encountered the ghost of Laura Bradford. "I found her remains beneath a stack of rocks behind the old house. I found this, too. It's the same jewelry she was wearing the last time we saw her. Laura didn't disappear back when we were in school. She was murdered."

The hurt in Terri's eyes convinced Elliot to take it one step further. "I didn't tell you earlier but I've recently seen Laura too. Think about it, Terri. When you saw her, did it feel right, or did it seem more than a little odd, even dream-like?"

Terri started to protest but a reflection of realization showed connections were starting to form and a painful question came across her face.

Elliot didn't want to answer it but he had to. "Laura stumbled onto some information someone was willing to kill to protect. Gerald knew something about it, too. Why the killer waited so long to go after him, I don't know. Someone must have started looking into it again."

With the help of tears that had started to form, Terri's fragile and caring face managed to show through her gothic disguise. "What about Gerald? Is he dead, too?"

"I'm sorry, Terri. But it's possible, even likely that he is."

"Why?"

"I haven't pieced it together yet, but it has something to do with Angela Gardner."

After a long period of silence, she said. "We need to find her, don't we?"

Elliot knew Terri had spent time and energy diverting her thoughts away from the past, and now here he was, bringing it all up again. "I already have. She's in the hospital. I tried to talk to her, but she kept drifting in and out of coherency. I got the feeling it was normal for her."

"Angela did it? She killed them?"

"I don't think so. It doesn't feel right."

Terri's pasty complexion lost a little more color. She nodded, a slow up and down motion. "It's Laura, isn't it?"

"Don't be ridiculous," Elliot said.

"I'm not. You said you saw her too."

"I'm a cop, Terri, a homicide detective. A job like that forces you to embrace the tangible side of life."

"Two of our friends are dead and another is in the hospital with mental problems. I get it now. You called this little meeting not to resurrect old times but to warn me that you and I could be next."

Elliot glanced at the table. "I don't want to make things more difficult for you, but the thought has crossed my mind."

"Have you talked to the police? I mean the local guys. They should know about this, right?"

"They know. I spoke with them earlier this morning."

"I don't know why I should worry about it anyway," Terri said. "I mean there's not much cops can do about our kind of problem, is there? Maybe we should call a priest instead."

"Come on, Terri. You're right. I didn't ask you here to talk about old times, and maybe it is a bit of a warning, but I need your help with this. You knew Gerald better than any of us. Is there anything you haven't told me?"

"What do you mean?"

"Did he ever mention archaeology, or Native American artifacts?"

"As a matter of fact, he was fascinated with such things, had a bunch of books and stuff."

Elliot pulled the photocopy of the Aztec knife from his pocket and smoothed it out on the table.

"Yeah," Terri said. "That's the kind of stuff he showed me, all right."

Elliot ran his finger across the photocopy, tracing the outline of the ceremonial knife. "This particular piece was important to Gerald. It was what drew him to Tulsa. Don't ask me how I know. I just do. Do you have any idea why such a knife would mean so much to him?"

"No, but he always got rather quiet, almost stoic when we talked about such things. I always wondered about it. I mean, shouldn't a hobby be something you enjoy?"

"I think it was an obsession," Elliot said. "A passion, not a pastime." He leaned back in his chair. "What about Professor David Stephens, did Gerald ever talk about his involvement, other than being Angela's teacher? No one seems to know where he is. The school's all hushed about it."

"Not that I can remember. Gerald was related to him, though."

Elliot leaned forward. "Related? In what way?"

"His uncle, I think. He wasn't real open about it, but yeah, he mentioned it several times."

Elliot sat back in his chair and stared at the photocopy. "You're right. He never talked much about his family. Did he ever mention anyone else, his mom, or his dad?"

Terri shook her head, a look of both bewilderment and realization coming across her face.

Elliot laid down enough cash to cover the tab. "I need you to do something for me. Go to the police and file a missing person report on Gerald."

"I thought you said he was...."

"I can't prove it yet. Maybe that will at least get them going. I don't think anyone else is going to do it, especially not his wife."

"But if you can't prove it, does that mean there's a chance he's still...?"

Elliot started to say no, but considering the way things were going, he'd gone back to not being sure himself. And if Gerald was still alive, what were the implications? He shook his head. "Anything's possible, but I wouldn't get my hopes up."

Terri's face looked as if she might crumple into tears. "I need to be going, Kenny. Thanks, though, for everything."

Elliot watched her until she disappeared from sight. With the elusive professor fresh on his mind, he called Buddy Wheeler, his old football coach, and asked him if he could dig up anything on David Stephens.

As the traffic rolled by outside the restaurant, he thought about Jake and how he'd seemed a little off the mark of authenticity.

Elliot left Joe's and drove back to the metal building where he and the biker had hidden. He arrived with some luck. The overhead doors were open and a car was parked in the drive.

Inside the metal building, a man stood at a workbench, grinding on a piece of metal.

"Excuse me," Elliot said.

He jerked away from his work. He tore off his goggles and tossed them onto the surface of the workbench. "Something I can do for you, mister?"

"Sorry about the intrusion, but the door was open. I'm looking for someone, a biker named Jake."

He glared at Elliot. "I don't know any Jakes."

To the right of the man, a sink, a refrigerator and a microwave oven made up a small kitchen area. On the other end of the garage, three vintage bikes, two Harleys and one Elliot wasn't sure about, an Indian perhaps, sat in various stages of restoration. "Tall, dude, rides a black Harley?"

"Like I said, I don't know the guy. I've been missing a few things around the shop, though. You know anything about that?"

Elliot shifted his weight to his left foot. Everyone seemed to be in the mood for a fight. "No. I don't."

The man stepped around the work bench and came toward Elliot. "I'm not sure I believe you." He reached out with his left arm, not a real punch, not even a jab, but an attempt to shove Elliot off balance.

Elliot stepped back and slid to his right, the opposite of what one would normally do when fending off such a lead, but the guy moved like a lefty and, if he struck again, it would be with a straight left or a left hook.

Sure enough, the maneuver took Elliot out of range, and the left hook breezed past his jaw.

The anger showing in the man's eyes said he would try again.

Elliot had to make a decision. It was either deck the guy or pull his badge. He showed his badge.

He hovered in attack mode a few seconds before lowering his hands. "You might want to start introducing yourself. I almost took your head off. But, now that you're here, maybe you could fill out a report for the stolen items I told you about."

Elliot tapped the badge, indicating it showed Tulsa. "I'm out of my jurisdiction. And I only do homicide."

"And you're here, looking for this Jake fellow?"

"That's right."

"Yeah, well I meant it when I said I didn't know him, but the description you gave got me to thinking. I've seen him around.

He stopped by a couple of times. It doesn't surprise me the law would be looking for him. I mean the looks of the guy for one thing, but he came in here asking about Indian things, wanting to know where he could buy arrowheads and stuff. Can you believe it? I mean anybody can see this ain't no gift shop. So when you came in, asking about the dude, well.... What I'm trying to say is I'm sorry I started a fight with you."

"Don't worry about it. If you could tell me where I might find the guy, I'd sure appreciate it."

"You might try Harry's. The place seems to draw them in, the crazies I mean."

Chapter Twenty-Seven

"You're looking good," Buddy Wheeler said, "like you could still play. Maybe I should put you out there, see what you can do."

After Elliot had left the cycle shop, he'd called his old football coach and asked him to have coffee. He and Buddy talked on the phone, even exchanged emails, but it'd been awhile since they'd actually seen each other. "You never played me much when I was there."

Wheeler laughed. "You had a lot of competition. What can I say? You were a good kid, though. I miss having you around."

Elliot studied the plastic top to the Styrofoam coffee cup. Buddy was a good guy, with his own share of problems, a wife with a history of medical problems and a mentally challenged adult son who still lived at home, probably always would. "How's the family?"

"They're okay. Betty's blood sugar's running a little high. She's pretty good about it though, could be worse. And Jimmy, he took a job at one of those donation centers. He seems to like it. I think it might work out. How about you? How's the cop business?"

"It has its days. Unfortunately, it's been awhile since I've seen one."

Buddy shook his head. "You always could make me laugh."

"It's never been much of a challenge. And I really don't want to change the subject, but were you able to find anything on Professor Stephens?"

Buddy sipped his coffee and stared into space. "I've been at the university going on twenty years now. It's different, working for a school you know. They have their own society, a city within a city more or less. And like any society, you got those who run below the surface of the system and those who try to fly above it."

"What are you trying to say, Buddy?"

"Well, you remember all of the ruckus and hoopla when it happened. Anyway, it quieted down for a while, but the police started coming around again, asking questions and all. Maybe they found some new evidence or something. Stephens became too much of an embarrassment, I guess. Anyway, the right people decided they'd had enough of it, and Stephens was asked to leave.

He tendered his resignation six years ago. The school kept it quiet. Far as I know, nobody's seen or heard from him since."

"Any idea what happened to him?"

"Nobody wants to talk about it. But there were rumors he went psycho or something, maybe even had something to do with the missing people. I'm not saying that's what happened. You know how stuff like that gets started."

"Well, get ready for it again," Elliot said. "I'm pretty sure the detectives will be coming around, asking more questions."

Elliot gave Buddy Wheeler a summary of what had happened since Gerald's phone call.

"No kidding. The nerdy kid you used to hang with?"

"That's right. And maybe by some miraculous stroke of luck you'll be able to tell me where I could find his family."

"I wish I could help you, kid, but I wouldn't even have remembered him if you hadn't brought it up. But with a name like Stanley Gerald Reynolds, how hard could it be?"

"You might be surprised," Elliot said. He finished his coffee and stood. "It's been nice visiting with you, Buddy, but I need to get going, lot of work to do."

Outside the coffee shop, Coach Wheeler said, "That's some fancy ride."

Elliot followed his line of sight to the engine of the bike. The fuel line had been disconnected.

Elliot slid his hand inside his coat and touched the handle of the Glock while scanning the area. He saw nothing out of the ordinary.

"Take it easy," Coach Wheeler said. "You look like a quarterback who's just met his replacement."

Elliot leaned over and examined the vandalism. Within the last twenty minutes, someone had walked up to the Harley and detached a key component, but that wasn't all. Wrapped around the gas line, like some kind of sleeve, was a piece of paper.

Elliot carefully removed the paper and unrolled it.

It turned out to be a note.

I'm taking a chance writing this. Disobedience is not tolerated. I can only ask that you stop what you are doing and go back to the world you inhabited before I, through actions not entirely of my own, gained the focus of your attention. I don't want to hurt you, but I can promise if you continue with your

present course of action, you will end up with more in common
with your friend Stanley than you would find desirable.

Elliot folded the note and an old memory buzzed through his
head.

He and Nick Brazleton had hiked up the grade behind their
houses. They called it a mountain, though even describing it as a
hill would have been a stretch. But it was their place to roam,
their sanctuary, and it was what they wished it to be. During a
particular excursion, they'd taken a new path and stumbled upon
a place where they had never been, a strange area chock full of
things to pique a twelve-year-olds' interest.

It was an old house site, though the only thing remaining was
the foundation. It was a fascinating discovery but not the best of
it. Occupying the property as well were two old cellars. The
dugout near the foundation was, in itself, an explorer's dream.
The door long since removed, its steps descended into the
darkness of a room where fruits and vegetables preserved in
mason jars still rested on dusty wooden shelves. However, it was
the other cellar-like structure that rose partially out of the earth a
few hundred feet from the house that had sent chills down
Elliot's spine.

The curved concrete roof with two small windows, one on
each end, protruded above the ground, while the rest of the
cellar, a small rectangular dungeon with walls of brick, was
buried beneath the earth. The macabre design included no
doorway. No way in, and no way out. The windows were much
too small to allow the admission of an adult, but were sufficient
for a child, if one so dared.

Elliot lowered himself into the darkness, and even before his
feet touched the floor, he sensed the foolishness of his decision.
The pit could have been squirming with snakes, or crawling with
spiders, or filled with God only knew what.

Elliot found the dark hole in the ground to be absent of
anything physical, but it was not empty. Just being there had
filled him with shame and a sense of wrong-doing. He knew he'd
picked up on a vibration, a reflection of the bad things that had
taken place there, and his feet were only on the dark soil for a few
seconds before he scrambled from the foul smelling enclave,
pulling himself back through the window at a much faster rate
than he'd entered.

Elliot slid the note into his pocket. It was during his short stay in the old cellar he'd first realized he was sensitive to things that most people were not.

Detective Ryan's voice cut through the air.

Coach Wheeler patted Elliot's shoulder. "Hey, I got to go. See you around."

By the time Ryan walked up, the coach had found his car and was driving toward the exit. Ryan put his hands on his belt, though he wore no firearm or police belt around his waist. An old cop habit. "I see you didn't heed my warning. You're still hanging around."

"I have as much right to be here as any other citizen."

"Yeah, but you don't have the right to be acting like a cop."

Elliot gestured toward Coach Wheeler's car. "I was just having coffee with a friend."

"Why don't I believe that?"

"Beats me," Elliot said. "But sooner or later someone's going to file a missing person report on Stanley Reynolds. You might want to check with his wife, Cheryl. She asked a local bozo named Darrel Bogner about the prospect of getting rid of her husband."

"Someone had a run-in with Bogner at a bar called Harry's, worked him over pretty good. You wouldn't happen to know anything about it, would you?"

Elliot reconnected the gas line then climbed onto the Harley. "It must have been somebody else."

"Don't toy with me, Elliot."

"Don't worry. It's not my style. Anyway, we're on the same side, or at least we should be."

Ryan exhaled heavily.

"The newspapers in the old house," Elliot said, "they're the reason Laura Bradford was here. You should reexamine your notes on those drifters. There should be some clues there."

"What are you trying to say?"

"I don't think they just moved on. I believe they were murdered."

"You're saying atrocities of that magnitude happened right here in my city, and I never knew anything about it? Doesn't say much for me, does it?"

Elliot looked away, observing the traffic. "I didn't mean it that way. I'm just trying to help."

Color flashed across Ryan's face. "Don't tell me what I should or shouldn't understand. I've just about had enough of you, Elliot. Maybe we should take off the badges and settle it right here."

Elliot tried to grasp what was happening. He'd seen some pretty hair-triggered cops, but nothing like this. He climbed off the bike and readied himself, aligning his left shoulder with Ryan's chest. In an effort to not mirror his adversary's aggression, he thought of Carmen, harnessing her influence to maintain control. "Don't do this, Ryan. You'll regret it."

As if someone had reached inside Ryan's head and flicked a switch, he'd become irrational, and now the switch was flicked the other way. As quickly as it had started, it was over

Ryan turned and walked away.

Elliot watched Ryan climb into his car. There was no denying what he'd just witnessed. Either Detective Ryan had a serious personality disorder, or the old case meant more to him than he was letting on.

Ryan's uncanny behavior still occupied Elliot's attention when his phone went off. It turned out to be Doctor Meadows, the Methodist pastor he'd asked to visit Angela Gardner.

Chapter Twenty-Eight

Doctor Meadows, the Methodist pastor, was sitting at the bedside of Angela Gardner, reading quietly to her, but he closed the Bible and placed it on the bedside table when Elliot entered the room.

"Thanks for coming," Elliot said.

"I'm grateful to be of service. And please, call me Tom."

Elliot glanced at the floor. Doctor Meadows had asked him before to call him by his first name, but it made Elliot uncomfortable, seeming to diminish the respect he felt he owed him.

Doctor Meadows smiled. "How about Pastor Tom?"

"I'll work on it," Elliot said. He glanced at Angela, who seemed to be sleeping. "I got here as fast as I could."

The sound of someone's shoes squeaking against the tiled floor echoed through the hallway. Seconds later, Doctor Shaffer came into the room and went to Angela's bedside.

"The doctor gave her something earlier," Pastor Meadows said. "I think she'll be ... resting for a while."

Pastor Meadows had avoided the term *all right*, but the question the words would have posed hung there, as if he'd added emphasis to them instead. He lowered his voice. "Miss Gardner said some peculiar things during our visit. She calls you her guardian angel, said she saw you on the other side, while she was out. Even in my line of work, I don't often hear that kind of talk."

Elliot glanced at Angela. In the last few days, he'd seen the ghost of someone who'd passed away, and the spirit of another who had, at the very least, brushed the gates of death. He decided to play it safe. "Angela's been somewhat delusional, but her concern for her spiritual welfare seems genuine. That's why I called."

He smiled. "You did well, son. We had a good talk."

Elliot considered confiding in the pastor. Such things often concerned him, wondering whether the source of his somewhat unusual abilities came from the right side of things. Carmen, the only other person he'd ever mentioned it to, said it was the nature of the individual that determined their effect, and not the other way around. Her wisdom had always inspired him.

Angela's eyes fluttered open. She rose partially out of bed and propped herself on her elbows. With a raspy voice she said, "Kenny?"

Elliot glanced at Doctor Shaffer.

The doctor nodded.

Elliot went to Angela's bedside and took her hand. It was almost as if she'd come to his rescue, helping him avoid what might have been an uncomfortable discussion concerning their relationship. "How's my girl?"

Angela managed a smile. "You know, it's kind of like hiding under the covers when you're a kid. You feel safe there, but if you ever stopped to think about it, what's a bunch of wool or a bit of cotton going to do?"

"I'm not sure what you're trying to tell me, Angela."

"Don't be silly. You're the one who showed me. We have a similar false sense of security when we try to hide from God."

Pastor Meadows came over. He put his hand on Angela's forehead. "Be at peace, my child. God is with you."

"My heart is stained but not darkened. I've done things which were not my own. The truth is hidden in my dreams, as well, but not so much that I can't recognize it. I've lived there, an inward quest of consumption. Knowing whether or not I am for that purpose alone will be my redemption, if not my damnation. In the end, we all have to pay for our sins, don't we?"

"Jesus paid the price for you," Pastor Meadows said. "All you have to do is believe and accept him as your savior."

Angela squeezed Elliot's hand and started to cry. "The girl with the dark eyes became the enemy, her sole purpose to destroy the vehicle, to remove the pathway it created. Her life was offered, not to me but for the darkness, though ultimately it was I who took it, with a blade of black glass. I killed her, Kenny."

Angela stopped speaking. She relaxed her grip on Elliot's hand and fell limply to the bed.

Doctor Shaffer ushered Elliot aside.

Other hospital personnel and people arrived, but among the faces that surrounded Angela's bed, two stood out. Elliot stared into the sad and knowing eyes of George and Emma Gardner. And though the room was filled with people, it was empty of conversation, with the only sound coming from the heart monitor as its mournful cry indicated a flat-line of the patient. Angela Gardner was gone.

Elliot responded to a tap on his shoulder and when he turned he saw Angela, scared and confused. If he had not seen her body on the bed, he might have thought she'd made a recovery and had gotten up to go to the bathroom or to get a glass of water. She had sought him out before. Why shouldn't she come to him now?

Elliot said nothing, but Angela seemed to catch the meaning of the words he would have spoken had he not been surrounded by others who would not understand. A peaceful look came over her as she fixed her gaze on something and she faded away.

A wave of dizziness came over Elliot. He reached for support, finding Pastor Meadows' shoulder and with the pastor's help, stumbled from the room.

Outside in the hallway, he leaned against the wall and drew his sleeve across his forehead to wipe away the perspiration. In a short amount of time, he and Angela Gardner had become close, forging a bond beyond the boundaries of friendship, even surpassing the rapport shared by family members.

Pastor Meadows squeezed Elliot's arm. "She found her way, son. She was right with God. I'm sure of it."

"Did you hear what she said?"

"I'm not Catholic," Pastor Meadows said, "but I've heard my share of confessions. People facing death seldom lie about such things."

"I didn't see it coming."

"It's easy to get caught off guard in such a situation. And the way she went. She seemed ill but...."

Elliot nodded. It was as if Angela had waited for his arrival, and after purging her soul had given up and let go of the life that remained in her. Facing the reality of her own demons had been too much for her.

"We need to talk more about this," Pastor Meadows said, "later, when you've had time to let it digest. Call, or come by my office."

Elliot put on his coat and started down the hallway, Angela's words still ringing in his head. *I killed her, Kenny.*

Angela's thoughts had been jumbled and her words cryptic, but the message had come through with clarity. She'd confessed to murder. Eight years ago, when they were still in school, she'd killed Laura Bradford.

Elliot reached the elevator and jabbed the button. He'd have to contact Ryan and let him know about this.

Chapter Twenty-Nine

Elliot had chosen the restaurant, a high-end hamburger joint on 71st Street. "How's this?" he asked, aiming the question at whoever might answer.

Wayne shrugged. "Okay, I guess. I don't think I've ever been here."

Carmen nodded her agreement as well.

At the hospital, Elliot had called Ryan and left a message, explaining that he needed to talk to him concerning Angela Gardner. After that, he'd driven home and spent a few hours repairing the flattened truck tires. It'd been good therapy. With his head somewhat cleared, he'd convinced Carmen to reschedule their date night, or just having dinner, as she put it.

After the waiter had taken their order, Elliot studied the black and white photographs decorating the walls, some reflecting streets and buildings from 1930's Chicago. He noticed Carmen watching him, so he brought his attention back to the table. "Thanks for rescheduling," he said. "It means a lot to me."

"Are you still working the case that has you so involved?"

She trailed the question off, her expression reflecting her dismay at having brought up the subject.

As if sensing his mother's discomfort, Wayne seized the opportunity. "Have you ever shot anybody, Mr. Elliot?"

"Wayne...."

Wayne's question, spoken with a volume typical of a boy his age, drew the attention of several nearby tables.

A vision of Ralph Kincaid's tormented face played through Elliot's memory. Of all the times he'd had to use his service weapon, that one haunted him the most.

His cell phone came to his rescue. He'd turned down the ring volume, but in the quiet that'd come over the restaurant, it still made a disturbance. The caller ID showed it was Detective Ryan.

"I really need to take this," he said. He wiggled from the booth and strode across the lobby. Outside, he brought the phone to his ear. "This is Elliot."

"Yeah, let's talk about why you called." Ryan's voice was quick, irritated.

"I have some information for you," Elliot said. "It has to do with the old case."

"Say what you mean, Elliot. I don't have time for games."

"This is no game, Ryan. I tracked down Angela Gardner. Check your notes. She was one of the students you interviewed while you were checking on Stephens."

"If there's a point to all of this, I wish you would get to it."

"Angela Gardner killed Laura Bradford. She confessed to it."

The phone seemed to go dead, but it was just Ryan, trying to find the words. "Do you have her in custody?"

"She's dead, passed away right after she told me."

"I'm sorry to hear that. But, hey, you found my killer for me. It's sad it turned out like this, but I can't deny my relief. It's time the old case was put to rest."

Elliot squeezed the phone. There was no question Ryan wanted all of this to go away. "The case isn't over, Ryan, not even close."

Elliot watched a couple teenagers dressed in baggy pants walk into the restaurant. Ryan hadn't replied, so he continued. "Angela killed Laura, but she didn't have anything to do with the other murders."

"Are we back to that again? What makes you so sure those drifters didn't... well, just drift off again?" Ryan's question sounded more like a plea than a belief, an expression of his desire for this thing to be over.

"I have my ways."

"Yeah, I'll bet you do. Now, if you have additional information pertinent to the case, I need to know about it."

"Not a problem."

"Come on, Elliot, you drop a bombshell on me and go silent? What are you saying, that Angela had an accomplice?"

Elliot watched the sloppily-dressed kids leave the restaurant and stroll across the parking lot. "In a manner of speaking, except it was the other way around. Angela would have been the accomplice."

"I still think you know more about all of this than you should. Putting that aside though, do you have any idea who it might have been?"

"My guess would be Professor David Stephens," Elliot said. "Do you know where he is?"

"What makes you think Stephens had anything to do with it?"

"You had him under investigation. A cop like you wouldn't do that without a reason. Now you get all defensive every time I bring up his name."

There was no answer.

"Come on, Ryan. What's up?"

Again, the phone was silent. Ryan had disconnected.

Elliot shoved the phone into his pocket and went back inside the restaurant.

The food had arrived, but neither Carmen nor Wayne had touched it.

Elliot slid into the booth. "Sorry about the disturbance. But you shouldn't have waited for me." He held the phone out so they could see him switch it off. "No more interruptions. I promise."

Carmen shook her head. "Your work is important to you. That is how it should be."

Elliot picked up his burger and had it halfway to his mouth when Carmen nudged him.

"Would you like to say the blessing?" She asked.

Elliot flushed. He put his sandwich back on the plate and wiped his hands. "Sure." He bowed his head and put together a short prayer. As soon as Elliot had finished, Wayne, who'd been showing obvious enjoyment over Elliot's predicament, began eating. It was nice, like being in a real family. "So how's school going?" Elliot asked.

Wayne shrugged. "Okay, I guess."

Elliot hadn't been around his son much, something he regretted, but still he could tell something wasn't right with him.

"What about the play?" Carmen said. "Why don't you tell...Mr. Elliot about it?"

Wayne's expression reflected apprehension. "Aw, mom."

"I have some friends who are involved with acting," Elliot said. "It takes a lot of courage and determination."

Carmen smiled at Elliot's attempt to encourage Wayne. "He wants to write and create screenplays someday."

"I've always thought it'd be cool to be a writer, too," Elliot said, "but so far all I've managed to crank out are a few police reports, and according to my captain I haven't done all that well with them."

Wayne made an effort to hide his smile.

"I'm proud of you, son. More than you'll ever know."

Wayne and Carmen exchanged glances.

Elliot wiped his hands on his napkin. He'd slipped with his word choice, and neither Wayne nor Carmen seemed comfortable with it. The episode left him feeling, and not for the first time, like an outsider. "Well," he said, "now that we're on the subject of screenplays, why don't we go see one, a movie that is? You can pick the flick, Wayne, if it's okay with your mother."

Carmen's expression showed she was uncertain about the prospect.

"That'd be neat. Could we, Mom?"

Carmen gave Elliot a look he could not read. She glanced at her watch. "I guess it would be all right. But we'll have to hurry. Wayne has school tomorrow. He shouldn't stay up too late."

Elliot signaled for the waiter and after settling the bill they left the restaurant. A few minutes later, they walked into the lobby of the theater, a cinema complex just off 101st and Memorial.

Wayne scanned the billboards and studied the digital display screens that showed an offering of animated stories, a couple of superhero flicks, and a few action-adventure stories. He kept looking until he found something that pleased him, a science-fiction film involving time travel.

The Parental Guidance rating concerned Carmen, but Wayne's pleading eyes finally won her approval. She glanced at Elliot. "It's what he likes."

"Can I have popcorn?"

"You hardly touched your dinner."

"I'm sorry. I wasn't hungry then."

Elliot gained Carmen's visual approval, dug a ten dollar bill from his pocket, and handed it to Wayne. "Go for it, sport."

A crowd of people buzzed around the concession area. Wayne would be a few minutes. As soon as the boy was out of hearing range, Elliot turned to Carmen. "Is something bothering Wayne? I realize he's uncomfortable around me, but he seems more distracted than usual."

She glanced at the concession area. "He's having trouble with all of this, trying to come to terms with your being his father. I should have told him sooner. I had no idea he'd take it so hard."

"You're doing fine. Nobody really knows how to deal with this kind of thing. Wayne will come around. He's a good boy. And he couldn't ask for a better mother. Anybody can see how well you've done with him."

She shook her head. "He says he wants to go and stay for a while with his father... Anthony, I mean."

Tears formed in her eyes but she fought them back. "I don't want him to go. He's all I have."

Carmen's words shot a current of pain through Elliot's chest. "I don't think he really wants to leave. His motivation is the same as when he ran away, to get things back the way they were, his family the way he remembers it. He thinks this might make it happen."

Carmen pulled a tissue from her purse and wiped her eyes. "I called Anthony and tried to talk to him about it. He wasn't receptive to the idea. I thought he might talk to Wayne, make him feel better about the separation. He wouldn't even do that. He doesn't want anything to do with us. As far as I'm concerned, it's good riddance, but Wayne doesn't feel the same way."

Elliot stared at Carmen, unsure of what to say, and whether it was the right time or not, he wanted to take her in his arms and tell her everything would be all right, but before he could act, Wayne came running over. He grabbed Carmen's arm and tugged her toward the theater. "Come on. We're going to miss it."

The film turned out to be one that left the room dark most of the time. Elliot thought it was a good thing, since the lack of light hid their emotions. About halfway through the movie, Carmen slipped her hand into his.

Elliot closed his eyes and prayed for it to be real, for Carmen to want him as much as he wanted her.

A little later, she leaned close and whispered, "You're a good man, Kenny Wayne Elliot."

Elliot meditated on her words, trying to determine what, if anything might be in them, all the while searching for something to say in return. "Then what's keeping us apart?" he asked.

Carmen didn't answer, but she didn't let go of his hand.

Elliot sank back into the theater seat, relishing for the moment the feeling of things being right in his world.

He should have known it wouldn't last. After the movie let out, he walked with Carmen and Wayne into the lobby where he saw a familiar face in the crowd, just a brief glance he caught before the guy, who looked and moved a lot like the biker from Stillwater, pushed through the doors and stepped outside.

Elliot thought about going after him, but the peaceful look on Carmen's face caused him to rethink his options. He hadn't gotten a good look at him anyway. It could have been anyone.

Near the exit, in a corner of the lobby, a coin operated photo booth caught Elliot's attention and he thought back to an earlier time.

Carmen's mother had taken them to the mall in Tulsa where they had come upon an older version of the device now in front of them. Carmen had begged Elliot to go inside with her to have pictures taken together. She'd hung those photos on the wall of her bedroom.

Elliot tugged at Carmen's arm and guided her toward the booth.

"What are you doing now?" Wayne asked.

Elliot stopped in front of the machine. "Your mother used to get quite a kick out of these things."

"Don't be ridiculous," Carmen said. She held her arms up as if measuring Elliot's shoulders. "I doubt you would fit anyway."

Wayne giggled.

"Laugh it up, sport. We're all three going in."

"You're on," Wayne said. "Could we, mom?"

Elliot fed some money into the machine, went inside and poked his head through the curtain. "Don't make me come out there."

Carmen shook her head but her resistance was superficial at best, and soon she relented and squeezed in as well.

With Carmen on one knee and Wayne on the other, Elliot pushed the ready button.

As soon as the process had finished, Wayne scrambled out of the machine and grabbed the snapshots. He laughed as Elliot and his mother struggled from the booth, though his smile went flat as he settled down and began to examine the photos.

A current of disappointment ran through Elliot. He'd hoped Wayne might find the experience interesting, a good thing, not something to further dampen his spirits.

Wayne removed his attention from the photos and handed the snapshots to Elliot.

Curious as to what had caused Wayne's sudden mood swing, Elliot examined the photos, and has he drew the glossy shots close and ran his gaze across them he began to realize the source of Wayne's reaction. He glanced at Carmen.

She held his gaze for a moment, closed her eyes and nodded.

Elliot had, of course, noticed the resemblance, but seeing the boy's face in close proximity to his own on the photographs was something he wasn't prepared for. He and Wayne were practically identical, adjusting for the age of course.

Carmen slid her arm around Elliot's. "We should be going."

Outside the theater, as they crossed the parking lot, the roar of an automobile that sounded a lot like the one Elliot had heard leaving his neighborhood after its driver had flattened his truck tires grabbed his attention. He thought of Jake, the biker from Stillwater. Was it possible he'd been following him? The idea made little sense, and yet Elliot couldn't bring himself to completely reject the notion.

Chapter Thirty

Somewhere around 9:00 PM, after dropping off Wayne and Carmen, Elliot rolled back into Tulsa. It'd been an uncomfortable ride, with long stretches of silence in between Wayne's questions about football and being a cop.

The evening left Elliot considering a lot of things, most of it dealing with family, which reminded him he needed to follow up on Shane Conley. Shane's connection to the case, if there was one, still had him baffled. Instead of going home, Elliot drove to Conley's neighborhood. However, as he neared the front door, he relived the events leading up to Sergeant Conley being shot to death by a madman named Ralph Kincaid. It happened every time he came here. He was about to turn and walk away, but before he could, the door opened and Susan Conley stood in front of him. "I've been expecting you," she said.

She appeared to be in better condition this time. "That's pretty good," Elliot said, "considering I didn't know I was coming until a few minutes ago."

"I guess I know you better than you realize. It isn't surprising. David talked of you often."

"Do you know why I'm here?"

Susan turned and walked away, disappearing into the house.

Elliot found her, sitting on the sofa in the living room. "Can I get you anything," she asked, "coffee, or a drink?"

"No, thanks," Elliot said. Her mentioning alcohol concerned him. He didn't want to see a repeat of her last performance. "I need to talk to Shane. Is he here?"

Susan's eyes showed her weariness. "All right, but before I turn him over to you, there's something you need to know."

"I'm listening."

"Shane's not easily impressed" she said. "He's hard for his age. I guess being the son of a cop will do that. He looks up to you, Mr. Elliot. I guess he sees in you something of what his father stood for."

"He certainly has a funny way of showing it."

"Shane's a hard person to understand. His capacity for respect is pretty thin. Try not to diminish it further."

"All right," Elliot said. Susan definitely wasn't mincing her words today. "I'll be as tactful as I can."

Susan stood and walked toward a hallway leading away from the living room. "Shane's waiting in his room. He wanted to be alone with you."

"How do you feel about that?"

She knocked softly and opened the door. "Whatever works," she said.

She walked away, leaving Elliot unannounced and standing in the doorway. Shane sat at a desk with his back turned.

Elliot rapped his knuckles against the doorframe.

"Yeah, come on in. Shut the door, too."

Elliot walked across the room and sat on the bed.

Shane's fingers worked the keyboard of a computer. "Are you a gamer, Mr. Elliot?"

"Not really. I usually have my hands full with the real world."

"Yeah, well that's kind of the point, leaving it all behind for awhile. You should try it."

"Maybe I have in one form or another. But the trouble with escapism is the real stuff's always still there, waiting for you when you get back."

"You sound just like my dad."

Elliot stared at the boy in front of him, not with anger but with a sort of pity. Even though Shane had had a hard life, he hadn't lived long enough to realize his view of the things bothering him now would not so much soften with age as they would from overcrowding. With so many other problems coming along, you just get numb.

"Mom don't get it either. She's nothing like she used to be. If I ask her for something, she gets it for me. If I tell her it ain't right, she just looks sad. She tries so hard to please me it gets on my nerves."

"Have you talked to her about it?"

"Sure I have. We just don't communicate."

"Would you like me to give it a try?"

"That's all right. I have a feeling it's not going to matter anyway, once you get through with me."

"You shouldn't jump to conclusions. Your agreeing to talk with me says a lot. Where we go from here depends on your level of involvement, if there is any."

Shane pulled a pack of cigarettes from a drawer of the desk and lit one up.

"What does your mother think about your smoking?"

"Like I said, she lets me do what I want."

"Yeah, but like you just admitted, that's not always a good thing."

"Whatever. Could we just get on with it?"

"All right. Why were you parked along 14th street near the old house Monday night? And don't try to deny it. I saw you. You were driving your mother's car."

"So what if I was?"

"So you had to have a reason. Let's hear it."

Shane took a drag on his cigarette. "It's my connection. He asked me to meet him. I think he lives over there somewhere."

"What kind of connection?"

Shane rolled his eyes.

Elliot rubbed the back of his neck and let out a sigh. The kid hadn't been involved after all. "I'll need a name."

"You know I can't do that. It's not just me."

Shane had a tell-tale look on his face. Elliot had seen it before. The kid acted tough, but he was in over his head and he was looking for a way out. "If you're being straight with me, I can help, and nobody's going to hurt you or your family. You have my word."

Shane worked the keyboard, acting as if he didn't care one way or the other. Later he stopped and said, "Skyler. They call him Skyler."

"Does Skyler have a last name?"

"That's all I know. I swear to God."

"All right, Shane. I'll take care of it. But you have to promise me you'll straighten yourself out."

"Yeah, yeah, same old stuff."

"Okay, so you don't care about yourself. What about your sister, Megan?"

Shane took a drag on the cigarette. "What about her?"

"She's going to end up just like you. She's already started down the path."

"I know what you think of me, Mr. Elliot. Just like dad, you only see what you want to see."

"I don't know any way to put it to you other than to just lay it out, but you got it all turned around. It's a cop's job to see the wrong side of people, and the cops who have the mettle to stick with it pick up on a few things along the way. You learn the ins and outs, just like any job. Learning how to read people is a fundamental necessity if you want to work the streets. And contrary to what the songs, and the poems, and the television programs try to ram down your throat, there are predictable patterns of behavior. To put it in simple terms, people who talk the talk sooner or later will walk the walk. So when you start to see those negative patterns of behavior developing in someone you care about, it tends to rip your heart out."

"So you're telling me I'm a born loser?"

"That's not what I'm saying. Your father was a good man and a good cop. Sometimes we don't get around to telling those closest to us how much they mean to us."

Shane nodded.

"That's why you went to the cemetery, isn't it, to talk to him?"

"Maybe."

"He loved you, Shane. And I promise you, he's up there watching over you right now. He's counting on you to take care of the family. So why don't you straighten up and make him proud?"

Elliot stood and started toward the door.

"Wait," Shane said. His voice was low, almost a whisper. "There's something else I need to tell you."

With reluctance, Elliot turned back. Had he been too hasty with his earlier assumption of Shane's innocence? The last thing he wanted to hear was a confession falling from the mouth of David Conley's son.

"I'm not sure how to put this. No matter how I say it, you're going to think I'm nuts."

"I'm listening."

"Before you get any ideas, I was straight. I hadn't taken anything yet. It's been running through my head since it happened, and I can only come to one conclusion. It was real, Mr. Elliot. I didn't imagine it."

Elliot readied himself for what was coming, a variety of demented scenarios running through his head. "Go on."

"I've heard stories about the old house, crazy stuff going on there."

"What kind of stories?"

Shane pushed his hair back. "People go in but they don't come out. It was good it burned down."

"I think someone was killed there, Shane. If you know anything about it, anything at all, you need to tell me."

His eyes grew wide. "I don't know anything for sure. I've just heard stuff. But I saw something the night you were there, and I can't get it out of my head."

Elliot had seen plenty of defiant people beaten by interrogation, and the look that came over them when they realized it was time to come clean. Shane had the look about him. "All right," Elliot said. "I'd like to hear about it."

"Don't play dumb with me, Mr. Elliot. Something ran out of that old house and you were chasing it. So don't tell me you didn't see it."

"I flushed someone out of there. You took off in your car right after, so I thought it was you."

Shane shook his head. "He ran right past me."

Elliot wondered if he could actually get a break this easily, if Shane could describe the suspect. "Did you get a good look at him?"

"Yeah, you could say that. Whatever it was, it came awful close to me."

"If we bring the guy in, could you make an ID?"

Shane stared at his desk, and when he looked up his complexion had turned the color of cement. "That's not going to happen, Mr. Elliot."

"What makes you say that?"

"Because there's no way you're going to put what ran past my car in a lineup."

"I'm not sure what exactly you're trying to say."

"Yeah, right. I'm not telling you anything you don't know. I mean you didn't have a chance the way that thing moved."

"If you're trying to tell me something, why don't you just go ahead and say it?"

Shane sighed. "I don't know if I can. I mean, there was something about the guy's face. It just didn't look right."

"Was it some kind of deformity?"

"I don't know. Like I said, it was dark."

"Was he tall, short, heavyset?"

"Sort of tall, I guess, and athletic. Yeah, anybody who could run like that would have to be in pretty good shape."

Elliot started to put his hand on Shane's shoulder, but changed his mind. He believed Shane was telling the truth, at least as he understood it. "Thanks for your help, buddy. I doubt you'll understand this, but I'm deeply relieved it wasn't you."

"Thanks."

"Could I offer a little advice?"

"Sure."

"I know it was just an expression, but it's not a good idea to swear to God. Try praying instead."

Elliot closed the door to Shane Conley's bedroom and as he walked down the hallway, he wondered where his words to the boy had come from. He'd never before lectured anyone on religion.

Outside, Elliot sat in his truck, staring into the darkness of the street that ran past David Conley's house. He was tired, but he'd made a promise. He grabbed his phone and called Bernie Sykes, an old friend who kept his ear to the street.

Bernie answered with a gruff, "Yeah, what?"

"I'm looking for someone," Elliot said, "and I heard you were a P.I."

"It kind of depends on who needs the service."

"A young dealer, goes by the name of Skyler, caters to the high school crowd. You know anybody like that?"

"Last time I heard, you worked homicide, so why are you asking vice questions?"

"I believe the dealer lives near the scene of a case I'm working, thought he might know something. It's important, else I wouldn't be asking."

"So why do I get the feeling you're not being straight with me?"

Sykes had been around the investigative scene awhile. He had instincts, and they were good. "All right," Elliot said, "I'll level with you. There's this friend of mine, a cop who's not around anymore. His kids need some guidance. Let's just say I feel responsible. Your boy's been peddling his wares in their vicinity. It's got me in a foul mood. Maybe I should come down to your place, talk to you about it."

"You're as comforting as a toothache, Elliot. Capone could have used a guy like you. Too bad you weren't born in his time."

"Just tell me where I can find this guy. Nobody will know where I got the information. You have my word."

"Too late, Capone's been dead for years."

"Okay, Bernie. Have it your way. I'll be there in a few minutes."

"Take it easy. I'm just having a little fun with you. There's this coffee shop in Brookside where you'll see more tattoos and piercings than you care to. You'll know it when you see it. I ain't saying that's where he is, but you never know who you might find there."

"Thanks, Bernie. If it works out, maybe I'll send you a box of chocolates."

"I'd rather you didn't."

Elliot disconnected, shoved the phone into his pocket and pulled the truck onto the street. Based on what Sykes had told him, he had a pretty good idea of where the coffee shop was located.

A few minutes later, he coasted to a stop near the curbside of a backstreet intersecting Peoria Avenue.

The murmur of conversation came from patrons sitting outside. In the misty glow of tiny lights strung across the patio, Elliot recognized someone. It was the familiar curve of her face and the shape of her lips, and though he realized her being there wasn't probable, he accepted the possibility that Cyndi Bannister had somehow breached the boundaries of her prison and even now leisured on the patio, sipping coffee.

The lady sensed his attention and turned toward him, the gaze of her brown eyes revealing in an instant her approval of the flattery and a cautious warning as well.

Elliot turned away. He was thankful he'd been wrong. It had only been a few months since he'd met Cyndi. He'd fallen in love with her, but some serious character flaws had gotten in the way. She'd been one of those frightening individuals who had no problem with killing someone if, in her demented way of thinking, it needed to be done. The lovely Cyndi Bannister exhibited the tendencies of a sociopath, and Elliot was the cop who'd put her away.

Elliot was still caught up in the past when the entrance to the coffee shop opened and three young men walked out, nearly colliding with him. Taking a step back, Elliot excused himself.

The one in the middle, a chunky kid with spiky, red hair said, "Hey, dude, what's your problem?"

"I'm looking for someone," Elliot said. "Maybe you could help."

"Do I look like a dating service?"

Chunky's friends laughed. One of them said, "Good one, Nate."

Elliot smiled. "He goes by the name of Skyler. Would that be you?"

The boy's expression went flat. "I don't know anybody named Skyler. Now get out of my face, dude."

He tried to push on past and continue his exit.

Elliot grabbed his arm and pulled him back. "I'm not through with you."

"Let go of me, dude. I'm warning you." He glanced around for support but his buddies had already cleared out. "What are you, crazy or something?"

"Most likely," Elliot said. "Now answer my question."

"I'm not saying I know anything, but you might check the dude behind the register."

"Would that be Skyler?"

The red-haired kid sighed. "Look, I don't need this kind of trouble. I did what you asked. Let me go, okay?"

"I'll be happy to. I just need you to do one more thing. Go inside and tell Skyler I need to talk to him."

"You don't know what you're asking. Come on, dude. You look pretty straight. What do you want with somebody like Skyler?"

"It's personal."

"You're making a big mistake. Anyway, I can't do it. Get somebody else."

"I don't remember offering you a choice. Do what I ask and you're free to go. But don't try anything stupid. I'll be right here, waiting."

"Don't make me do this. I'm asking you nice."

With his free hand, Elliot opened the door to the coffee shop and shoved the red-haired kid inside. "Send him out here. And don't worry. He won't bother you. I plan on occupying his full attention."

Elliot stepped back into a darkened area near the street and waited.

Later, he checked his watch. He toyed with the idea of going inside, but decided against it. He didn't want to get arrested, and creating a disturbance with the patrons looking on could lead to that. He was about to give up and walk back to the truck when the door banged open.

Someone burst out of the coffee house holding what looked like an axe handle.

Elliot had expected a kid, but this was a man, taller than he, and nearly as broad.

He saw Elliot and charged. Brandishing the weapon like a backstreet thug, he swung the handle in a wide arc. It whipped past Elliot's face, missing by inches.

Elliot tried to gather himself. If the maniac dazed him with a blow or knocked him to the ground, he would beat him senseless.

Elliot raised his right arm and caught the next attack on his forearm.

Pain arced through his arm but he didn't have time to worry about the injury. The next swing was already in progress. It caught him on the left shoulder.

The man repositioned his grip and swung again.

It was the break Elliot needed. He ducked beneath the path of the weapon and drove his hand into his attacker's throat. He followed with an overhand right, catching the man square behind his ear. He stumbled backward, his equilibrium disturbed by the shot to his head.

Elliot wrenched the axe-handle from the man's grip and tossed the weapon into the street.

The man stared at the weapon as if he might go after it, but lunged forward instead.

Elliot hooked a body shot, nearly lifting his attacker from his feet then drove a hard right into his face.

He dropped to his knees and continued his descent, ending up face down by the curbside.

Seconds later, he lifted himself off the ground, but only to his knees. "Who the hell are you?" he asked.

"That's not important."

"Well what do you want with me?"

"It involves a mutual acquaintance, a kid named Shane Conley."

"Who?"

"Skinny kid with big eyes and curly hair?"

"What's it to you, anyway?"

"I want you to stay away from him. If I catch Shane with drugs again, or if anything happens to him or his family, I won't bother asking questions. I'll just assume it's you and come looking for you. It won't go so easy the next time. Do you understand?"

"Whatever you say."

Elliot grabbed a wad of the man's hair and yanked his head up. "You need to be a little more convincing, Skyler."

"Stay away from Shane Conley. I got it."

Elliot released his grip and walked away.

Chapter Thirty-One

The clock showed 4:00 am when Elliot gave up on sleep and rolled out of bed to take a shower. The bruises he'd suffered during the fight with Skyler throbbed, but that wasn't what kept him awake. The conversation he'd had with Shane Conley had acted as a catalyst, causing him to follow a line of logic he'd been avoiding. A disconcerting theme had begun to claim commonality with the details of the case. Angela had indicated she'd taken the life of Laura Bradford with a blade of black glass.

Elliot poured a cup of coffee and walked into the spare bedroom where he kept his computer. He switched it on and fed some key words into the search engine.

Doctor Cramer at the museum had described the artifact as having a blade of obsidian, essentially volcanic glass. The strange knife, Gerald's obsession, an artifact created to inflict death, indicated a disturbing possibility. If he knew more about the history, if there was ritual involved, maybe he could understand it, and know what to look for.

Elliot couldn't visualize Angela Gardner willingly doing such a thing, killing somebody in an ancient ritual. In addition, Shane Conley had seen something odd run past his car, and he'd indicated the suspect to be tall and athletic. Angela had been small and frail. And she'd certainly been in no shape to check out of the hospital and drive to Stillwater to fasten a note to the fuel line of the Harley. She had, however, been a student of archaeology, a science dedicated to the study of ancient civilizations and analysis of the material its people left behind, including religious artifacts. More importantly, Professor David Stephens had been her mentor.

Elliot scanned the monitor as the results of his search came into view from the typical people-finding sites. He chose one he'd used before and plugged in the name *Stanley Reynolds*.

The program pulled up two pages indicating various versions of the name.

However, when Elliot refined the parameters to include only those individuals named *Stanley Gerald Reynolds* the results narrowed significantly, down to three to be exact; Elliot's old buddy Gerald, and his two predecessors. Strangely enough, Stanley Gerald Reynolds the II turned out to be Gerald's grandfather. His father had been named Samuel. A generation, as far as the name was concerned, had been skipped.

A few minutes later, after digging into the family history, Elliot found the connection Terri Benson had mentioned. David R. Stephens, better known as Professor Stephens, turned out to be the son of Gerald's great aunt Julia. The *R* stood for Reynolds. However, the uniqueness of the family name failed to render the results Elliot had hoped for. Gerald's grandparents and great grandparents were listed as deceased while his mother and father still lived somewhere in the south of France.

An hour later, Elliot shut off the computer. The phone numbers he'd found were all disconnected or belonged to someone else. Directory assistance yielded the same results, as did the wireless companies. The chances of that being a natural occurrence were pretty slim. It appeared as if Gerald's family had intentionally gone underground.

Elliot pushed away from the desk to get a refill of his coffee, but a sound from another part of the house, like liquid being poured from a bottle, caused him to rethink his actions.

Someone was in the house. Elliot reached for his service weapon but found only his ribcage. Of course he didn't have it on him. He wasn't dressed, wasn't ready for work. He edged toward the bedroom doorway and peered outside the room.

There was no one in the hallway.

Elliot slid through the doorway and ducked into the laundry room.

The holster was there, on the hook where he'd left it, but the Glock was gone.

Elliot leaned against the wall of the laundry room and ran through his options. He considered the door from the laundry room into the garage but dismissed the idea. He didn't have his phone. It was on the charger in the kitchen. And if he tried to exit through the garage, the only way out was the overhead door, and using it would make a lot of noise. He wanted to catch the prowler, not scare him off.

Elliot left the laundry room and crossed the hall, leaned into the bathroom, and flipped on the light.

His reflection in the mirror caused him to jump, but no one else was there.

He eased out of the bathroom and crept down the hallway to the spare bedroom across from the office. He rarely used the room, keeping it closed until he had guests. He opened the door and found the light switch.

No one was there.

Elliot stepped into the room to check the closet. If someone was inside, there would be no need to exercise caution or worry about alerting them. In such a confined area, like a caged animal the prowler would be ready to retaliate, maybe with the Glock. Elliot slung the door open.

No prowler stared back at him.

Elliot left the spare bedroom and eased up the hallway, stopping close to the edge of the wall where the hallway opened into the living room. From there, he made his way to the front entrance and turned on the light.

The room was as quiet and peaceful as it had ever been.

He checked the coat closet near the front entrance then went back through the living room and into the kitchen. He removed a knife from a drawer and crept toward the master bedroom.

Elliot eased into the room, and immediately a familiar scent of sweat and fermented fruit invaded his senses. It was the same odor that had hung like a cloud around the homeless man he'd questioned at the old house.

Elliot ran his hand along the wall and flipped on the light, the action leaving him in direct confrontation with the source of the odor. He'd half expected to find the old beggar, standing in the room, but he did not. What he saw instead could only be described as odd. He had made the bed but the covers were now disturbed, though only slightly where the weight of several items caused an indentation in the bedspread. Piled in the middle of the bed was the Glock, a half empty bottle of wine, and a business card.

Elliot placed the knife on the dresser, gently lifted the Glock from the bed, and checked it.

The weapon was loaded and ready, just as he'd left it, though it was now wet where the contents of the bottle had been poured onto it.

Elliot searched the entire house again, including the garage and the attic.

The doors were locked. The windows were secured. No glass had been broken. Someone had gained entrance to his home, showed they could take his weapon and destroy his property, and they had accomplished it without alerting him to their presence.

Something like that shouldn't have happened, and yet he held the proof in his hand. The business card was one of his, more specifically, the one he'd given to the homeless man.

Elliot stumbled back into the living room and lowered himself into the recliner, though any relaxation he might have gained through the experience was not to be. A feeling of being watched came over him.

The patio door drew his attention. The blinds for the glass door were open.

He jumped from the chair and strode to the patio door where he pressed his face against the glass and peered into the darkness of the backyard.

He saw no one, but the sensation of being watched did not subside.

He flipped the switch for the outside light.

A soft glow spread across the patio and some of the yard and in the illumination, something was there, but only for an instant. In a blur of movement, a subtle change in the formation of shadows, the silhouette of something streaked past the door.

Elliot still had the Glock in his hand. He checked it, hoping the wine dousing wouldn't cause it to misfire. He unlocked the patio door and slid it open. Holding the weapon in front of him with both hands, he stepped outside, and though he figured the action would do little good, he shouted, "Halt."

He saw nothing that should not be there, and he heard only the sounds of the early morning.

Stepping from the patio onto the grass, Elliot walked quickly across the yard, looking from left to right, holding the Glock like a shield. The thought that he should have grabbed a flashlight went through his head. The area behind his house, enclosed by a six foot stockade fence, had a lot of shadowy areas. The prowler had been moving from west to east. That part of the yard held the least likely prospect for someone to hide. There were no sheds or outbuildings, and it didn't take long to determine no one was there.

Elliot gave up the search and stepped back inside the house, the smell of wine reminding him the events of the morning were all too real and not the product of his imagination. The business card had been intended as a message. Exactly what the intruder was trying to tell him, Elliot didn't know.

Outside, an automobile fired up and roared away.

Elliot grabbed his keys and scrambled into the garage. Finding the homeless man would not be easy but he had to try.

A few hours later, Elliot pulled onto another street where the downtown buildings loomed in the darkness before him. The city exhibited a different flavor in the early morning before the traffic started to build along the main thoroughfares and the side streets relinquished their hold on the shadowy quietness of the night. Elliot searched these areas but his luck ran thin. The street-people didn't want to talk to him. They turned their backs and walked away.

Elliot headed north when he saw another prospect, a man in a tattered navy coat leaning against the black iron fence just across from the Ambassador Hotel on 14th Street.

The man in the navy coat turned his head when he heard the slamming of the truck door, and when he saw Elliot he pushed away from the fence and began walking away, heading west.

Elliot crossed the street and went after him.

The man quickened his pace, but his age and condition left his efforts with negligible results.

Elliot caught up with him and blocked his path. "I'm not here to hurt you," Elliot said. "I'm looking for someone. I was hoping you might be able to help."

"You got the wrong guy, sir. I don't know nobody. I'm not from around here anyway. Ain't staying long neither. Just taking a little break, know what I'm saying, a rest before I hit the highway."

"All right," Elliot said, "but this is important. He's a tall fellow with an army field jacket, walks with a limp?"

"Hell, that sound like half the people I know."

Elliot smiled at the ragged man's sense of humor. He pointed to the area where the old house had been. "I talked with him a few days ago. He was staying just down the street from here."

The man stared at the vacant lot. "He your kin or something?"

"Let's just say he helped me out once, and I want to return the favor. I've been asking around, but I haven't had much luck."

"Maybe I know who you're talking about. And if you're who I think you are, the guy you're looking for, Jeremiah's his name by the way, was expecting a little help all right. I guess you're a little late, though. The people, they're moving out of here, finding different parts of the city. Me, I'm leaving the whole thing. I might even leave the state. Ain't nobody going to tell you nothing cause they scared they be next. The city knocked down that old slaughter house, but it didn't stop the killing, no sir. People be leaving all right. Jeremiah, he gone and he ain't coming back."

A curious expression waved across the old guy's face. A reflection of pity showed in his eyes. He shook his head but continued his journey down 14th Street.

The helpless feeling residing within Elliot grew more substantial. A subculture of the city, a population of lost souls who embraced anonymity, was being singled out, its members subjected to brutal murder only to have their remains secreted away, leaving their deaths as opaque to the eyes of everyday people as their lives had been.

A disturbing concept ran through Elliot. Psychopaths who commit murder on a grand scale typically thrive not only on the act itself but also on the attention and fear it draws. That did not appear to be the case in this situation. The killer seemed to covet anonymity, committing murder for murder's sake or for some unknown agenda.

Elliot went back to the truck and headed north on Main, but when he glanced in the mirror a knot formed in his stomach. The grey Infiniti had fallen in behind him.

Elliot gripped the steering wheel. It was time to put an end to this little game. He turned east on 15th, picked up some speed, and caught the next street going north. When he reached 11th, he hung a right. Seconds later, he pulled into the parking lot of the Home Depot that'd been constructed behind where the old Warehouse Market used to be.

The increased speed coupled with some quick turns had given him a slight lead. A little luck was on his side, too. An old blue Chevy, 1980's vintage, was in the parking lot, and it appeared to be unoccupied. Elliot came to a stop near the old car and scrambled from the truck. He squatted out of sight in front of the old Chevy, raising his head just enough to peek across the hood of the car.

The grey Infiniti pulled into the lot, cruised past, swung back around and stopped beside the truck.

Elliot worked his way around the Chevy and crept toward the truck, working his way behind the tailgate where he could observe his pursuer without being seen. The driver of the Infiniti did not exhibit the patterns of someone trained in the art of covert operations. Anyone with experience would have driven past, as if they had given up the search, but would come back and watch from a distance.

The driver leaned to his right and studied the truck through the passenger window. He opened the driver's door and eased himself onto the pavement.

Even in the partial darkness, Elliot recognized the driver of the Infiniti. He stepped from behind the truck and strolled toward him, the fingers of his right hand brushing the handle of the Glock. He shoved the man into the side of the pickup with his left forearm, pinning him against the vehicle. "Nice disguise."

Fear showed on the biker's face. "I can explain."

"That'd be a good idea."

The biker had lost the Harley and traded the leather for a business suit and neatly trimmed hair.

"I knew something about you wasn't quite right," Elliot said. "What are you, someone's attorney, a high-priced P.I.?"

The biker shook his head.

Elliot pulled the Glock from its holster. "I'll let you in on a little insider secret, Jake. If you're going to tail someone, you should do so as inconspicuously as possible. Not only is your ride too fancy, it has a distinctive sound. I should know. I've heard it often enough lately. Now that we've established that fact, the question begs to be posed. Why are you following me, Jake?"

"It's a complicated issue."

Elliot nudged the barrel of the Glock against the biker's head. "Your complication is about to escalate into a crisis. Tailing me is one thing, but breaking into my home, that's taking it way too far. Now I need some answers."

"I've been following you, but breaking and entering is not my style. You got the wrong guy."

"So you know the lingo. You a cop?"

The biker shook his head. "No, nothing like that."

"Why are you hanging around a college town pretending to be someone you're not?"

"Like you, I'm trying to figure things out, only I'm doing it undercover."

"Who're you working for?"

"Nobody. It's personal."

Adrenalin surged through Elliot. He shoved his forearm against the biker's throat. "Twice now someone's broken into my house, and you were in the vicinity both times. I saw you. If you didn't do it, who did? You were there. You must have seen them."

"I didn't see anything, except for you when you came tearing out of the house."

Elliot eased the pressure of his chokehold. Logic seemed to be missing from the equation, but he believed Jake was being honest with him, at least on the point of the break-ins. "Why have you been following me?"

"It's because of the questions you've been asking around Stillwater. It seems we have a common interest. Since you're a cop, I thought you might lead me in the right direction."

Elliot eased back on the pressure. "What sort of common interest are we talking about?"

"My brother and me," Jake said, "we always looked out for one another. We got separated when I was young, but he stayed in touch, wrote me letters, just about every month. Something I could count on."

"What does that have to do with me and Stillwater?"

"Corey, my brother, attended school at Oklahoma State, but it didn't work out. He fell in with some people who lived in a commune near there. He thought they were kooky, but they treated him with respect and let him stay there until he could get on his feet. That was eight years ago, and it was the last I heard from him."

Elliot thought about the newspapers he'd found in the old house where Laura Bradford had lived. *The Gazette* article had only mentioned several people had gone missing, downplaying the incident by emphasizing they were a group of drifters with histories of moving in and out of locations without notice. Gerald had taken a more sinister approach, though his reputation for tabloid style writing had acted to soften its impact. One of the names mentioned in Gerald's article had been Corey Sherman. Elliot slid the Glock back into its holster. "What can you tell me about the commune where your brother was staying?"

"It was located on private property, just north of Stillwater."

"Have you been out there?"

"Yeah, but I didn't find anything. If people had been living there, it'd certainly been cleaned up. I got to feeling guilty, not having permission or anything, so I didn't stay long."

Elliot ran Jake's explanation through his head. Maybe he was finally getting somewhere. "Do you know who owns the property?"

"Yeah, I managed to find out. His name is David Stephens. He used to teach at the University."

Connections were starting to fall into place. Elliot was starting to like this guy.

"Someone showed up while I was out there," Jake continued. "He came out of nowhere, asked me what I was doing there. He didn't look too happy. I told him I was a treasure hunter, and I'd heard stories about an old tent camp located in the area. I got the idea from my mom's boyfriend. He used a metal detector, was always looking for places like that. He took me with him a few times."

"Did this guy give you a name?"

Jake shook his head. "He seemed to buy my story, so I did what he said and took to the road. 'Get the hell out and don't come back' was how he put it. If he'd known what I was really up to, I might not have made it out of there so easily. I figured it was Stephens, the property owner."

Elliot wondered if that could be the case. It seemed unlikely. "Could you describe him?"

"He was kind of big, like you, but a little older."

"Greying blond hair and blue eyes?"

"That's the guy. You know him?"

"It wasn't Stephens."

"How do you know?"

"I was a student at the university when he was teaching there, had a couple of run-ins with him. David Stephens is about five foot six, with dark hair and dark eyes."

Jake shook his head. "Maybe this guy works for Stephens?"

"Maybe," Elliot said. "Anything's possible."

"He might have been with him," Jake said. "He'd parked on the road about 400 feet ahead of me. I thought I saw somebody in his car."

"Are you a Christian, Jake?"

The biker's face went blank. "I guess so. I mean, I'm not anything else. Why do you ask?"

"Before my mother lost her soul to drugs, she read scripture to me, told me everybody had a role to play, a purpose if you will. This is mine, Jake. It's what I do. I appreciate your help, but this is the part where I tell you to drop the investigation and go on back home."

"You're creeping me out."

"I hope I'm getting my point across. I've been on some strange cases, but I've never seen anything like this before."

"Yeah, it's strange, all right," Jake said. "So give it to me straight. Is there any chance my brother could still be alive?"

Elliot leaned against the truck. He'd begun to like this guy, and he knew what it was like to be alone. He doubted after eight years there would be much hope, but he said, "Anything's possible. I'll do what I can to find out."

Elliot watched Jake Sherman climb into his car and drive out of the parking lot. He hoped the biker would leave this thing alone, but he didn't think it would play out that way. He hadn't told Jake, but he knew who'd run him off Stephens' property. Greying blond hair, blue eyes. It was Ryan, and he worked for the Stillwater Police Department.

Elliot climbed into his truck and rummaged through the glove compartment until he found Ryan's business card. When he dialed the number, he reached a Sergeant Westlake.

"Detective William Ryan, please."

"He's out of the office right now. Could I take a message?"

Elliot loosened his grip on the phone. Westlake's voice sounded tentative. "Do you know where I can find him? It's pretty important."

"I could be of more help if I knew who I was speaking with."

Elliot stared through the window into the nearly empty parking lot. "The name's Elliot, Tulsa Police Department."

"Tulsa? You guys working on something together?"

"You could say that, but it's kind of unofficial."

"That's our boy," Westlake said. "Or at least it used to be."

"What do you mean?"

"He turned in his badge this morning and walked out. I haven't seen him since."

"You've got to be kidding me."

"I wish I was. He won't answer his phone either. I went by his house twice, but he's not there."

Elliot squeezed the phone. The tone of Westlake's voice said this thing was bothering him. "Why would he do something like that?"

"I can't figure it. He's a different sort all right, but I've never known him to pull anything like this."

"Do you have any idea where I might find him?"

After a pause, Westlake said, "I wouldn't ordinarily give out personal information, but I'm really worried about the guy. I was going to swing by there after work anyway, to check on him, and make sure he's okay."

Chapter Thirty-Two

A few miles west of Stillwater, somewhere near Lake Carl Blackwell, Elliot turned off of Highway 51 and headed north. Following the instructions Sergeant Westlake had given him, he found Ryan's cabin sitting about one hundred feet from the roadway on a wooded lot.

About five hundred feet up, another house peeked around the corner. The noticeable lack of noise played around the edges of Elliot's nerves. The smell of burning wood wafted through the air, but no smoke came from the chimney.

A thick layer of oak leaves announced Elliot's progress as he made his way around the house toward the back of the cabin where he found Detective Ryan sitting in a lawn chair with his feet propped against the railing of a wooden deck. He had a breakfast sandwich in one hand and a Styrofoam container of coffee sat within reach on the side railing. The smoke came from a campfire where Ryan had constructed a ring of sandstones on the ground in front of the deck.

"Nice place," Elliot said.

A blank expression came over Ryan's face. He'd taken a bite of sandwich and he forced the food down his throat, grabbing the coffee to wash it down, all the while keeping his gaze fixed on Elliot. He began to laugh, not an expression of humor but an outpouring of cynicism. Regaining control, he said, "The harbinger of death arrives at my doorstep."

Ryan didn't appear to be drunk or under the influence of drugs, but he trembled, barely able to drink his coffee without spilling it.

"You could be right," Elliot said, "if you don't start playing it straight with me."

"Big city cop, you think you know it all. You know nothing."

"You've been uncooperative, even defensive. What would you think if you were me?"

"Good point," he said. "I guess I'd look suspicious, maybe even guilty."

"Are you?"

"Not really. Not in the way you think, anyway."

"If you're telling me the truth, what are you afraid of?"

"I could tell you, but you wouldn't believe me."

Elliot climbed onto the deck, stopping near Ryan's chair. "Why didn't you tell me about Corey Sherman?"

"How do you know about Sherman?"

"Big city cop, remember. I'll tell you something else. Corey didn't disappear and neither did the people he was with. They're dead and buried on the commune where they lived on property owned by David Stephens. Somebody killed them. Where do you fit in, Ryan, murderer or accomplice?"

Ryan removed his feet from the railing and put them on the deck. "You have no idea what you're getting yourself into."

"Why are you protecting Stephens?"

"I'm not."

"You've been a cop for a long time. That's not something you just walk away from. Your connection must be pretty deep for you to turn in your badge over it."

Ryan tried to stand but his trembling legs wouldn't allow it. Halfway through the maneuver, he gave up and dropped back into the chair. "For God's sake, Elliot, can't you see what this has done to me? Leave it alone."

"People are dying. I want to know why."

"You'll find out soon enough. Seen anything outside your windows lately, shadowy forms hiding in the darkness?"

Elliot thought about what he'd seen moving past the patio door in his backyard. "Funny you should ask. Was it you?"

"It only gets worse. Soon you'll begin to hear things, sounds coming from inside your house, an intruder, but one you'll never catch. God help you if you do."

"Come on, Ryan. You're talking crazy."

An expression somewhere between worry and sympathy crawled across Ryan's face. He pulled a small black book from his shirt pocket and held it out.

Elliot took the book and glanced through it. It was an address book, though the pages were empty except for one, which contained a string of numbers written in black ink.

"You will begin to feel it in the night," Ryan said, "hovering in the darkness just inches from your bed. There might still be time for you to stop it, but you have to drop the investigation, and you have to do it now."

Ryan continued to speak but his words softened, fading to background noise as the campfire again drew Elliot's attention.

The fire had grown, the circle of its heat stretching out to include the deck where Elliot stood. The warmth fell across his skin, scattering his thoughts in multiple directions.

As if she were a neighbor come to visit, Elliot's mother appeared from around the cabin and climbed onto the deck. She kneeled in front of Elliot, and using blood that'd fallen from the syringe in her hand, she traced designs across the floor of her room, misplaced emotions embedded in her stare as she squiggled out the word, *sustenance.*

A soft voice came from somewhere, and Elliot accepted the embrace of a young girl, a disturbing version of Cyndi Bannister, a woman he had once loved, the child, in fact, from the photograph in her father's study. She reached into her pocket and when her hand was once again revealed to Elliot it held a note, its diction scribbled in pencil, from which came a message: I love you. The girl stood on her toes, bringing her face close to Elliot's and she kissed him, the soft touch of her lips brushing against his until he pushed her away.

Elliot was alone in the room and when he turned to see his reflection in the mirror above his mother's vanity, he saw that he, too, was a child.

A chill ran through him, and he realized the fire had gone out, and he was once again standing on the deck of Ryan's cabin.

He quickly surveyed the premises, studying the trees with their absence of birds and sounds, but in particular he became aware of no ring of stones, no smoldering wood, and no ashes. If there had been a campfire, no indication of it now existed. Also, Detective Ryan was gone, as was the lawn chair where he'd sat and the cup of coffee he'd placed on the railing.

Elliot walked across the deck toward the cabin and tried the door.

He found it locked. He thought about the front entrance but suspected it would be secured as well. He pressed his face against the small rectangle of glass on the backdoor.

Worn, comfortable-looking furniture occupied the room. Pinewood paneling covered the walls, stained in a few areas by smoke that'd come from the fireplace: A Norman Rockwell scene, its picturesque essence obliterated by the corpse of Detective William Ryan, which appeared to levitate above the floor.

Elliot kicked in the door, but as soon as he confirmed what he'd suspected, that what had happened was long past his being able to do anything about it, he pulled his phone and punched in the number for the Stillwater Police Department.

Westlake answered.

Elliot had hoped he would. "You need to get out here," he said. "Ryan's dead. He hanged himself."

Elliot broke the connection with Westlake. Some paperwork scattered across the floor of the cabin caught his attention.

Being inside Ryan's place, let alone sifting through his personal belongings, put a knot in Elliot's stomach, but he pulled a pen form his pocket and shuffled through the papers, reading enough to get the gist of it. The documents amounted to a recent transaction between Ryan and the Trustee Department of the Bank of Oklahoma. The business acted to transfer, to the bank, Ryan's power of attorney over the estate of David Stephens. The professor, if the documentation was accurate, now resided at Woodland Estates, an upscale senior living center in South Tulsa.

Elliot stood and walked outside. Money had been involved, but from the look of things, Ryan hadn't taken any of it. He'd used the funds to care for Stephens and nothing else.

Elliot used his phone to find the address of Woodland Estates and as the number appeared on the screen, his mouth went dry. It was the same number that had been written across the pages of the address book Ryan had handed him as they'd talked on the deck of the cabin.

Chapter Thirty-Three

Several hours after he found Ryan hanging from the ceiling of his cabin, Elliot stood in a common area at Woodland Estates, the senior living center indicated in Ryan's paperwork. The receptionist had sent him to the skilled nursing wing where he found a trembling and frail man slumped in a wheelchair. The invalid was not alone. An attendant, a slender man of African descent, sat beside him.

The invalid in the wheelchair was David Stephens.

"Can he get out of the chair," Elliot asked, "walk around if he needs to?"

"Oh no, sir, nothing like that," the attendant said. He leaned over and stared into Stephens' face. "Most times, he don't know where he is, much less what he's doing. It kind of comes and goes. Won't let nobody but me help him. Don't know why."

"How long has he been like this?"

"Ever since I've been here, going on seven years now would be about right. Are you family or something?"

"No, just an old acquaintance."

As if acknowledging Elliot's presence, Stephens raised one of his hands slightly from the arm of the chair.

"The way I understand it," the attendant said, "I'm the closest thing he's got to family. Like I said, he comes around, not so much anymore, but we talk now and then, he tells me things."

"What kind of things?"

Stephens made an effort to move, his actions becoming somewhat successful as he reached from the wheelchair and grasped his attendant's hand.

"Would you look at that," the man said. He leaned close to Stephens. "He wants to know who you are. I understand you told me already, but he wasn't listening, know what I'm saying?"

"The name's Elliot. I attended school at the university while you were teaching there."

"Student?"

Surprise showed on the aide's face. The word had come from Stephens.

"Not exactly," Elliot said. Of course he'd been a student at the university, but Stephens was talking about students who had taken his classes. "I knew Angela Gardner," Elliot continued. "She told me about your classes."

Stephens raised his head, some of the haze clearing from his eyes, his recognition of Elliot now showing on his face.

"What happened to Corey Sherman, Professor Stephens, and the rest of those people who lived on your property?"

Elliot didn't like being so blunt, but it was why he'd come to Woodland Estates, and the question needed to be asked.

A tremor started in Stephens' neck and worked its way to his feet. He freed his hand from the attendant's and began to slap the arm of the wheelchair. "Don't touch the knife. Don't touch the knife."

The man rubbed Stephens' shoulders. "It's all right, now. Everything's all right." To Elliot he said, "Maybe you ought to get on out of here. It ain't good for the Professor to get all worked up."

The attendant seemed like a good man and Elliot didn't want to make life hard for him, but he had a job to do. "You've shouldered the burden long enough, Professor Stephens. Tell me what happened while you were teaching at the university."

The aide came from behind the wheelchair and started toward Elliot, shaking his head.

Elliot showed his badge. It seemed the only way.

The man examined the identification and backed away.

Elliot unbuttoned his jacket exposing the Glock hanging in the shoulder holster, an old interrogation habit. It was possible Stephens had something to do with the missing drifters in Stillwater, but it was a pretty sure bet he hadn't killed anybody in Tulsa. "Whatever you let loose eight years ago has found a way to come back, Stephens. If you know how to stop it, or corral it in anyway, please tell me."

Stephens opened and closed his mouth, like some kind of demented fish, though he could not speak, and when he'd managed to regain a small amount of control, he squeezed out one word and said "Reynolds."

Elliot leaned closer to Professor Stephens. "Are you talking about Stanley Gerald Reynolds who wrote for the school newspaper?"

Stephens slumped over, his head hanging nearly to his chest. The nurse shook his head. "The professor's gone back to wherever it is he goes."

"How long will it last?"

"Hard to say. Could be hours, could be days. The fellow he mentioned, though, I'm pretty sure he's some kind of kin. He talks about him. I gather there was some kind of dispute, something bad enough to tear the family apart. That's why nobody comes to see him, the way I see it. This Reynolds he keeps talking about, you know the man?"

"He was Stephens' nephew."

"I see. You know I hate to pry into other people's business, but with Mr. Stephens being under my care and all, I'd sure appreciate knowing what brought you here."

Elliot glanced at the floor. The man had been cooperative, allowing the questioning of his patient. Answering his question was only fair. "Something odd went down a few years ago in Stillwater while Stephens was teaching at the university, people gone missing, that sort of thing. I suspect Stephens knows something about it."

"I'm not an educated man," the attendant said, "but I know people. It's something God gave me. The professor here, he's sure enough got some problems, but he's not a bad person. No, sir, I can't see him killing nobody. You find this Reynolds fellow he keeps talking about and maybe you get some answers."

Elliot thanked the attendant for his time and cooperation then turned and walked away. The man's advice carried an element of logic, but as Elliot left the senior living center, he began to entertain a line of reasoning. The commonality linking the murders was not the killer himself, or herself, but the type of victim and the manner in which their lives had been taken. Laura Bradford had known that as well, and her understanding of the problem had drawn her to Stillwater.

Elliot grabbed his phone. He had a hard time understanding how someone like Detective Ryan, who had been, at least on some level, a kind and caring person, could have taken his own life. However, suicide by its nature would involve some level of premeditation. Ryan had made sure David Stephens would be taken care of. It was possible, after Elliot had showed him the remains that he'd done the right thing and contacted Laura Bradford's next of kin as well.

Elliot called Sergeant Westlake and explained the problem. A few minutes later, Westlake gave him the name of Nathaniel Parker, Laura Bradford's grandfather. The address was in Spiro, Oklahoma.

Chapter Thirty-Four

The address in Spiro turned out to be an old singlewide on Dogwood Street. A tall Native American with long, grey hair stood on a small wooden deck attached to the mobile home.

At the foot of the steps leading to the deck Elliot stopped and said, "The name's Elliot. I called earlier. I'm looking for Nathaniel Parker."

He smiled. "It looks like you've found him."

He invited Elliot inside, and once they were seated, he said, "I spoke with Detective Ryan yesterday. He told me you were the one who found my granddaughter and called the police. It was a good thing you did."

Elliot started to speak but nothing seemed appropriate, so he just nodded, a gesture that was also insufficient to express his feelings.

"I have a question," Nathaniel Parker said. "You seem like a nice person, but not so much that you would drive to Spiro just to offer your condolences to an old man who you don't even know. Why are you here, Mr. Elliot?"

Elliot leaned forward in the chair, a brown leather model with wagon wheels on the sides. "I knew your granddaughter while she was in Stillwater, long enough for us to become friends."

Mr. Parker nodded. "She was like that."

"Yes. She also gave me the impression she'd come to the school for a reason, something more significant than hanging out with a bunch of college kids. When she stopped coming around, we were all curious as to why she might leave without saying anything, but we didn't take it any further. I'm sorry. We should have done more."

"Did you suspect at the time that she might be in danger?"

Elliot shook his head. "Although, looking back, it's difficult to understand why I wasn't more concerned."

"Don't be so hard on yourself. If what you say is true, you did not know what had befallen Laura."

Elliot sat back in the chair. Nathaniel Parker was much like his granddaughter, possessing a mysterious yet kind and respectful nature that gave him the resonance of an old friend. Elliot told him everything, beginning with what happened in Stillwater while Laura was there, and ending with what had transpired since Gerald called him a few days ago. He didn't skirt the issue of murder, and unlike the abridged version he'd given to Dombrowski, this account held back nothing.

Mr. Parker's dark eyes studied Elliot. Later he said, "You should let go of the guilt. You were young and did not know."

"That's good advice. But I'm not very good at letting things go."

"Tenacity is a good character trait for a police detective. It's also part of why you are here."

"I checked the records. Laura wasn't a student. The content of an article published in the school paper concerning the drifters drew her to Stillwater, but she could have known something, picked up on a part of the article the casual reader would not have. Do you know why your granddaughter went to Stillwater, Mr. Parker?"

Nathaniel Parker leaned over and switched on a lamp, sending a soft glow across the room, not enough to eliminate the darkness created by heavy shaded windows, but sufficient for a commingling, a tolerable dilution, like a campfire in a dark wood. "Do you believe in God, Mr. Elliot?"

"Yes, sir, I do."

"Good. I've been a member of Oakwood Baptist Church here in town for more than twenty years. I also remember and respect the ways of my people. We all have darkness in our hearts, some more than others. I used to wonder if agrarian societies bred superstition, you know, like the book by Stephen King, *Children of the Corn*, I think it was."

Elliot smiled. It was difficult to imagine Mr. Parker kicking back in an easy chair and reading horror novels.

"But I finally decided it was more a matter of time."

"Come again?"

"I think it's why my people hold in such high esteem the balance of nature and the sanctity of the hunt. When having to use the bulk of your faculties just for survival, a certain purity of the soul results. It's when we have the time to sit around and think about what we are doing that we get ourselves into trouble."

"I've never heard it put that way before," Elliot said, "but the concept carries a fair amount of logic."

"You have a strong spiritual nature, Detective Elliot. This is the impression you give me. But it causes you discomfort because you don't understand it. You lean toward the pragmatic world in which you live, but your spiritual gift refuses to relinquish its hold. Laura was like that, too, and she cared for our culture, a rare quality for someone as young as she was."

"You have a gift as well, Mr. Parker. You look inside people and understand them."

Laura's grandfather smiled. "Let me tell you a story. Long ago, even before the white man, a stranger came to a village of my ancestors. He tricked them by saying he was lost and hungry. In truth, he was an outcast, an evil shape-shifter, driven from his homeland by his own people. This was found out later. As it was, he came to live among the villagers who took him in.

"As time passed, being clever and deceitful, the stranger convinced many of the villagers he had power and would make a good religious leader. He promised he would bring prosperity and much food. He gained many followers who fell under his spell and were blinded to his true nature. Soon he began to hold ceremonies in secret, where he and his followers would offer blood sacrifices, cutting out the hearts of prisoners from other villages with an obsidian blade. Carved into the handle was the likeness of his god.

"This angered and troubled the elders, so they held council and decided the visitor should be made to leave the village. Having been around the people, though, the stranger had many followers and he refused.

"Soon the skies dried up and the crops began to wither. The elders knew it was because of the stranger and the bad things he did. Again they held council, and this time they prayed to the spirits of their ancestors so they might help them.

"The next day, a princess came to the village and said she would help the elders with their problem if they would promise to leave food for her on occasion in the forest where she lived. The elders agreed they would do this.

"When night came, the princess caught the eye of the stranger and she lay with him. When he was asleep, she took the knife with the blade of obsidian and killed him with it.

"Early the next morning, the princess was gone, and before anyone else awoke, the elders took the body of the stranger and sealed it along with the knife in a tomb on which they put a curse so no one would open it."

A knot formed in Elliot's stomach as he thought of Gerald and his obsession with Native American artifacts. "Would the tomb happen to be what is now called the Spiro Mounds?"

"Yes, that is the story as it has come down to me."

"The mounds were reopened in the 1930's."

"Yes. By the white man."

"What does any of this have to do with Laura, Mr. Parker?"

Nathaniel Parker's eyes looked as distant as the time period of which he spoke. "Do you believe in genetic memory, Detective?"

"I never gave it much thought."

"Even as a child, Laura would ask me about the legend. I would say it was an obsession, but it goes deeper than that. Laura knew the desire of our ancestors to put an end to the curse. She was wise," he said, "and knew things her years should not support. She told me of a vision she had, and its meaning was clear to her. The visitor, who had long ago brought trouble to our people, had been possessed by a darkness that did not die with him. It had been imprisoned in the tomb, but was set free when the tomb was breached.

"The next morning, I found her room cleaned and her bed nicely made, but Laura was gone. The note she left said only that it was time for her to be on her own, and that I should respect her wishes and not try to follow her. She said she loved me and she would be back some day. It wasn't until yesterday that I learned what had happened to her. I always knew, though. I think I knew."

Elliot took a deep breath and let it out slowly. The rhythm and cadence of Nathaniel Parker's words had him mesmerized. "Thank you," he said, "for sharing the story with me. I know it must be hard for you."

"The job you keep carries honor, though many in such positions are not honorable people. With this case, you lack the support of your superiors and even, or so it sounds, those close to you, and yet you sacrifice your time and the respect of those who do not understand in order to continue your mission. Simply having the ability and the strength to impose your will does not make you a warrior. There are those who stand tall among their nations because they refuse to lose dignity and humanity for the sake of vague ideals. These are the true warriors of the world. You and I, Detective Elliot, we are warriors.

"Laura brought hope and filled this old trailer house with happiness. For an old man who had looked forward to only alcohol and sin, she was a savior. Let me show you something."

Nathaniel Parker led Elliot through the back door and down a set of steps to a small backyard where an old swing set occupied an area sectioned off and filled with sand. The grass, though cut and trimmed, had for the most part reclaimed the play area.

"I come here when I want to remember how it was when Laura played in this yard. She liked to dance and she was good at it, practicing almost daily the meaningful movements of our ancestors. They have been covered over by the seasons, but if you look closely you can still see her footprints in the sand, footprints of a dancer.

"Laura did not explain to me the complete meaning of her vision because she was trying to protect me, but now I understand. She believed she could stop the darkness. I think she is still trying, Detective, and she brought you here, to her grandfather, so I could tell you that she needs your help."

Chapter Thirty-Five

Elliot's visit with Nathaniel Parker, Laura's grandfather, changed forever the way he would think about the Spiro Mounds Archaeological Park. It would be closing in less than an hour, and he had no idea of what he hoped to accomplish there.

Elliot passed a couple of tourists who were on their way out, and a portion of their conversation drifted his way.

"Well they're not very big, are they?"

The tourists were talking about the mounds. The grassy hills that now rose up from the earth were reproductions. The original mounds constructed by Native Americans had been torn down in the 1930's, tunneled into and blasted by a venture known as the Pocola Mining Company, and later completely leveled by State Archaeologists. It wasn't until the 1970's that the mounds were reconstructed, using, in all probability, some of the same dirt, but the fact remained they were not the real deal. The knowledge of this weighed heavily on Elliot's mind.

A rustling sound like dried leaves scraping across a hard surface filled the air, and just at the boundaries of his vision Elliot caught a suggestion of movement, a subtle blurring of the landscape as something traced across it.

Elliot studied the mounds, the area from where the disturbance had come. He forced his attention away from the distraction only to confront another problem. He was not alone. He stared into the lovely eyes of Cyndi Bannister.

Cyndi wrapped her arms around Elliot, and while her breath fell warm against his face and the scent of candied grapes clung to her hair and filled his senses, she pressed her lips against his.

It did not seem like fantasy, though Elliot knew it must be since Cyndi now resided in prison. At the moment, though, his thoughts stemmed not from a place of logic but from desire, and he longed to again experience the heat of Cyndi's passion. He ran his hand down the small of her back, pulling her closer and straying even further, caressing the softness of her buttocks before regaining a portion of his senses.

Elliot brought her hair to his face to again relish her sweet scent. He had to remind himself she was an evil killer, capable of atrocities without remorse, had in fact taken the lives of her parents. He closed his eyes and when he reopened them Cyndi was gone.

Before Elliot could recover from the vision, or mental lapse, or whatever he'd just been through, someone spoke.

"You all right, sir?"

It was one of the park rangers.

"I'm fine," Elliot said. "The lady I was with, did you happen to see where she went?"

"No, sir. But you've been standing in the same spot for a few minutes, so I thought I'd better check. You never know how these old mounds are going to affect people. Anything I can do for you?"

Elliot gathered his senses. "I'm interested in the history of the mounds. I've read a few books, looked over most of what's on the internet, but I've yet to find exactly what I'm looking for. Would you know where I might get some information that's not so well known, maybe even a little offbeat?"

The ranger stifled a laugh. "I knew there was something different about you, more than the average tourist, I mean. You're one of those tabloid writers, aren't you, looking for spooks and curses, that sort of thing?"

"Not exactly. I'm..."

The ranger waved his hand. "Don't worry about it. If you promise not to mention me or any of the other park employees, I've got a lead for you, one that'll probably give you what you're after."

* * *

The sign painted across the window read *Spiro Research Center.*

Inside the shop, a small man with black, oily hair sat behind the counter, flipping through the pages of a book. The front entrance had been equipped with a bell, but he gave no indication he'd heard the warning.

Books lined the walls, and thousands more occupied inner shelves, creating dark hallways through the store. The silence was broken only by a slow turning ceiling fan that was slightly out of balance, its long chain knocking against the motor housing in a rhythmic clicking.

"Excuse me," Elliot said.

He looked up from his study. "Hey there. Sorry. Didn't hear you come in. Must have been caught up in my reading. Happens all the time."

"I'm looking for information concerning the mounds. I was told you might be able to help."

The bookstore owner glanced at a wall clock. "Oh, well I'm afraid the park would be closed now. You could try tomorrow. Directions, is that what you need?"

"I know where the park is. What I'm after is history, something a little more in depth than what's readily available."

He stood and touched his forehead with his fingertips, as if he were trying to extract something. "In depth?"

Elliot followed the man as he left the counter and started down one of the narrow, isles. "Got a few books," he said, "should be something here. Are you looking for dates, when and how the mounds were constructed, time periods, who occupied the area?"

"Do you have anything concerning the destruction of the mounds in the 1930's, and what was found, specific artifacts, that sort of thing?"

"Specific artifacts?"

"One of the park rangers thought I might find what I'm looking for here."

"A ranger?"

"He thought I wrote for the tabloids. I don't, by the way."

"Why would he do that?" Answering his own question, the man said, "Questions. The questions you asked. Tall lanky guy, smiles a lot?"

"That's the one."

He nodded, incorporating both his head and his shoulders. "Okay, who are you for real?"

Elliot extended his hand. "Name's Elliot."

"McKenzie, Doctor McKenzie."

"I'm an investigator, Doctor McKenzie. But the unusual nature of the case I'm working suggests I play things a little differently. I'm unofficial, on my own time."

"Unofficial?"

"I'm in the process of compiling evidence."

A tentative grin spread across McKenzie's face. "Investigating the paranormal would be my guess. Are you a ghost hunter, Mr. Elliot?"

Elliot's stomach tightened. In a very real sense, that's exactly what he was. "The information I need could stray in such a direction."

"Well, Mr. Unofficial Investigator, the generally accepted theory is that the mound area was inhabited by people of Caddo influence, a pre-Columbian, Mississippian culture that occupied the site from roughly 850 A.D. to 1450.

"What Pre-Columbian really means is before the occurrence of significant European influence. The Vikings reached Newfoundland about 500 years before Columbus stumbled upon the islands he called the Indies, and it's been suggested the Irish might have landed in North America 400 years before that. In addition, there's the Chinese, Polynesians, Greeks, yadda, yadda. I guess you could say Columbus rediscovered the new world, but he wasn't the first and neither were any of the other groups I rattled off."

"Interesting," Elliot said. "But what does any of that have to do with Spiro?"

"The mounds... right. It all relates. But I can see where you might think I lost focus. You wouldn't believe what goes on. Anyone who attempts to go against the popular theories is literally attacked by the archaeological establishment. Unless they have something to hide, why would they do such a thing?"

"It's all very interesting," Elliot said. "But I don't think we're on the same page here."

McKenzie touched his forehead. "Wait. What exactly are you looking for?"

Elliot pulled the photocopy of the obsidian knife from his pocket and held it out.

McKenzie studied the photo briefly. The expression on his face said it all. "What does this have to do with the mounds?"

"I was hoping you could tell me."

McKenzie blinked several times. "Most archaeologists don't believe there was significant interaction between Mississippian and Mesoamerican cultures. Some say none at all. That's ridiculous. Trade goods from all over the country, including Mexico, have been found at the mounds. Of course there was contact."

McKenzie led Elliot to the rear of the shop and into a storage room. A bright, bare bulb dangled from the ceiling, its glow revealing an area with large metal shelves lining the walls. An old wooden desk occupied the corner closest to the door. McKenzie rummaged through some items in a box, pulled out a framed photo.

The 8 x 10, black and white photograph the doctor handed Elliot depicted two men standing near a crude wooden table scattered with various artifacts. In the background, open tunnels snaked into the northern-most cone of the Spiro Mound complex. The experience of the photographer showed through, rendering the subject matter in clear, distinguishable detail. Among the artifacts displayed on the table was a knife made of obsidian. It looked, in every detail, exactly like the one in the photocopy he'd found in Gerald's car. The knife might have been of Mesoamerican design, as Doctor Cramer at the museum had indicated, but in the summer of 1935 it, or one just like it, had been excavated from the earthen mounds located near Spiro, Oklahoma.

Elliot suspected the men in the photo were members of the Pocola Mining Company, the company that had leased the property and tunneled into the mounds to get the artifacts. "Do you know who these people are?"

Doctor McKenzie shook his head. "There are no names on the back, but check this out."

McKenzie pulled a magnifying glass from the top drawer of the desk and handed it to Elliot. "Look at the upper left corner."

Elliot studied the photo. He hadn't noticed it before, the strange obsidian knife having garnered his attention, but standing off to the left, almost out of the camera's field of vision, a man dressed in black leaned against a tree.

Elliot's fingers went slack and he nearly lost his grip on the magnifying glass. The man in the photograph looked like his old buddy, Gerald. "He's wearing a Roman collar."

"Interesting isn't it?"

"Why would a Catholic priest be at an archaeological dig?" Elliot asked.

"I know. You never know what you might run across."

"How did the photograph come to be in your possession?"

McKenzie shrugged. "I pick up things as I run across them."

Elliot thought about the man in the photograph, the elongated shape of his face, the way his eyes sat deep in their sockets. He looked too much like Gerald not to be related. "Is there a Catholic church in town?"

An understanding look crossed McKenzie's face. "Yeah, but it's only been here since the 1970's. The closest one back then would've been in Poteau. It's still there. I mean, I guess it's the same one. I don't know what kind of records they would keep, but I guess it'd be worth a shot."

"Thanks," Elliot said.

"Sure. Let me know what you find."

Chapter Thirty-Six

In the dim light of the overcast evening, the Immaculate Conception Church appeared stoic, even foreboding, as if it were a miniature castle lifted from the foggy moors of Scotland, a country manor where one did not go without proper invitation.

Father Williams came out of the darkness of the chancel, his pace slow and deliberate until he stopped a few feet away.

The nearly expressionless face of the priest did little to alleviate Elliot's apprehension, though he'd called ahead so his visit would not be a surprise. "I appreciate your seeing me on short notice."

"Of course," the priest said. "However, I do have a prior engagement. If this is nothing more than a genealogical quest, I'll have to decline the interview. Otherwise, I can only offer a few minutes."

Elliot pulled his badge. A need to be completely honest pressed heavily on his conscience.

Father Williams examined the credentials and handed them back. "Why would a homicide detective from Tulsa be interested in the archives of a Catholic church in Poteau, Oklahoma?"

The atmosphere inside the church should have been peaceful, should have been quiet, though the tension in the nave and the unnerving sound of wind blowing outside the building worked hard to undermine such a state. As if he understood what Elliot was thinking, the actions of Father Williams, his glancing at the windows and constant straitening of his clothes, indicated this was not, at least in total, an often occurring ambiance.

"I can't tell you that the case is official," Elliot said, "but I can tell you it's extremely important."

"Please make your point, Detective."

"Of course. In the summer of 1935, something happened in Spiro, an event connected with the removal of ceremonial objects from the mounds."

The priest studied Elliot's face. "Your regret is understandable. What the miners did was wrong. There's no doubt about that. However, it's prudent to keep in mind that what you speak of was a depression-era venture, the goal of its members certainly being to make money, and during a time when there was little of it to go around."

"Thank you, Father. And forgive me for speaking in such general terms. My concern has to do with a particular artifact the priest I'm inquiring about was associated with."

Father Williams frowned. "I hope it is not your intention to cast doubt upon the Church."

"No, Father. On the contrary, I believe the priest's role would have been directly related to his faith, his Christianity."

"In that case, unless you are being less than honest, and acting only to gain my favor, please continue."

The sound of the wind increased, though it did not seem to be leaking through the windows or any other openings in the structure.

"Oh, I am being honest, Father. Some might say it's not in my nature to be otherwise. I won't ask for much of your time, just the name of the priest who would have presided over the parish during the time period."

Again, Father Williams glanced at the windows.

"Unusual weather we're having," Elliot said.

The priest nodded. "Although your request is rather unusual, I'm inclined to align my decision based on your sincerity. While you were en-route, I looked up the information you inquired about. The priest's name was Father Reynolds."

"Thank you," Elliot said. "Would you happen to know the complete name?"

"Yes, of course. It was Stanley Gerald Reynolds."

The name delivered confirmation of what Elliot had expected. In the photograph McKenzie had shown him, the priest hadn't looked exactly like his old college buddy, but there had been enough family resemblance for him to make a tentative assumption. Now, upon hearing the name, he had no doubt. The man, dressed in Catholic clothing and standing in the background of the photo was Stanley Gerald Reynolds I, Gerald's great grandfather. "Is there anything else you could tell me about him?"

"What do you want to know?"

"Let's just say I went to school with his great grandson."

Father Williams frowned and glanced at the floor. "The records indicate he resigned his position that same year. The reason given was he'd become dissatisfied and disillusioned."

"Thanks," Elliot said. "I appreciate the information, and your time."

Elliot turned and started toward the exit. He still had questions, but Father Williams seemed anxious to get on with his business. At the door, however, Elliot turned back. The priest's answer begged for another question. "Do you know what happened to him?"

"The subject was, for many years, the source of rumors I do not wish to perpetuate. The truth is no one seems to know the exact fate of Father Reynolds after he left his post. Perhaps he simply left town, started a family as you indicated and lived out his new life in another community."

Elliot left the church and descended the steps into a windless day, as serene and commonplace as it had been when he'd arrived. No leaves dotted the lawn, and no branches had broken free from the trees. A wind of the magnitude Elliot had heard from the nave should have left a reminder of its presence, but it had not.

Elliot reached for the door of the pickup and again the wind began to blow, and though it arrived with no perceptible disturbance of the area, it raked across his skin like currents of water, cooled from unimaginable depths of darkness.

An understanding of an impending change in his surroundings blossomed in Elliot's mind. Where there had been cars, there were none, where there had been people, no one strolled the sidewalks. The buildings and houses were still there, occupying their sections of Oklahoma soil, but Elliot suspected that, like plastic replicas in a kid's playhouse, they were empty. On Bagwell Street, just down from the Church of the Immaculate Conception, Elliot stood in a lifeless vacuum that, seconds earlier, had been an ordinary town.

A scream, not unlike the unnerving sound Elliot had heard the night he'd last seen Gerald, cut through the air.

Elliot scanned the area, his gaze fixing on the church.

Father Williams had come outside onto the lawn that ran beside the church. The priest stumbled and dropped to his knees.

Elliot grabbed his phone and punched in 911 as he ran to Father Williams.

Blood striped the left side of his face while a similar wound ran across his chest, his shirt shredded in a matching pattern. His eyes begged for Elliot to come closer so he could speak.

Elliot lowered himself to the priest's side to hear the words he was forming.

* * *

About an hour later, Bill Ludlow, Poteau's Chief of Police, crossed the room and poured himself a cup of coffee. "Tell me again why you were at the church."

"Come on," Elliot said, "you've been around law enforcement long enough to know I didn't carry out the attack. There's no blood on my clothes. I don't have a weapon which could have inflicted that kind of damage. Anyway, all you have to do is ask Father Williams."

"Yeah, well I'm way ahead of you. By the way, what was he saying to you when we arrived?"

"He kept repeating the name of Father Reynolds."

"That mean anything to you?"

"It ties in with an unofficial case I've been working. Father Reynolds used to be a priest here in Poteau."

Chief Ludlow's face showed interest. "Is that right? Well, where is he now?"

"The way I understand it, he disappeared in 1935."

"Are you trying to play me for a fool, Elliot?"

"The thought never entered my mind."

"Yeah, I'll bet. What's a Tulsa police detective got to do with all this?"

Elliot briefly explained what had brought him to Poteau, leaning it more toward a missing friend rather than murder. It just seemed like the thing to do.

Chief Ludlow went behind his desk and lowered himself into his chair. "Let me ask you something. Coming from a place like Tulsa, you've probably seen it all, not much left that might surprise you. What's your take on this?"

Elliot considered his answer. He didn't want to be misleading, but he didn't want to be led into a trap either. "With your being from the country, you should have more experience with animal attacks than I would."

"You sound pretty convinced that's what it was."

"What else could it be?"

"Maybe you're right. But you said you didn't see or hear anything."

"I heard Father Williams' scream."

"What kind of animal do you think could do that," Ludlow asked, "inflict that kind of damage yet come and go without being seen?"

"I don't know."

Chief Ludlow rubbed his forehead. "Word travels fast in a place like this. I know what kind of questions you've been asking around town. I've lived here long enough to have heard the stories. I don't want folks getting all stirred up over some hoodoo nonsense associated with the mounds."

"That was never my intention."

Ludlow's flat, grey eyes studied Elliot. "What are your intentions? My instincts tell me there's more to this than a missing friend."

Elliot stared back at Ludlow. For rumors to have been powerful enough to last all these years, one had to wonder if any substance was behind them. "What about Father Williams?" he asked. "What was his *take* on what happened?"

Ludlow's face remained flat, unreadable. "That's all I have for now, Detective. But don't go getting any ideas about questioning Father Williams. I've posted a guard."

"I won't bother him," Elliot said. "I hope he recovers quickly."

As Elliot walked out of Ludlow's office, he wondered what, exactly, had happened after the miners removed the obsidian knife from the mounds, and what kind of archives the town newspaper might keep.

When Elliot found the office of the *Poteau Daily News*, the lights were on and a car was parked in front, so he pushed through the door and stepped inside.

A man came through a door near the back of the office, wiping his hands on a rag he'd pulled from his pocket. "Langley Peterson," he said. "Make it quick. I've got work to do."

A shock of silver hair protruded from beneath Peterson's folded, paper hat. He'd walked in a stooped manner and remained slightly bent as he stood waiting.

Elliot decided to get right to the point. "What can you tell me about the summer of 1935?"

"That's a pretty broad subject."

"Let me narrow it down," Elliot said. "I'm looking for information about Stanley Gerald Reynolds, better known as Father Reynolds."

The newspaper man's jaw tightened, wrinkles creased his forehead. "You don't strike me as the kind who would walk in off the street, thinking he might get lucky. What makes you think I might know anything about something that happened so long ago?"

"Who says anything happened, out of the ordinary I mean? Maybe I'm just a guy on a genealogical quest, or a curious history buff."

Peterson ambled over to an office chair and lowered himself into it. "I heard about Father Williams. You know what they say about small towns. You're a cop from Tulsa. So cut the crap and tell me why you're here."

Elliot gave the newspaper man a brief and guarded run-down of what had brought him to town.

Langley Peterson stroked his chin. "I was just a kid at the time, and knowing that what's in my head was filtered through the mind of a child has been a blessing, a sort of buffer between the lie of reality and the truth of fiction, if you know what I mean."

"That's an interesting way of putting it."

A hint of suspicion flickered in the Peterson's eyes. "You're not one of those tabloid writers, are you?"

"Don't worry," Elliot said. "You had it right the first time. Name's Elliot. I'm a detective."

"I shouldn't know much about it, mind you. Good folk wouldn't talk nonsense in front of the kids in those days, had to put them to bed first. I learned to feign sleep and keep a sharp ear open. Most of it was just *when's it going to rain* and *how are we going to pay the bills*. Not much interest to a six year old. But it was the occasional verbal wondering of *why is this happening to us*, and *maybe there is something to what folks have been saying about the world coming to an end* that got my attention."

"They say most rumors have an element of truth behind them," Elliot said.

Peterson leveled his gaze. "You're right, Detective. There was something going on all right. People started disappearing, whole families mind you. I was terrified. My folks would have croaked if they knew I was listening."

"We're talking about the middle of the Depression," Elliot said, "and the Dust Bowl. People were doing that weren't they, packing up and leaving their homes, going out of state?"

"That was the Sheriff's explanation. The paper went along with him. And yeah, plenty of folks got their fill of it and moved on, but they'd talk about it first, tell somebody what they were planning. They didn't just disappear during the night, leaving everything behind, including supper on the table. There was talk they'd found the Johnston family, buried in the floor of their barn."

A disturbing thought snaked through Elliot's head. Serial killings had patterns and this series was no exception, even though the murders spanned a time period of nearly eighty years, with victims chosen from the ranks of the homeless in Tulsa, a band of wanderers in Stillwater, and down-and-out Depression era families in and around Spiro. "When did this happen?" he asked.

Peterson stroked his chin. "I reckon it was right around the time the Pocola Mining Company busted into the King's chamber, out at the mounds. The diggers said they heard a hissing sound when they breached the tomb walls and not long after a musty odor seeped out of the ground. The air rushing in to fill a 700 year old vacuum was what they said, and maybe that's what it was, but I figure something more than a bad smell came out of the ground that day."

Elliot leaned back in his chair. Neither Peterson's expression nor his body language indicated deception. "What about Father Reynolds? How does he fit in with this?"

"There was talk maybe the young priest had gone mad, and that maybe he had something to do with the disappearing people. Some said he wasn't a normal man at all, but had the ability to change into some sort of animal, a big cat."

"What do you think?" Elliot asked.

Peterson hands began to tremble. "When those miners dug into the tomb, they released some kind of curse. And I'm not the only one who believes that."

Elliot pulled out one of his business cards and gave it to Peterson. "I should be going. I'd like to talk more about this, but it's getting late."

"You don't know me, Detective, but folks around here will tell you I'm a rational, conservative, church-going man."

"There's no need to justify yourself," Elliot said. "I understand, and I appreciate your input."

"There's something else I need to tell you."

"Go on," Elliot said.

"My uncle on my mom's side, Charles McDugan, who lived down the street from us, he was one of those miners."

"He worked for the Pocola Mining Company?"

"That's what I'm saying. Uncle Charlie, he had always been a kind and generous sort, but he turned mean, wouldn't come out of the house or let anybody in."

"Do you think he had something to do with the disappearances?"

"I don't know, but I overheard Mama saying Charlie had found something out at the mounds, something he didn't tell the other miners about. A few weeks later, Mama found him out back in a shed. He'd wrapped a length of baling wire around his neck and hung himself."

A vision of Detective Ryan hanging from the ceiling of his cabin formed in Elliot's mind.

"I saw a priest," Peterson continued, "over at Uncle Charlie's place a day or two before that. I suspect it was Father Reynolds. Not long after that, people stopped disappearing. I don't know why."

Elliot's stomach tightened. The man in the photograph Doctor McKenzie had shown him, standing behind the table that held the obsidian knife, must have been Charles McDugan. "Thank you, Mr. Peterson. You've been most helpful."

Elliot walked out and as he climbed into the truck, he thought about the fearful look that'd shown on Peterson's face when he'd brought up the subject of the Spiro Mounds.

Elliot pulled his phone and punched in Carmen's number. She answered on the third ring.

"It's good to hear your voice," she said. "Is everything all right?"

"Sure," Elliot said. But he was hiding the truth, and he suspected Carmen could tell. He scanned the dark streets but saw nothing out of the ordinary. "How's Wayne?"

"He thought it might be fun if you could come over this weekend, maybe grill some hamburgers. He wanted me to ask you about it."

A smile spread across Elliot's face. "I can't think of anything I'd rather do."

"There's something you're not telling me, Kenny. What is it?"

Hearing Carmen's voice settled Elliot's nerves, though his troubles did not slip completely into the background. "It's the case," he said. "I've never run across anything quite like it before."

"I spoke with Captain Dombrowski."

Elliot's hold of the phone went slack, and though Carmen's words raced through his head, he could not come up with a logical response.

As if sensing the question, Carmen said, "He called."

"I didn't know he had your number."

"He's worried about you. So am I. He wants you to come back to work. Maybe you should, Kenny. Maybe you should come home."

Elliot squeezed the phone. He wasn't sure what Carmen meant exactly when she used the word *home*. It sounded inviting, though in his tired and confused state, he could be reading more into it than was actually there.

Before Elliot could complete the thought, something slammed into the passenger side of the truck.

Elliot dropped the phone onto the seat, pulled the Glock, and stepped outside. The streets were empty and the only sound he heard was Carmen calling his name over the phone, asking him what was wrong.

Keeping the weapon in front of him, Elliot used his free hand to fish the flashlight from his jacket pocket. He swept the beam across the area.

Nothing.

He made his way around the vehicle, and when the light fell across the passenger door, it revealed a concaved area about the size of a basketball. Holding the weapon and the flashlight together at arm's length, Elliot walked around the front of the vehicle and when he reached the driver's side he climbed in.

Carmen was still on the line.

"Sorry about dropping the phone, like that. I thought I heard something outside the truck. Things are happening that I don't understand."

"Maybe you should leave it alone for a while."

Elliot started the truck and pulled onto the roadway, then turned onto Highway 59 and headed north. Carmen knew him well enough to understand he couldn't walk away from this. "It's something I have to see through."

"I will pray for you."

An empty stretch of road unfolded in front of the truck, and as Elliot drove into the darkness outside the town, he said, "I love you, Carmen."

Through the static, Elliot could not make out Carmen's reply, but he knew it would do no good to ask her to repeat it. The phone had gone silent. That'd never happened before. Sure, he'd had dropped calls but this was different. It was as if the phone had experienced an instantaneous power drain.

The cab of the truck grew cold as the headlights revealed a car parked alongside the road, about fifty feet ahead. When Elliot's truck drew near the car, a man stepped from behind the vehicle and ran into the road. He stopped directly in the pathway of the truck and waved his arms.

Elliot crammed his foot against the brake pedal.

Displaying an eerie confidence, the man did not move but kept his ground, and as he basked in the beam of the truck's headlights, a smile spread across his familiar face. Standing on the roadway was Elliot's old friend, Nick Brazleton.

Elliot backed off the roadway, jumped out of the truck, and pulled Nick back to safety alongside his vehicle, a red 1957 Thunderbird. Nick had always talked of owning one.

"What do you say, Bulldog?"

Elliot stared at the man in front of him. No one called him that anymore. It was Nick all right, though nothing about the encounter made sense. "What are you doing out here?"

"Thought you might need my help," Nick said. "I guess it turned out to be the other way around, though."

Elliot glanced at Nick's car.

A flat tire on the front caused the vintage ride to lean toward the driver's side.

"You still carry the heavy artillery around with you?"

"Yeah," Elliot said, "I got it." He kept a floor jack in the bed of the truck when he travelled, but he hadn't been aware that Nick knew about it. And why would a trained mechanic not have a jack of his own?

Elliot retrieved the jack from the truck and carried it to the Thunderbird where he positioned it beneath the vehicle. As he pumped he handle, it occurred to him he'd seen no other vehicles on the roadway, not an impossible situation but unlikely to be sure. He wondered if he was actually in the company of his old friend, or if he was, in fact, alone. He raised the car until the damaged tire was just touching the ground then went back to the truck for the lug wrench.

He didn't see Nick. He grabbed the four-way lug wrench from behind the truck seat and started back toward the Thunderbird. As he neared the vehicle, he heard shoes crunching in the sand and gravel, but distant and hollow, as if echoing through a tunnel.

He turned as Nick's dark form approached.

"Nick?"

"Hey, old buddy."

A bead of perspiration trickled down Elliot's back. "What's going on, Nick?"

"More than you'll ever understand." Nick reached into his coat and pulled out a knife. "You remember that old bloodhound Clarence Moore kept down the street from us? Well, you're a lot like that. Once you catch the scent of something out of kilter, you just can't let it go. I'm sorry it had to come down like this."

He raised the knife and lunged forward, swiping the blade in a downward arc.

Elliot stumbled to his left, the knife blade ripping through his jacket on his right shoulder.

Nick swirled the knife in a tight circular motion. "You've always hated me, haven't you, old buddy?"

"You know that's not true."

"You blame me for all that went wrong in your life."

"You're talking crazy."

"Am I? If you won't be truthful, allow me the luxury."

"Nick, don't do this."

"I could have made Carmen happy, but you were always in the way, always hurting her. Now look at her. You gave her a kid, but you didn't stick around to help her raise him. I won't be like that. I'll treat her right."

Elliot clinched his hands but fought off the urge. "If Carmen feels the same way about you, I won't stand in the way."

A grin spread across Nick's face. "That's good to hear, because I intend to take her tonight whether she wants it or not."

From somewhere inside, a portal opened and darkness pumped into Elliot's veins. He didn't like hearing Carmen threatened that way. But still, the feelings seemed foreign, as if he wasn't thinking them. They were just there. He balled his hand into a fist and busted Nick square on the chin.

Nick wiped blood from his lip and smiled.

Elliot stepped back. He outweighed Nick by fifty pounds. That shot should have taken him off his feet.

Even if it didn't knock him down, it did something to him. Nick's eyes looked as distant as those of an animal. Cool now, he cradled the weapon in his hands and held it out.

Elliot recognized it now. It was the obsidian knife, the artifact that had destroyed Gerald's family.

"Take it," Nick said. "Release me. Free me from this evil."

Elliot stared into Nick's eyes and he began to understand the source of his dark logic. It was the knife.

Chapter Thirty-Seven

Nick Brazleton ran his hand across the fender of the Chevy Malibu sitting in the garage bay. Wasn't much he could do until the fuel pump came in from Tulsa.

He walked out of the garage, turning off the lights as he left, and plopped down in the office chair. He propped his feet on the desk, worked his phone out of his pocket and scrolled down the list until he found Linda Cook. She and Tom had busted up a few months ago, and lately she'd been coming by the shop, wanting to talk, doing everything but flat out asking Nick to call her sometime.

His thumb hovered over the call button, but he couldn't go through with it. He laid the phone on the desk.

Through the plate glass window, Nick saw the old Ford in the parking lot. With the dim glow of the garage sign softening the car's reality, it was easy to imagine how it might have looked off the assembly line decades ago. It was no '57 Bird, but that didn't bother him much anymore. He'd grown used to falling short of his desires.

He grabbed the phone from the desk. Spending time with Tom Cook's ex wasn't exactly his idea of a peaceful way of avoiding loneliness, but it was better than going home to an empty house. Staying at the garage until he was exhausted so he could go home to sleep only to get up and do it all over again was a strategy he'd grown tired of.

He found the number and pressed the button, but something he saw outside the shop caused him to end the call prematurely.

Carmen Garcia had come out of the darkness and now stood at the door, pressing her face against the glass.

Nick wondered if Carmen could've had a change of heart. Maybe she'd begun to love him as he'd always loved her. She could keep it hidden no longer, and had come to tell him this.

Carmen folded her hand into a fist and pounded on the door.

Nick scrambled from the chair, unlocked the door, and swung it open. "What a pleasant surprise."

Carmen Garcia stepped inside. "I hoped I would find you here. I went to your house but there was no answer."

Nick wished he could tell Carmen how he felt, but she'd made it clear they were just friends. "Sorry. Just finishing up some work. I'm glad you came by, though."

A guarded look made its way across Carmen's face. "I need to ask a favor."

"Sure. Anything."

"It's Kenny."

Nick turned away and went back to the chair and sat down. Kenny. It was always Kenny. But he didn't hold it against him. On the contrary, if there was anyone he cared about as much as Carmen, it was Kenny Elliot. "What's he gotten himself into this time?"

Chapter Thirty-Eight

Elliot was in darkness, and something was out there, moving toward him. That's all he knew.

He tried to focus on his surroundings but could grasp only emptiness and an overpowering sense of being in a place—though it seemed to have no real sense of place—where he did not belong.

From inside his pocket, Elliot's phone vibrated against his skin, and a streak of light cut through the darkness.

He brought his hand up to shield his eyes from the brightness, and with dead-on accuracy, his sense of place returned to him. The interior of his pickup wrapped around him, and through the windshield he saw the front of another vehicle and the fear-twisted face of its driver. He'd drifted across the road and into the path of the oncoming traffic.

Elliot grabbed the wheel of the truck and steered hard right. The old truck lurched to the right, slamming Elliot's shoulder into the driver's side door.

Turning back left, into the slide, Elliot brought the truck back in line.

Moments later, he leaned his head against the steering wheel, still reeling from the near-collision. Somehow he'd made it off the road and onto the shoulder where he'd shut off the engine.

His phone was still going off.

He fished it from his pocket and brought it near his face, and through the speaker of the phone, he heard the voice of Nick Brazleton.

"Hey, old buddy."

Elliot checked his watch. Twenty minutes had passed since he'd talked with Carmen. He wondered if he'd come to his senses, or if this was merely an extension of the nightmare. "Nick?"

"Carmen's worried about you, sport, asked me to call. What's up, old buddy?"

Elliot stared into the night. He was parked alongside the highway, the vehicle he'd nearly taken out miles away by now, but the uneasiness he'd sensed, the unnerving suspicion that something was out there waiting in the darkness lingered. He strained his eyes, looking for Nick, or the old Thunderbird. "Where are you, Nick?"

"You remember when Coach Sims told us we didn't need to leave town to find whatever it was we were looking for? I think he was just trying to make us feel better. Don't guess I'll ever know anyway. Doesn't look like I'm going anywhere. I'm at the garage. Where else would I be?"

"I was thinking maybe just outside of Sallisaw on Highway 59."

"Yeah, well, I hope that makes sense to you, old buddy, 'cause it sure don't to me. I don't know what you're up to, but it's got Carmen all upset."

Elliot leaned back in the seat. If Nick was telling the truth, there was no way he could have made it from Porter to Sallisaw and back again. "Is she there?"

"No. She had to get home to Wayne. Maybe you should give whatever's going on a rest, come on back here and take care of things. You're never going to find anyone else like her, Kenny. Don't mess it up this time."

Elliot reached inside his jacket and ran his fingers along the handle of the Glock, holding on, in a manner of speaking, to something real. Had he seen Nick earlier, helped him fix a tire alongside the road, then been slashed at by his old friend, or had Nick's call saved his life? He checked his coat but there were no rips in it.

"How's the bird running? Nice looking car, by the way."

After a pause, Nick said, "We always understood each other pretty well. No secrets, remember? You can talk to me, Kenny. Hell, you know that."

A synopsis of his and Nick's troubled childhood played through his mind. Nick was right. If a couple of outsiders like them couldn't trust each other, what chance did they have?

"Kenny, are you drinking again?"

Elliot squeezed the phone, a fair question from an old friend. He almost wished he had been. "No, Nick, it's not that, but something's going on for sure."

Once again, the call had been dropped. "Nick, are you there?"

Elliot tried recalling, but it was as before, as if the phone had become a useless piece of plastic. He reached for the ignition switch. He was not completely alone, like before, but in between the sporadic pockets of traffic, and the uneasiness he'd sensed, the unnerving suspicion that something was out there, waiting in the darkness, lingered. It had happened again, his mind taken...

somewhere. And what had happened while he was away? Had he driven the truck in a trance-like state, or had his reality been altered? He dropped the phone onto the seat, and as the interior of the cab seemed to grow smaller, he lowered his defenses and allowed himself to entertain the idea that he was in over his head this time. He closed his eyes and began to pray. He prayed for forgiveness and for strength. He asked that if the visions and clairvoyant thoughts were not from God that they stop. If his abilities were from God, he begged for the wisdom to use them wisely.

Later, he twisted the key in the ignition, half expecting, like a scene from a late-night movie, the old buggy to not start, but the truck fired up with no problem.

Elliot pulled onto the roadway and started toward Sallisaw. He wouldn't go home tonight. He was tired and his nerves were shot.

Chapter Thirty-Nine

The brick structure reminded Elliot of the University of Oklahoma, though he was neither in Norman, nor traversing the sidewalks of a university.

During the night, as he'd jolted in and out of sleep in the cab of the pickup, a tenuous understanding of various aspects of the crimes unfolded. Taking into consideration the chaotic state of mind he'd witnessed in those who'd come into possession of the knife, and his own delusions apparently brought about by nothing more than association, he'd come to realize how the influence of the knife might drive one to madness. In some, though, it might also inspire a desire to escape.

The 1935 murders had not begun with the resignation of Father Reynolds. On the contrary, by and with his disappearance he had executed a stay upon the atrocities. He had been, Elliot suspected, a man of great faith. If such a priest had come under the persuasion of evil, he might have sought respite and solitude with God through a life inspired by monastic ideals.

Elliot walked the grounds of St. Gregory's Abbey in Shawnee, Oklahoma, searching for a name among the rows of small headstones in a cemetery located on the grounds of the monastery.

A police car pulled up behind the pickup, and an officer climbed out. He looked up and down the street and started toward Elliot. Stopping a few feet away, the officer said, "Something I can help you with, son?"

"No thanks," Elliot said. "I'm just having a look around, that's all."

"Is that right? Well, I don't mean to be rude, but if you don't have business here, I'm going to have to ask you to move along."

"I never said I didn't have business here."

The officer motioned toward the street. "That your truck?"

Elliot nodded.

"Not from around here, are you?"

"No, just visiting."

"Been in town long?"

"I'm only guessing," Elliot said, "but I'm betting tourism isn't very high on your list of economic stimulus factors."

The officer smiled. The joke seemed to lighten his mood. "Well I wouldn't say that, but when I see an out of town vehicle with the driver sneaking around on private property not more than two blocks from a break-in I just responded to, it tends to stir my curiosity. You wouldn't happen to know anything about that, would you?"

"About what," Elliot asked, "your curiosity?"

"Your cavalier attitude is going to get you into trouble one of these days. Maybe today's the day."

"Too late," Elliot said, "That day's long past."

The officer put his hands on his belt. "Got any ID on you, son?"

"What seems to be the problem, Thomas?"

Another voice had joined the conversation. Elliot turned and saw a tall, slender gentleman dressed in a black robe, a habit, standing before him.

"Father Davenport," the officer said. "I found this guy wandering around the grounds. Thought I should check it out."

"You did well. However, there is no need for alarm, for I have been expecting this gentleman."

The officer glared at Elliot. "Why didn't you just say so?"

Elliot didn't know why Father Davenport might stick up for him, but he decided to play along. "Sorry. I guess I just wasn't thinking."

"So," the officer asked, "everything's all right here?"

Father Davenport stepped closer and draped a frail arm around Elliot's shoulder. "Everything is fine, Thomas. But thank you for being vigilant. God will bless you for giving of yourself in such a risk-filled profession."

The officer studied Father Davenport's face, shot a glance toward Elliot, then turned and walked back to his patrol car.

Father Davenport watched the officer drive away. "All right, young man, you may go now. God has shown you grace today. You would do well to express your gratitude through seeking his forgiveness."

"I'll do that, Father. And thanks for helping me. However, I do have a reason for being here."

"I see. And what might that be?"

Elliot wondered how he should proceed. Getting right to the heart of the matter seemed best. "Does the name Stanley Reynolds mean anything to you?"

The old monk's expression remained stoic, though moisture showed in his eyes. "If, indeed, I had knowledge of such a person, how would such information benefit you?"

Elliot pulled his badge. "I'm a police detective, Father. However, I'm working independently, on a private matter. Father Reynolds had a great grandson, Stanley G. Reynolds III, who was a good friend of mine. He's gone missing, and I fear his fate might be even worse."

Father Davenport studied the identification and nodded, but his eyes held a question.

Elliot's instincts told him Father Davenport was of a deep spiritual nature. It would afford him an advantage in relating to the problem at hand. "Bad things are happening, Father, and I believe they tie back to Father Reynolds, not that he had anything to do with it. The source was something he was hiding, perhaps protecting would be a better word."

"Come," Father Davenport said, "let me show you something."

He led Elliot through the small graveyard, stopping at the headstone of Father Stanley Gerald Reynolds I.

Elliot decided not to hold back, but to explain the situation the way he understood it. "Numerous murders have occurred throughout the years, related to a dark force that I don't understand, though I have experienced what I believe to be the outer edges of it. I have reason to believe Father Reynolds experienced it as well."

Father Davenport looked away, his gaze becoming distant as if to study the grounds of the monastery. He returned his attention to Elliot. "In the summer of 1935, I found myself alone. Not knowing where else to go, I sought refuge at St. Gregory's. It was Father Reynolds who convinced Father Abbot and the brothers to take me in."

"You must have known him quite well," Elliot said.

"He was the best friend I ever had, a brother and a father, and all from the same man. However, he was a troubled and desperate soul who tried to find peace here. I'm not sure he ever did."

"Based on the evidence I've uncovered," Elliot said, "Father Reynolds appears to have been a rare and caring individual, always placing the needs of others ahead of his own. He withdrew from society and the parish he loved to protect the people."

"From the evil you described?"

"I know it sounds incredible, but I believe it to be true."

Father Davenport did not seem surprised, but rather as if he'd come to know, at least in part, the trouble Elliot alluded to. "What do you hope to accomplish with the knowledge you seek?"

"Lives are being lost," Elliot said. "I want to put a stop to it."

Father Davenport's face lost some of its color. "Father Reynolds was, indeed, a good and humble soul, a credit not only to the Abbey but to our faith as well. However, with respect to a certain possession, he was secretive, sharing little of the details even with me."

Elliot studied the grounds of the monastery, going over the words of Father Davenport. "Could you tell me more about this guarded possession?"

"It was a small rosewood chest he kept hidden and draped with the cross of St. Benedict."

"Were you privileged to know the contents of the chest?"

"Father Reynolds insisted it be kept secret. He said if anything should ever happen to him I was to guard it, but not open it, and never, under any circumstances was I to remove the protective crucifix."

"Is it still here?"

"A few years ago, a man, whom I suspected to be the son of Father Reynolds came to the Abbey. No one knew Father Reynolds had a son, except for me, and they could not see the resemblance as I could. Before coming to the Abbey, Father Reynolds had resigned his position that he held at a small church in Poteau. I suspect it was the contents of the rosewood chest which drove his decision to do such a thing. He even found a wife and got married. He and his son visited alone in Father Reynolds' quarters, and a few hours later, they left St. Gregory's, claiming they were to have lunch and get better acquainted. They never returned. Later, we got word Father Reynolds had been in an automobile accident, and he and his son, whose name also turned out to be Stanley Reynolds, had been killed."

Elliot stared at the grave of Stanley Gerald Reynolds I. The date of death showed the events spoken of by Father Davenport had occurred eight years ago, approximately one month before the murders in Stillwater.

With Gerald's great grandfather and his grandfather both losing their lives on the same day, their wills, if there had been wills, would have dictated the distribution of their possessions, passing them on to the next of kin, which should have been Gerald's father. But, had it happened that way? With Gerald's father having been denied the family title, a rift could have occurred. Gerald was related to Professor David Stephens, and it was possible Stephens had come into possession of the artifact.

Gerald had written about the missing drifters in the school paper. His obsession with Spiro Mounds artifacts suggested he knew about the knife and its entanglement with his family history. He must have suspected his uncle, David Stephens, had come under its influence.

"Following through with what I'd promised, doing what I'd been asked to do," Father Davenport continued, "I went to the quarters of Father Reynolds to retrieve the rosewood chest, but I did not find it."

"He must have taken it with him," Elliot said.

"Indeed," Father Davenport said. "And a few months after we interred the body, someone named McDugan came to the Abbey to inquire about the possessions of Father Reynolds. Father Abbot was gracious and showed the young man his quarters, but I already knew there was nothing there. Curious, wouldn't you say?"

Elliot thought about Langley Peterson in Poteau and his story about Charlie McDugan being found dead in 1935, having hung himself in his cabin. It seemed the murders only occurred when someone was under the influence of the knife. Had the curse of Laura's ancestors, the ancient Caddo, backfired and given life, or a pathway of existence to the very evil they were trying to destroy? The tainted knife was once again in circulation. The question was: Who had taken it from Gerald? "It is," Elliot said, "and the name McDugan has come up before in my investigation."

"If you intend to see this thing through," Father Davenport said, "you will need some help." He removed the crucifix he wore around his neck and offered it to Elliot. Embedded in its center was a medallion. "The cross of St. Benedict," he said. "It carries my blessing. I hope it will offer you protection."

Elliot slid the crucifix around his neck. The cross was a possession surely dear to Father Davenport's heart. He would not have given it or his blessing without reason. "Thank you," Elliot said. "I'm honored to have gained your trust."

Elliot turned and walked away. The newspaper man from
Poteau had said he'd seen Father Reynolds at Charles McDugan's
house before he'd been found dead. Elliot decided to call him, to
tell him what he'd found.

Someone answered, but the voice didn't sound right. "Mr.
Peterson?"

"Who wants to know?"

"Detective Elliot. We talked yesterday."

After a pause, the voice said, "This is Chief Ludlow. Where are
you, son?"

Elliot watched a couple cars drive by. "St. Gregory's Abbey, in
Shawnee. Where's Peterson?"

"How long have you been in Shawnee?"

"About an hour, I guess."

"What time did you leave here last night?"

"Around 8:00. Why?"

"That's pretty much what Dick Hamilton said. He was across
the street from the newspaper office, saw you leave."

A sick feeling crawled through Elliot's stomach. "What's this
all about, Chief?"

Ludlow cleared his throat. "Peterson's dead. He called this
morning, carrying on, nearly incoherent. I found him in his chair
in the front office."

Dizziness swept over Elliot, blurring his focus, threatening to
again derail his reasoning. And Ludlow seemed unsure of
himself, coming across as part interrogator, part confidant. "How
did it happen?"

Ludlow didn't answer.

"Let me guess, an animal attack."

"He left a note," Ludlow continued, "put it where he knew I
would find it. It says to tell Elliot it's Jeremiah. Does that mean
anything to you?"

The name resonated through Elliot's memory. "I can't place it,
but Peterson talked about the old days, and about his uncle,
Charles McDugan."

"Always told myself," Ludlow said, "I wouldn't get caught up
in all the mumbo-jumbo. I'm not so sure anymore. I don't know
how much Peterson told you, but his Uncle, McDugan, had a wife
and son. They didn't stick around after the trouble started,
packed up and moved away."

Elliot squeezed the phone. He'd just met Chief Ludlow, but he knew veteran police officers didn't rattle easily, and this man was scared. "What does that have to do with anything?"

"All caught up in the mumbo-jumbo," Ludlow said. "The boy's name was Jeremiah McDugan. He was Peterson's cousin."

A chill went through Elliot. "Do you know where I can find him?"

"Do you think he had something to do with the death of Langley Peterson and the attack on Father Williams?"

"It's starting to look that way. And to set the record straight, Father Reynolds didn't kill Charles McDugan. He tried to save him."

"From what, selling a few trinkets on the side to feed his family?"

Elliot found the crucifix beneath his shirt and wrapped his hand around it. "Charles McDugan pulled more than a trinket from the mounds in the summer of 1935, much more, in fact, than the curiously out of place Aztec knife it appears to be."

"That was a long time ago," Ludlow said, "and if what I've heard about his age at the time is correct, Jeremiah would be in his eighties now."

"Maybe so," Elliot said. "But I suspect McDugan's son came into contact with the artifact, enough to be influenced by it. Could be he made it his life's goal to find it, reclaim it for the family, a quest he recently succeeded in satisfying."

"We're starting to sound like the old timers around here, obsessed with burial mounds and curses."

"Langley Peterson's childhood fears were well founded, Chief Ludlow. What's more, the source of it all, the knife his uncle dug out of the ground, is still out there and back in circulation, as is the malevolent force that seems to be attached to it."

When Ludlow spoke, his voice echoed the stress he'd been under. "Karen McDugan had family in Sand Springs," he said, "up near your neck of the woods. I suspect she took Jeremiah and moved up there."

Chapter Forty

The house, rather drab and unimposing, sat atop a small hill alongside an asphalt and gravel road, just another sleepy bungalow in an aging neighborhood, a suburb west of Tulsa.

Elliot took his foot off the accelerator and eased the truck to a stop. A little work checking the records had paid off. He'd found the address where Karen McDugan had taken her son after leaving her husband and the trouble he'd embraced nearly eighty years ago. A gravel drive curved in an s-shape from the road to the doorstep, though no cars were parked there.

Elliot pulled in, shut the truck off and stepped out. As he neared the main entrance, a sensation of being watched crawled over him and, though he knew it to be impossible, the thought that the house possessed perceptual abilities played through his head, and that it was watching him, following his movements, anticipating, hoping even he might find his way inside.

Elliot climbed the stairs and stepped onto a small landing, but as he prepared to knock, a reflection of light coming from the back of the property caught his attention.

Constructed of wood that had long since turned a color just this side of charcoal, an outbuilding sat about fifty yards behind the house with a set of double doors large enough to accommodate farm equipment.

An uncomfortable notion crept across Elliot's senses, telling him he should get back in the truck and drive away from this place, but instead he stepped off the landing and started toward the outbuilding. When he reached the double doors, he stopped and studied the structure.

The hasp that held the doors was secured, but the padlock that ran through it had not been fastened, but merely aligned to look as if it had been.

Elliot surveyed the rest of the property. No one seemed to be around. He had no warrant, but he wasn't on official business in the first place. He'd gone too far to stop now. He removed the lock from the hasp, pulled his service weapon and slowly opened one of the doors.

The barn had no windows, and the sunlight that came through the open door did little to alleviate the darkness, but even in the dim light, the shape of a familiar automobile became visible.

Elliot's knees grew weak. Holding the Glock in front of him, he crept into the dark confines of the barn. A few steps later, with his left hand holding the weapon cocked at a right angle, he ran his free hand across the car's fender.

No doubt about it. He'd found Gerald's Cadillac.

Along the south wall of the barn, an old workbench supported a large vise bolted to the wooden top. Fastened to the wall above the bench, a pegboard held a few tools. Near the workbench was a stack of bricks.

Elliot made his way to the driver's side door of the Cadillac.

The keys dangled from the ignition.

Again the sensation of being watched came over Elliot, and he wondered if his arrival had been anticipated. He shook off the notion and opened the door to the Cadillac.

The smell of old carpet and well-worn leather wafted out of the interior. Gerald had probably loved the old car. Elliot leaned over and removed the keys from the ignition. Keeping his vigil, he made his way to the rear of the vehicle where he inserted the key into the slot and triggered the latch. With a steady motion, he raised the trunk lid.

Elliot uttered a prayer of thanks. Sitting in the center of the cavernous trunk was a small, rectangular box, but neither Gerald nor his remains had been stored there.

Elliot exhaled some of the breath he'd been holding. He pulled the flashlight from his jacket pocket and ran the beam of light around the interior of the trunk.

The material from which the box had been made, along with the intricate designs carved into it, left little doubt in Elliot's mind as to its nature. Father Davenport had described it perfectly. It was the rosewood chest, the keeper of secrets for Stanley Gerald Reynolds I.

Elliot stowed the flashlight and lifted the lid from the box.

Inside, coiled upon a bed of blue velvet, was a chain of gold and attached to it a crucifix embedded with a medal.

Elliot pulled the cross Father Davenport had given him from beneath his shirt. It was the same as the one in the box, the cross of Saint Benedict. The special crucifix had not been the intended contents of the box but had been employed to offer a measure of protection against what had been in it. It was here, inside the chest of rosewood, that Father Stanley Reynolds had kept the knife of obsidian he'd taken from Charles McDugan.

A sound like people gathered in a hallway and whispering filled the corners of the barn.

The hair on the back of Elliot's neck stiffened as he remembered a book he'd read where people had been driven insane by something similar. He stowed the crucifix inside his pocket and dropped the lid of the chest into the trunk. Stepping away from the car, he quickened his pace as he crossed the floor.

The muffled voices started again, resonating now, as if coming from all directions.

Elliot tightened his grip on the Glock, eased through the door, and stepped outside.

The voices abruptly ended.

Elliot studied the area, methodically and incrementally looking in different directions. His emergence into the open had interrupted the menagerie of whispers, and that meant whoever or whatever was behind it was also aware of his location. A disturbing thought swept through him. The source of the strange sound could have been inside the barn all along. He turned toward the doorway.

A swath of daylight cut through the opening revealing a misshapen, triangular portion of the dirt floor, but it was something beyond that which grabbed Elliot's attention. A pair of luminous eyes, like those of an animal, floated in the darkness.

Elliot backed away, mesmerized by the intensity of the disembodied gaze.

A wave of heat raked across his back and a force shoved him forward. He stumbled into the barn, the momentum taking him to the floor, knocking the Glock from his hand.

The dirt floor oozed a thick aroma, like a garden shack that'd been closed up for years. Elliot scrambled for the Glock, lurched to his feet, and swept the barn, his finger on the trigger.

The barn doors slammed shut, the hasp fell into place, and the lock snapped into position.

Elliot ran to the exit where he pressed his face against the doors and peered through the cracks between the planks.

The rough wood scraped against his face like sandpaper. Part of the yard and the back of the house came into view, but nothing else.

Elliot lowered his shoulder and thrust his weight against the door.

Dust belched into the air, but the heavy planks held firm.

Elliot looked wildly into the shadows, fear mounting as he wondered what to do next. He considered taking another run at the wooden barricade but abandoned the idea. Instead, he placed the Glock where he thought it would be most effective and fired two rounds into the wood. A hard right kick did the rest, and the doors swung open.

Elliot stepped outside and did a quick three-sixty, the Glock held in front of him with both hands.

Along the street that skirted the front of the property a car glided past the house and disappeared from view. From somewhere in the distance, the sound of a leaf blower droned on. Just another peaceful day in suburbia, until the grass near Elliot's feet moved and something slithered past.

Instinctively he stepped away, ignoring the fact that whoever had shoved him into the barn was probably still around.

A brown, cord-like vertebrate continued its movement through the grass. Near the barn doors, several more of them wiggled free from a burlap bag while others, having already found the opening, slithered in the dirt.

Elliot's pulse quickened. The place was swarming with Copperheads. Elliot backed away and ran toward the house. It looked no more welcoming now than it had earlier, but Elliot suspected whoever was behind this was probably in there. When he reached the steps, he climbed onto the landing and banged on the door.

The lock disengaged and the door began to open, not quickly but a few inches at a time.

Elliot leaned forward and peered through the open doorway. Like the barn, the house smelled of decay and lacked light, as if all places where light might have gained entry had been blocked and sealed off. "I know you're in there," Elliot said. "Why don't you come on out, so we can talk about it. You're not in trouble. Nothing's really happened yet."

No answer.

"If I have to come in after you, all bets are off."

"You surprise me, Detective Elliot. I didn't take you for someone given to gambling."

It was a voice tinged with age. Elliot could almost place it, but not quite. "Who are you?"

A hand shot from the doorway, clamped around Elliot's wrist, and yanked him forward, into the house. Just as quickly, the door slammed shut, closing off the light. In a near simultaneous action, something banged against his right hand, and the Glock fell from his grip and thudded to the floor.

Elliot went after the weapon, but he didn't make it far.

A fist caught him on the forehead and he stumbled backward. With the quickness and skill of a cop, someone yanked Elliot's arms behind him, wrapped them with a sticky binding, and forced him to sit. Using more of the tape, he bound Elliot to the chair. With the job finished, the captor walked away, his footsteps echoing through the black void.

Elliot tested the bindings. They were tight, but he could move his hands and wrists slightly. If given time, he could work them free. He wanted to ask questions, but feared the action might cause the assailant to tape his mouth as well. For what seemed a long time, he sat in darkness, struggling against the bindings. It was working. He'd gained some slack.

"Stop moving around."

Elliot put his escape efforts on hold. Hearing the man's voice after such a long period of silence surprised him. He'd even entertained the thought that he'd been left alone. The vaguely familiar voice had come from maybe ten feet in front of him, but he couldn't see anyone. The darkness was just too thick. He decided to chance a question. "Why are you doing this?"

"I should have killed you when I had the chance."

Elliot ran several recent arrests he'd been involved with through his memory, trying to imagine who the assailant might be. "Why didn't you?"

"I do what I'm told. Works better that way."

Elliot resumed his struggle with the tape. "So you're telling me you're not responsible for all of this, that you're just the messenger?"

Elliot waited for a reply but none came.

"This guy who's putting pressure on you, telling you what to do, maybe I can help."

"You don't know what you're saying, have no idea what you're offering."

Elliot worked one hand free. "Don't be so sure. I'm a cop, and I'm pretty good at what I do."

"I'll bet you are. But this is different."

"How is it different? Maybe you could explain it to me?"

After another period of silence, he said, "That would be the worst thing I could do, worse even than killing you."

Elliot wondered if this was the son of Charles McDugan, and if he'd been exposed to the same thing as David Stephens and Angela Gardner. "Is it the voices," Elliot asked, "the ones inside your head?"

"If you know about that, it's already too late. I'd thought about letting you go, persuading you to forget about all this and go on about your life. That's not an option now. In fact, I suspect you'll welcome my killing you."

Elliot removed the remainder of the bindings. The voice had moved behind him. He stood and turned toward the area from where the sound had come.

A small flame appeared in the darkness, the self-appointed warden of this prison having lit a match. He lowered it to a candle, and when the wick caught fire, its light revealed a man of medium build, about five foot eight in stature. The lone candle, though seemingly bright in the instant it had broken the darkness, did not remove enough of the gloom for Elliot to identify his captor.

The man's next move was not completely unanticipated. He hadn't dragged Elliot into his world and tied him to a chair merely to observe his reactions.

He came forward, the Glock Elliot had lost held in his right hand and pointed at Elliot, though judging from the lack of rigidity in the aim of the weapon, Elliot did not think he intended to kill him with it, at least not yet.

He continued across the room, walking slowly in what seemed an almost non-deliberate manner, as if even he were unsure of his next move.

As he closed in, the barrel of the Glock grew larger, and at a distance of about six feet, he stopped.

From this proximity, even though the candlelight was partially blocked by the man's body, Elliot now recognized him. He thought of the grizzled, almost ghostly face he'd encountered at the old house in Tulsa where Gerald had disappeared.

Elliot fought to gather his senses. The man confronting him did not look old enough to be the son of Charles McDugan. "I guess you gave up stealing motorcycles in favor of taking up kidnapping, not exactly a good career move, if you ask me, Jeremiah. It is Jeremiah, isn't it?"

The son of Charles McDugan, if indeed that was who he was, did not reply, and when he brought from behind him his other hand, it held the obsidian knife, its jagged blade glistening, even though the light was dim and coming from a distance behind Jeremiah, who now raised the artifact above his head.

"That's a fancy weapon," Elliot said. "Where did you get it?"

"It is sacred to me. You have no right to doubt its power or to blaspheme its purpose."

"It belonged to your father, didn't it? But that meddling priest tricked it out from under him. I suspect, though, had you anticipated the consequences you would have left it alone."

He didn't answer.

"I have to hand it to you, McDugan. Tracking the knife down after all those years must have been difficult."

"I knew the name of the Catholic who secreted the *tecpatl* away. It was simply a matter of waiting until it showed up at the right time and place."

Elliot grabbed the chair he'd been bound to and thrust the makeshift shield between himself and Jeremiah McDugan.

"Your spiritual presence is strong. Submit to me and I will make you a powerful priest in my name."

"I think I'll pass."

McDugan's face remained passive, his eyes reflecting no passion, and he did not bring the ancient weapon slashing down upon Elliot. Instead he gently lowered the relic and held it out, as if it were a peace offering.

The words of Professor David Stephens ran through Elliot's head. *Don't touch the knife.* He took a step back. "I've got an idea," he said. "Why don't you put the gun and the artifact on the table, and you and I can have a little talk about your father, Charles McDugan."

"My father's dead. Now take the knife. It is the reason I'm here, and the reason you've made it your quest to find me. Come on. Just think how easily you could kill me with it. That's what you want, isn't it?"

"You've got it all wrong," Elliot said. "I'm here to help you."

McDugan laughed. "Don't pretend you're different. You're all alike. You'll do anything to save yourself, anything at all."

Elliot took a step back. "I've seen the results of the knife's influence. Losing my sanity and sense of self-awareness doesn't appeal to me."

"Careful," the McDugan thing said, "you wouldn't want to disturb my little servants."

From every corner of the room, they emerged from the shadows, slithering, tongues darting, their bellies whispering across the floor.

Elliot's throat tightened. He slammed the chair down and jumped onto it, his stomach churning at the thought of having sat in the dark with those things crawling around. "You're nuts, McDugan. What makes you think your little friends won't turn on you?"

Like a child playing with a toy airplane, McDugan moved the obsidian knife through the air. "They're even more afraid of me than you are. And your fear runs deep. I am given to pity, something of a rarity I assure you. If you wish that I should take your blood instead of your life, I'll make it so. Get down from the chair and lie on the floor."

McDugan's voice had turned softer, almost consoling.

Elliot glanced around the room, and as he considered his options his hope that both he and McDugan might make it out of the house alive evaporated. He decided to jump from the chair. His sudden weight upon his adversary would be considerable. He could knock him off his feet and make a dash for the door. If he could avoid the snakes, he would be free.

He studied his adversary, who now stood motionless, as if he were calmly awaiting Elliot's decision, his hands held loosely at his sides, the knife in one and the Glock in the other.

Elliot shifted his weight to prepare for the attack, but before he jumped, the room again went dark. He had thought he and McDugan were alone, but something had doused the candle.

Elliot recoiled at the tickle of fingers groping at his throat, and it was then that the cross of St. Benedict was ripped from his neck.

Chapter Forty-One

Elliot reached out, trying to locate McDugan, or whoever had taken the cross. He found only emptiness, nearly falling from the chair for his efforts.

Perspiration broke out across Elliot's forehead, though this was followed, not by a sense of calmness but of reassurance in his belief that if the crucifix afforded protection, it came not from a loyal follower, but from the one whose death and resurrection it symbolized. However, if McDugan, or what he'd become, feared the cross and was now, in its absence, more willing to do whatever he had planned for Elliot, that was something to consider.

Listening to McDugan's footsteps as he moved about the room, Elliot reminded himself that McDugan did not seem to want to kill him, at least not yet. He could have done so several times. The knowledge of this did not bring Elliot comfort. He began to conjure up all sorts of alternative fates, most of them dealing with torture.

Elliot groped his jacket pocket for the flashlight but found that it, too, was missing. He'd probably lost it in the same manner as the Glock.

He decided to stay on the chair for the time being. He had a pretty good idea where the front door was, but with snakes crawling about in the darkness, his chances of escaping were not good. McDugan was not near. His footsteps had come from the area where the candle had been.

In the darkness, a low, guttural growl, the kind a predatory cat might make, evolved into the voice of Jeremiah McDugan.

"No one knows you're here," he said. "Last anyone heard, you were somewhere in Eastern Oklahoma."

Elliot waved his arms to regain his balance but remained silent and as still as he could. Certainly McDugan knew where he was, but any bit of doubt would work in his favor.

McDugan was much closer now, his voice a whisper in Elliot's ear. "I've been waiting a long time for someone like you."

Elliot's skin prickled beneath the moist heat of McDugan's breath upon his neck, and even though the voice had been soft, his ears rang, as if he'd chosen a seat too close to the speakers at a heavy-metal rock concert.

Elliot squeezed his hands into fists and lashed out in different directions, hoping to get lucky and land a shot, knock McDugan off his feet.

He found only emptiness, though the sensation of McDugan's presence remained strong.

He felt a vibration, though it came not from his surroundings but from within, originating in his throat and lungs, a silent scream, not unlike the tormented cries that had torn open the evening in Poteau, during the attack on Father Williams.

Elliot looked around the room. It had been he who had growled, and with it something within him had changed. The darkness had not been removed or lessened to any appreciable degree, but there was no denying he now sensed, in detail, what was around him. More than his intuition was at work here.

McDugan stood near the doused candle, still and lifeless, his eyes empty, as if he were not a man at all but an elaborate suit of armor designed to mimic a real person.

An expanse of the hardwood flooring was cleared, the snakes having wiggled into rows on either side, creating a pathway, leading to McDugan.

Elliot lowered one foot from the chair then the other. He stepped onto the pathway and began walking toward McDugan, slowly at first but gaining in both speed and confidence. It appeared his adversary was unaware of what was happening.

Without warning, McDugan raised the Glock and fired.

Elliot dove for the floor, the slug whizzing past his head. He caught his breath and scooted toward McDugan, hoping to reach him before the wiggling wall of copperheads changed their minds and decided to attack.

McDugan fired another shot.

The projectile hit the floor, splintering the wood just inches from Elliot's head.

To Elliot's left was a sofa and a coffee table. He got to his hands and knees. McDugan had missed, and at that distance it was more than could be accounted for by a lack of experience with firearms. He had heard Elliot coming, but he had not known his exact location. Elliot didn't analyze the disturbing indications of why his senses had been heightened while his adversary's had seemed to fade. McDugan would fire again, and he might not miss the next time.

Elliot rose to his feet and brought his forearm down against McDugan's hand.

The Glock hit the floor, but Elliot didn't have time to retrieve it. McDugan came toward him, slashing wildly with the obsidian knife.

After the physical contact McDugan had honed in on his location. In addition, the snakes had closed the pathway behind him.

The blade caught Elliot's shirt, ripping a long slash across the material.

He didn't think the blade had touched him. He felt no pain.

McDugan readied the knife for another attack, his eyes as flat and lifeless as those of a sightless animal.

Elliot jumped for the coffee table, his right foot catching the edge, though he managed to balance and stay atop it.

Adjusting for what Elliot had done, McDugan, like an automaton under someone else's control, altered his course and again came toward him.

Elliot transferred his weight to his left foot and delivered a kick to McDugan's chest.

He kept coming.

Elliot kicked again, landing a well-placed shot to the Jeremiah's forehead.

Jeremiah McDugan did not fall but the action caused him to halt his progress. As if trying to gather his senses, he stood nearly motionless.

Elliot seized the opportunity. He grabbed the wrist of McDugan's knife hand and bashed it hard against his knee.

The obsidian knife dropped and thudded heavily to the top of the coffee table where Elliot stood.

He and McDugan stood in motionless silence, neither seeming to know what might come next. Elliot ended the standoff by reaching down and taking the knife, not quickly but slowly, gingerly running his fingers around the handle.

The action was not without effect. The room went black and Elliot began to lose his balance, swaying as if he might fall from the table.

Chapter Forty-Two

It was the cold that brought Kenny out of his sleep. He reached for the covers but there were none. Pain shot through his leg and he realized it had fallen asleep, and that something was beneath him, causing this to happen.

He found the object, pulled it from under his leg and brought it up where he could see it.

It was the BB gun Nick had given him just a few days ago for his ninth birthday. He must have been sitting on the floor, cleaning the gun or something, and had fallen asleep, leaning against the wall. He couldn't remember ever having done that before. He must have been awfully tired.

Something didn't seem quite right, though. He couldn't put his finger on what it was, or why he might feel uneasy. The bed was where it was supposed to be, still made and not slept in, the old dresser with a broken leg that Maggie, his mom's friend, had given him, a pile of dirty laundry in the corner. Nothing seemed any different, and yet he couldn't shake the feeling he didn't belong here. Being an outsider was something he'd grown used to, but still, everything seemed foggy, like he'd just come out of a dream that'd lasted forever. He didn't think that was possible, though his stomach told him he hadn't eaten in a while.

He got to his feet, but the effort made him dizzy and he had to put his hand on the wall to keep from falling. He guessed being hungry could do that to a kid. He walked out of his room and went down the hallway to where his mom slept.

The door was closed, but that wasn't unusual. He knew well enough about Mom's privacy. He pressed his hand against his stomach to quiet the growling, and again he wondered how long he'd been asleep. He thought about knocking on the door but decided against it and walked up the hall to the kitchen.

Inside the refrigerator, a carton of milk sat on the top shelf, but other than that it was empty.

Kenny brought the carton of milk near his face, something he'd learned to do, but quickly jerked it away. It'd gone bad. He took the milk to the sink and poured it out. Afterward, he climbed onto the cinder block he'd found in the backyard to use as a step and checked the cupboard where the food was kept.

It was empty.

He couldn't remember that ever happening before. There was always something, a can of beans, some corn, even some cereal on occasion, but not this time. He checked the other cabinets but found only dishes and stuff.

Going over to Nick's house occurred to Kenny, to see if Nick had anything, but he wasn't sure he wanted to. Nick's dad kept a roof over Nick's head, and made sure he had something to eat most of the time, but other than that, Nick's life was nothing to envy. He sure was hungry, though, and getting something to eat was worth taking a chance at getting yelled at, or maybe even worse. As he started toward the door, he realized he didn't know what time it was, what time of year even, and if it was hot or cold outside.

The thought of his memory being all messed up put a knot in his stomach. If something weird had happened to him, and he had slept far longer than usual, what about his mom?

He ran back to her door, having to fight the fear to knock, softly at first, but when she didn't answer, he rapped his knuckles hard against the wood. Having completed the knocking, he pressed his ear against the door and listened.

He heard nothing.

He tested the door. It wasn't locked so he eased it open. When the gap was wide enough, he poked his head through and peeked inside.

Mom was on the bed but she wasn't moving, and the soft snoring sound that usually accompanied her sleep was missing.

Kenny wondered if she'd stopped breathing. He stepped into the room and tiptoed to her bedside. In a voice somewhere between normal and a whisper, he said, "Mom?"

She made no indication she'd heard him.

All sorts of thoughts spun through Kenny's head and suddenly he wanted to be out of there, to run from the room and get away, and he had to fight the urge. He put his hand on her shoulder and gave her a small shake.

Still she did not answer and did not move.

Kenny glanced at the dresser along the wall beside the window.

The needle was there along with the other stuff his mom used. She looked awfully pale.

Kenny leaned closer, his face near his mom so as to hear any sound she might make. He shook her again.

Her eyes flew open and she grabbed his wrist, digging her fingernails into his skin. "What are you doing in here?"

"I didn't mean to bother you. I'm hungry that's all. I need something to eat."

"Get it yourself."

"There's nothing to get. If you give me some money, I'll go to the store."

"Give me this, give me that. Do you know how tired I am of hearing your whining?"

She paused, and when she spoke again her voice had softened. "I don't have any money, Kenny. I've been sick, haven't been able to work."

Kenny knew what he was going to say wasn't what his mom wanted to hear, but something had to be done. "What about Maggie?"

"Oh, that's the answer, isn't it? Go get Maggie. Maggie walks on water. Well I don't see her hanging around, doling out any food, do you?"

"I know where she lives. I could go there. She'd help. I know she would."

"Oh wise up, Kenny. The old bat's a nut case. You ought to know that by now."

"She is not. Besides, what if she is?"

Again her face softened. "Let's not fight. Listen, if you'll help me, I'll get up and find some food somehow."

Kenny wondered what she meant by that. He had a feeling it wouldn't be good. "Maybe you should stay in bed. I'll find something."

She managed a smile. "My medicine. I don't know why I left it there. Just bring it to me, okay?"

As quickly as his appetite had erupted, it began to deteriorate. He knew he should have left her alone, let her sleep. "No, Mama, it's what's making you sick."

She squeezed harder on his wrist. "Don't you dare take that tone with me. I'm still your mother. Now do what I tell you."

Kenny shook his head, even closed his eyes, hoping that somehow everything might be okay when he opened them again, but that did not happen.

His mother now had a needle in her hand, one she'd pulled from the drawer of the nightstand beside her bed. She pushed the plunger and watched as a small amount of the liquid squirted into the air. "You think I don't know you look down on me, like I was a piece of garbage you just scraped off your shoe? Well that's fixing to change, sonny boy. Now give me your arm."

Kenny pulled back, but his mother's grip was firm. "No, Mama, don't make me sick, please don't."

"Shut up, you ungrateful brat. It won't hurt much. This time tomorrow, you'll be asking me to do it, begging to put the needle in you one more time."

Her lips curled into a smile as she plunged the needle downward.

Kenny closed his free hand into a fist and brought it down, like a club, against his mother's arm.

She let out a sound unlike Kenny had heard before, like a scream and yet not like that either. The needle fell to the floor.

"I'm sorry," he said, "sorry I had to hurt you."

He tore free from her grip and ran from the room.

As he crossed the hall and entered the living area, he chanced a look back and again he saw his mother. She had gotten out of bed and was coming after him, dragging one leg behind her as if it had become paralyzed. When she spoke, it was not the strained voice she'd used before, but one with power, and the words were not her words, but something foreign.

Kenny reached the front door but it was locked, and there wasn't enough time to open it. Continuing to spout words he could not understand, his mother kept coming, and as she drew near she held the needle like a weapon, raised high above her head.

Wondering if he would have to fight his own mother, Kenny backed away, his eyes and hands frantically searching for a way out.

His mother's eyes grew wide and she screamed as she stabbed with the needle.

Kenny ducked, stepped around his mother and ran toward the windows. He picked up as much speed as he could and aimed for the middle window, tucked into a ball as he jumped the couch, smashed through, and ran as fast as he could.

"You better stop while you still can."

His mother's voice sounded like she was right behind him. He didn't know how that was possible. He was pretty fast, and before today it was all she could do to walk to the bathroom. When a familiar car pulled up, he opened the passenger door and jumped in.

"Go," he said. "Get me out of here."

Marcia Barnes put both hands on the wheel and floored the Mustang. The tires squealed and the car shot forward, picking up speed quickly as she kept her foot in it.

Kenny checked the side mirror and saw his mother in the middle of the road, walking after them, dragging one foot behind her. "Man, am I glad you showed up."

Marcia eased up on the gas and turned toward Kenny, her long blonde hair falling across her shoulders. "What was that all about, anyway?"

Kenny took a breath and let it out slowly. He didn't usually allow thoughts of what happened at home to roll through his head. He'd always thought it best to keep it private. But now, he wanted to tell Marcia about it, wanted to let someone share in his personal grief, though what he wanted to say seemed out of place somehow. "It's Mom," he said. "She's been acting..."

Marcia leaned against the car seat, "Are you sure you're all right?"

"I don't know. It's been a weird night."

"Seriously, Kenny? Your mom?"

Once again, he checked the side mirror. This time he saw only the open road behind them. "I know I don't talk about her much, but I need to right now. I thought maybe you'd understand."

"Your mom's dead, Kenny. At least that's what you told me."

Kenny turned away and stared through the windshield. Marcia was right. How could he have forgotten? His mother had died from a drug overdose. It'd been nine years ago. He'd had a lot on his mind lately. He suspected the stress had finally gotten to him. Out of a desire to change the subject, and a bit of true curiosity, he asked, "Where's Johnnie?"

With a look somewhat like a parent who'd given up on an unruly child, Marcia shook her head. "You're kidding, right?"

He shrugged.

"You're something else, Kenny. When a guy asks a girl out, he doesn't usually want the boyfriend to come along, too."

"I didn't mean it like that. Johnnie loves his car, and I've never known him to let anyone else drive it."

"You're not making this any easier. Don't you think I have any feelings at all?"

She smiled and wiped her eyes. "I like you, Kenny. A lot. I always have, else I wouldn't be here, wouldn't be doing this."

Even as he leaned across the car seat and kissed Marcia's cheek, glimpses of events of which he understood neither their significance nor their sequence in time ran through his head. Had he just dreamed he was nine years old again? It certainly hadn't felt like a dream, but it must have been. He was a senior in high school. "I'm sorry. I'm definitely not myself today."

Marcia slowed the car and pulled onto a dirt road that meandered through a wooded area at Murphy's Point. Near a clump of oaks, she brought the car to a stop and shut off the engine. In the patches of moonlight filtering through the foliage, her complexion looked almost ethereal. She leaned across the seat and pressed her lips against Kenny's.

Kenny pulled back and gazed into her eyes. "I don't know if we should be here, Marcia."

She turned away and flopped against the car seat. "Okay, Kenny, last chance. What's going on, what are you up to?"

He tried to sort through his thoughts, but nothing seemed to make sense. "I don't know how to explain it, but something bad is about to happen."

"You're not the same boy I talked with at school today. I wish I could understand, but I don't."

Kenny noticed his class ring suspended from a gold chain and hanging from the car's rearview mirror, and as it twisted in the semidarkness, catching the light of the moon and sparking like some distant star, he knew that he had lived this moment before. He glanced in the mirror and saw the blood smeared words written across the back window: *Johnnie Boy was here.*

"We have to get out of here," he said. But his words would have done just as well to have remained unspoken, for they were eclipsed by a scream from Marcia.

Kenny followed her line of sight and saw the source of her terror, something grotesque, not an animal but not quite human either, standing outside the car.

The door flew open and the thing leaned into the car, grabbed a handful of Kenny's shirt and jerked him from the vehicle.

"My Dear God. What have you done, Kenny? My God, what have you done?"

Kenny glanced into the car.

Marcia Barnes stared back at him, her eyes, though lifeless and unmoving, asking the same question, her body sprawled across the driver's seat, a steady flow of blood seeping from her throat and staining the front of her dress.

Kenny shook his head. "It wasn't me. I didn't do anything."

It was Chief Johnson. It had been he who had pulled Elliot from the car. "How do you explain that, son?"

Marcia's blood covered Kenny's hands and the knife he held, a knife with a shiny blade of obsidian.

Kenny shoved Chief Johnson aside and ran, bolted into the darkness and the covering of trees. For a while, he could hear Johnson's voice, calling for him to come back, but eventually it faded and Elliot continued tearing through the trees and the brush until he was completely alone and hidden in the thickness of the woods.

Later his lungs began to burn so he slowed his pace, and when he came upon a large rock, he sat down to rest.

At the sound of someone calling his name, Elliot opened his eyes into the light of a cold but sunny day. He had fallen asleep, he suspected, and lost track of time. Again, he heard the voice.

"Kenny, are you all right?"

Elliot turned toward the sound of his name and looked into the cold-reddened but lovely face of Cyndi Bannister. His first inclination was to hold her, to know that she was real and not some false memory or an illusion brought on by the stress, the source of which was also just out of grasp. He seemed to be caught up in a place where time had no meaning. He attempted to stand but an onset of dizziness changed his mind. "Thank God you're safe and unharmed," he said.

The words had formed in his head though it seemed as if someone else had spoken them.

Cyndi's eyes glistened. "I thought I was going to have to call an ambulance or something. I shook you but you wouldn't come out of it, like you were dazed or in a trance."

A walking trail, lined with dormant azalea bushes, meandered in front of Elliot. As if trying to apply logic to the fading remnants of a dream, he struggled to recall how and why he'd come to be in Tulsa, at Woodward Park. "How long have I been here?"

"I'm not sure," Cyndi said. "I saw you sitting on the rock, so I came over."

Cyndi took Elliot's hands and gently coaxed him to his feet then put her arms around him and rested her head against his chest. She wore a gray, wool coat with a red scarf thrown around her neck that not only complemented her complexion but tugged at Elliot's memory as well. The smell of her perfume filled his senses and he began to remember.

Cyndi had been missing and Elliot understood nothing more, only that her absence had caused him pain. Had he reached a point of not knowing what was real and what was not? He drew her close and kissed the top of her head.

"I'm so sorry," she said.

A few more memories fell into place. Elliot had purchased a ring and arranged for them to meet. He would have asked her to marry him, but she never showed. Even more, he had not been able to get in touch with her, had not seen her in several days.

"At first I thought you'd changed your mind," he said, "But when I couldn't find you, hadn't heard from you, I thought something terrible had happened. Being a cop will do that to you. It's hard to get close to people."

"Oh, Kenny, I got scared that's all, and I didn't trust my feelings. I left town for a few days to think things over. It was wrong of me. I shouldn't have put you through that."

Elliot studied the walking trail and the barren azalea bushes that would bloom lush in the spring. "Do you trust your feelings now?"

Cyndi wiped a tear from her eye. "I'm happy when I'm with you. I want that to continue."

Elliot pulled her close. Her answer had been evasive and yet it filled him with... He wanted to say hope but desire was closer to the truth. He'd never really understood the nature of their relationship, and yet there was no denying the attraction, a feeling so powerful it left not a trace of doubt in it being mutual. And how rare was that, when you thought about it?

Elliot tried to understand what was happening, and why he was confused, and it occurred to him it must be his feelings for Carmen. He still felt like he belonged to her, and yet he'd neither seen Carmen Garcia nor heard from her since high school. It was time he let go of her memory. "I'm willing to take it one step at a time," he said, "if you are?"

Cyndi grabbed the lapels of Elliot's jacket and smiled. "I've talked to my parents about it. They want to meet you."

Elliot brushed a loose strand of hair from Cyndi's face. In a few seconds they'd gone from one-step-at-a-time to meeting-the-parents. But he'd spent a lifetime blowing chances. "All right," he said, "I'd like that."

Cyndi pulled away and straightened her coat. "I was hoping you'd want to. Let's go."

Elliot didn't see his car, and he still wasn't sure how he'd gotten there, and now they were preparing to leave. "Where are we going?"

A curious look crossed Cyndi's face. "To meet my parents."

"Right now?"

"Is that a problem?"

"I guess not. Do they know we're coming?"

Cyndi shrugged. As her breath condensed in the cold air, Elliot noticed, and not for the first time, just how beautiful and sensuous her mouth was.

He pulled his sport jacket together and buttoned it, wondering why he had not dressed more warmly. "All right," he said, "let's meet the parents."

Cyndi slid her arm around his waist and they walked in silence to the parking lot. Once there, she dug her keys from her coat pocket and unlocked her car.

Elliot put his hands in his pockets. They were empty, no keys, no change, nothing. Again he checked the parking lot. He would have to ride with Cyndi, and though the question was on his mind, the words he spoke were different. "I've been thinking," he said, "about my occupation, whether or not I should give it up, try something else."

Elliot thought he saw a glimmer of hope cross Cyndi's eyes.

"You know how I feel about it. But I won't ask you to do that. I love you, Kenny. Cop or not, that'll never change."

Elliot leaned against Cyndi's car. Had she just told him she loved him? Yes, he thought she had. He pulled her close and brought his lips to hers, lingering in the warm pleasure. When he pulled away, he said, "I love you, too."

"Kenny, you're so honest it's almost scary."

Cyndi's remark seemed strange, but everything about this day was murky at best. "I've never thought of honesty as being frightening."

"You wouldn't, would you? You're a most unusual man. But you belong to me now, and that's forever."

Once again, Elliot experienced a bout of dizziness, and during the interlude he thought Cyndi's eyes had changed, that their shape had altered, and her pupils had become like those of a cat.

When he regained his balance, he shook off the ridiculous notion and walked around to the passenger side and climbed in.

If this seemed unusual to Cyndi, she showed no sign of it. She watched Elliot fasten his seat belt, then started the car and backed out of the parking lot.

George and Evelyn Bannister lived near the university where Mr. Bannister had worked. The red-brick house, an old bungalow of eighty years, preserved by hard work and diligent maintenance, looked as if it could have been constructed yesterday. The driveway, consisting of parallel strips of concrete separated by a strip of grass, ran beside the house and ended at a one-car garage, also immaculately maintained—the nice but modest home of a college professor.

Elliot took Cyndi's hand and together they walked to the door and rang the bell. Once inside, Elliot stood beside Cyndi while Mr. and Mrs. Bannister hovered near by.

Elliot felt like a teenager who'd brought his date home past curfew. The Bannisters seemed kind, even gracious, yet Elliot detected a hint of sadness behind their smiles. He'd seen the look before, and he wondered what kind of private pain they might be hiding.

Cyndi put her hand on Elliot's shoulder. "Mom, dad, this is Kenny, the guy I've been telling you about."

Mr. Bannister, who wore a tweed jacket with leather patches on the elbows, was lean with blue eyes and greying hair. He stepped forward and shook Elliot's hand. "Call me George."

Elliot wondered if the garage at the end of the drive housed an old British sports car. "Nice to meet you," he said.

Like members of a bluegrass band taking turns at the microphone, Mr. Bannister stepped aside and the missus came forward for her turn in the spotlight. She took Elliot's hands and squeezed them. "Why, you're a fine looking lad, Mr. Elliot."

"You're too kind," he said, trying to place her accent, Scottish, he thought, though years of American influence had eroded it to the point of being only slightly detectable.

She spun around and led Elliot into the living room. "Come, sit with us and we can talk."

In the area where they sat, two couches faced each other in front of a fireplace where a yellow blaze flickered. On a coffee table, an English teapot with matching cups sat beside a tray of cookies. Evelyn Bannister filled one of the cups and offered it to Elliot.

Elliot took the tea and glanced at the cream and sugar, the room becoming void of conversation as the soft tinkle of spoon against china filled the air. A few uncomfortable moments later, Mrs. Bannister raised her shoulders and smiled over her teacup. "True love is forever, wouldn't you say, Mr. Elliot?"

Elliot rested his cup and saucer on his knee, hoping his nervousness would not cause the pair to rattle. Mrs. Bannister's loaded question had caught him off guard. "Yes," he said, "I believe you're right."

Mr. Bannister, who had remained standing, sat his cup on the fireplace mantle. "Come with me, Mr. Elliot. I've something to show you, if you don't mind."

Elliot followed Mr. Bannister out of the room. The preliminary was over and the inquisition was at hand.

Inside Bannister's office, shelves stuffed with books went from floor to ceiling, lending the space a crowded, claustrophobic atmosphere. A two-sided desk made of mahogany sat in the middle of the room, with brown, leather chairs on either side of it. Bannister pulled out one of the chairs and lowered himself into it, then opened one of the drawers and pulled out a pipe and tobacco. He packed the bowl and struck a match, hovering the flame over the tobacco until it lit.

Elliot sat in the chair on the opposite side of the desk.

Bannister cut to the chase. "I take it Cyndi's rather serious about you." He paused and drew on the pipe. "How do you feel about her?"

"I'm in love with her," Elliot said, though the words felt strange as he spoke them.

Bannister held the pipe with his teeth and spoke around the stem. "I'm inclined to believe you, but there's something you need to know. Out of all the rooms in the house, she fancied this one as a child, always in here, always reading. She's a spirited woman, Mr. Elliot, and quite intelligent."

Elliot tried to imagine a young Cyndi and what books she might have chosen. "I think it's part of the reason I'm attracted to her."

From around the pipe stem, Bannister's lips curled into a grin, and when he spoke his voice had taken on a raspy, unholy quality. "Indeed. But are you worthy of the revelation, or prepared to bear the weight of its significance?"

Elliot wiped perspiration from his forehead. Though the temperature was winter-like outside, the room had grown unbearably warm. A desire to leave this uncomfortable meeting began to form in his mind. "I'm not sure I'm following you."

Bannister reached into the desk and when his hand was once again visible, it held a silver frame which contained a large photograph. He slid it across the desktop.

Elliot stared at the photo. It was not something he thought a family might cherish, but a thing that should be hidden, even thrown away. It was a snapshot of a jungle setting, clearly and graphically depicting a large cat, a jaguar, Elliot thought, feeding on a fresh kill, blood dripping from its fangs.

Elliot pushed away from the desk. What kind of sick person was Bannister, anyway? He'd had enough of this. He found his footing and started toward the door.

Bannister was already there, blocking the exit. In one hand, he held the photograph of the jaguar, and in the other he had the relic, the ceremonial knife with the blade of obsidian.

Instinctively, Elliot reached for his service weapon, but found only emptiness where it should have been. He remembered having checked his pockets at the park. He had nothing, no keys, no change, not even a wallet.

Bannister readied the knife and came toward Elliot. Bannister was not alone in the attack. Evelyn Bannister and even Cyndi had come into the room. The knives they carried were not made of obsidian, they had come from the kitchen, but the dingy steel of their blades would inflict sufficient damage. They formed a circle around Elliot and they began to chant in a language he could not understand.

Elliot studied his surroundings and decided to make a run for it, dash for the door and hope to knock one of the three down and buy enough time to clear the exit and make his way out of the house.

Seeming to read his mind, Cyndi stepped between Elliot and the door.

Elliot lunged toward her.

Pain shot through his left shoulder and across his back. One of the blades had found him. He kept going, colliding into Cyndi as he forced progress.

Cyndi screamed and dropped to the floor but she was not finished. She wrapped her arms and legs around Elliot, trying to bring him down.

Elliot wrenched free from the entanglement and stumbled into the hallway.

Fire climbed the walls and ran in streamers along the wood flooring. The curtains on the windows in the living room exploded into flames.

Chapter Forty-Three

At the end of the hallway, a ghostly figure that resembled McDugan emerged from the smoke and flames.

Elliot began to grasp the outer edges of what had happened. Going against Professor Stephens' warning, he'd touched the obsidian knife, and its poison, its curse, had affected his mind. In whatever place he had been, as real as it had seemed, it existed only in his imagination.

He saw the Glock lying on the floor near a bunch of wiggling snakes. As if someone had poured gasoline onto their backs and tossed a match onto the mix, the snakes squirmed and writhed as the fire consumed them.

Elliot was no longer an unwanted guest at the modest home of George and Evelyn Bannister but had been transported back to Sand Springs and the previously dark house of Charles McDugan. It no longer lacked illumination. The fire had changed that.

McDugan ambled closer, seemingly oblivious to the fire.

Elliot jumped back as a flaming rafter crashed in front of him. He fought to get oxygen into his lungs but gagged at the hot smoke. He brought his arm up and covered his face with the sleeve of his jacket. With McDugan behind him and flames to his left, there was only one way to go. He stumbled to his right, though his feet responded sluggishly as if mired deep in mud. Fatigue set in. Smoke and hot air clouded his senses. He pushed forward but his progress was short lived.

McDugan clamped a hand around his throat.

Elliot jabbed backward with one elbow and then the other but neither connected.

The grip around his throat tightened.

Elliot struggled to breathe, to again pull the smoke-tainted air into his lungs. He flailed behind with his arms and finally grabbed the arm that held him.

McDugan refused to let go.

Maintaining his hold on McDugan's arm, Elliot summoned the remainder of his strength and spun to his left. Following the momentum, he leaned into his attacker.

The twisting motion combined with Elliot's change of direction worked, and he twisted free. Not wasting the opportunity, he grabbed McDugan by the shoulders and slammed home a head-butt.

The impact jarred Elliot all the way to his toes, but had little effect on McDugan. He wrenched free from Elliot's grip. In the final seconds, Elliot had held in his hands skin that seemed to be covered with fur, and though McDugan had retained some of his characteristics, what Elliot saw disappearing into the darkness was not human.

Elliot set his focus on the exit and began to force his way toward it.

When the sound came, Elliot wondered if it was the roof collapsing, or if the fire had found a renewed source of oxygen and rapidly expanded to feed on it, but in his heart he knew it was nothing so benign. It was a cry, an animal's scream, and with it came a pain that raked like a band of razor blades across Elliot's back.

Elliot began to lose consciousness, but he refused to go down. He held his jacket to his face, trying to filter out some of the smoke. His chances of surviving another attack were not good.

Another section of roof gave way, providing a burning blockade between him and McDugan.

Elliot grabbed the opportunity and scrambled away, climbing over piles of debris toward the exit. Once there, he slung the door open and stumbled outside into the cool, clean air. After a gagging and coughing fit, he drew in as much fresh air as he could and went back inside the burning house. He could not go through with it, could not walk away, knowing the evil he'd encountered was left to go its way. He had to stop it.

Elliot groped the area where he'd last seen the Glock and located the weapon lying on the floor. He could not see McDugan but he had no doubt he was close by. He had made no attempts to escape the fire. Elliot could only assume McDugan did not fear it. The implications of that buzzed through his senses, and he wondered if the Glock would do any good. His lungs craved oxygen, but his throat refused to take in the hot air.

Recalling his training, he got down to the floor where the air would be fresher, dropping first to his knees then to his stomach.

Tears and smoke blurred his vision, but he saw McDugan lurch forward.

He aimed the weapon, but it was too late. McDugan grabbed him and flipped him over onto his back.

The beast stood over Elliot, and though it walked on two legs and retained some of the features of Charles McDugan, the head protruding from its shoulders was that of a jaguar, and what hung from its arms were claws. The beast dropped down over Elliot, pinning him to the floor. With its buttocks against his torso, its knees clamping his arms, it withdrew the ceremonial knife and lowered the blade to Elliot's chest. The beast reared back and let out a primeval cry, the same death-scream Elliot had heard a few days ago coming from the abandoned apartment house in Tulsa.

It was then that Elliot remembered the other crucifix, the one he'd found in Gerald's Cadillac. He worked his left arm free, drove his hand into his pocket, and pulled out the crucifix. His pockets had been empty when he'd been with Cyndi, but that had been something other than this reality.

The beast stopped howling and turned its eyes down upon Elliot.

Holding the cross suspended by the chain, Elliot shoved the crucifix toward the face of the beast.

The thing growled and pulled back.

Elliot freed his other hand, a short burst of relief flaring through his senses as he squeezed the handle of the Glock. He jabbed the cross of Saint Benedict against the chest of the beast, slammed the barrel of the Glock behind it, and squeezed off three rounds.

Elliot got to his knees and crawled to where the beast had fallen.

He found Jeremiah, who now looked merely like an old man. The power of the knife must have given him youth. He checked for a pulse but there was none. Whatever had been inside of Jeremiah McDugan, life and all, it was gone.

Elliot grabbed the obsidian knife and crawled to the exit. He rolled through the opening and onto the small landing. Later, he crawled down the steps and onto the driveway. His thoughts came in jerky, fragmented pieces and a deep-rooted sickness ran through him, but he clung to consciousness. The job was not finished. He got to his feet and staggered across the yard, falling several times before he reached the barn where Gerald's car was hidden.

Inside the barn, Elliot went to the workbench where he'd seen the tools. He placed the obsidian knife into the vise and cranked the handle until the jaws held the relic in place, though at that point he stopped and went no further.

He needed to think this through. He carried around a lot of pain and he'd felt the power of the obsidian, knew firsthand what it could do. For fear of losing his sanity, he'd continually reminded himself his excursions into the past lives of loved ones had existed only in his mind, but in his heart he wondered if he'd experienced times and places that had been more than flights of fancy, had been, in some unknown intersection of time and place, quite real.

The temptation of preserving the knife flowed easily through Elliot's mind and grew with dimensions of feasibility, but his hands, as if acting independently of his senses, had continued to turn the handle of the vise. As he watched in a near state of disbelief at what he'd done, he quickly cranked the vise tighter.

The handle of the relic, the image of an Aztec god, busted into several pieces, but the blade of obsidian, having been freed by the action, fell to the floor.

Still operating in a mode somewhere between coveting power at will, and fear of where it might lead, Elliot retrieved the blade and placed it back into the vise and closed the jaws around it.

The shiny glass-like material busted into fragments and fell onto the workbench, some bouncing onto the floor.

Elliot gathered the remains and placed them into a pile. He grabbed a hammer from the pegboard, raised it into the air and brought it down, pounding again and again until he'd pulverized the shiny chunks into a near powder-like state. Afterward, he brushed the powdered obsidian into his hand, being careful to get it all.

Elliot carried the powder to Gerald's Cadillac. He leaned inside the car, opened the glove compartment, and pushed the button to release the latch for the fuel door. He stumbled around the vehicle, opened the fuel door, and removed the gas cap. Steadying his hand, he poured the powdered obsidian into the tank.

The keys to the vehicle dangled from the trunk latch. Elliot grabbed them, and after picking up one of the bricks alongside the wall of the garage, he climbed inside the car.

He inserted the key into the ignition switch and with a flick of the wrist completed the circuit, causing sparks of electricity to jump between the gaps of the plugs, igniting the fuel-air mixture gathered in the cylinders, and the old V8 sprung to life.

The barn doors were open.

Elliot dropped the Cadillac into gear, eased it from the barn, and coaxed it across the yard toward the burning remains of the house where Charles McDugan had lived. As Elliot maneuvered a turnabout on the lawn, positioning the Cadillac so it looked as if it had come to its senses and was now driving away from the carnage, he thought of Gerald. Wherever his old friend was right now, he would be offering a nod of approval at what Elliot had in mind.

Elliot left the car running but shoved the gear selector into park and climbed out. He leaned back inside, placed the brick against the accelerator pedal, dropped the car into reverse and jumped out of the way.

Seeming to welcome its part in the plan, the Cadillac drove itself through the back wall of the house and had made it through the kitchen and into the living room before it exploded into flames.

Elliot turned away and started toward his truck. A feeling of triumph weaved through him, but somewhere between the truck and the driveway, his consciousness began to fade and everything went black.

Chapter Forty-Four

Carmen Garcia saw that Wayne had noticed her pacing the floor of the waiting room. She could have stepped into the hallway, where there was more room and walked there, but she did not want to be missing if someone came with news about Kenny.

She found a magazine she'd only been through once and sat down and started flipping through the pages again.

Wayne was trying to be strong for her. They had been at the hospital for hours and he had not complained, or even asked when they might be going home. Some might think she should not have brought him there, and that he would have been better left with a friend or relative, but Kenny was his father, and she thought Wayne should be there. Judging by his behavior, she thought he wanted that as well.

Kenny's Captain Dombrowski was there also. Each time Carmen glanced in his direction, she found him looking at her and this made her uncomfortable. She did not think he was that kind of man. He was just concerned and unsure of what to do.

Carmen lowered the magazine to her lap and looked at Wayne. "If you want, we can take a few minutes and go to the cafeteria to get some lunch."

Wayne shook his head. "I'll be all right. I don't feel much like eating anyway."

Carmen noticed someone's shadow on the floor and looked up to see Captain Dombrowski standing in front of her.

"I could go down to the kitchen and bring something back for you," he said.

Carmen was about to tell Captain Dombrowski she did not think it was allowed when someone called her name.

It was Doctor Hopkins, the physician that had been attending to Kenny. The doctor smiled, but his demeanor said he was tired. "Mr. Elliot is doing well, considering what he's been through. I was there when he stumbled into the emergency room. I'm not sure how he managed to get himself here. He'd lost a lot of blood, and his attempts at explaining had been incoherent. But he was clear about one thing. He gave me your name and phone number, wanted me to call you."

Carmen fought back the tears. "Can we see him?"

"His signs have stabilized. It shouldn't be a problem. Are you a relative?"

"I am," Wayne said. "He's my dad."

As was often the case, Wayne surprised Carmen with his compassion, and his ability to assess a situation. "I am a friend," she said. "But we are close, and he needs to see me."

Captain Dombrowski said something as well, but Carmen was too focused on the doctor to make out what it was.

The doctor turned and started down the hallway.

Carmen took the doctor's actions as a sign of affirmation and followed him.

Chapter Forty-Five

Elliot leaned back in the chair in Pastor Meadows' office. A month had passed since he'd showed up at St. John's, and the wounds he'd suffered, the physical ones anyway, were mending ahead of expectations. The doctor said he wasn't ready for active duty with the police department, and for once he agreed with them. He suspected it was Carmen Garcia's presence that got him well anyway, having more to do with his recovery than all the medicine he had to choke down. Not a day of his recuperation went by that she wasn't there. She'd often run her fingers through his hair and say, "It's the only part of you that isn't damaged." Elliot's love for her was indescribable, but he doubted she knew how close to the truth her assessment had been.

The pastor had asked him why he'd come to see him. Elliot wasn't quite sure how to respond, so he settled on a reflection of the guilt that had coiled up inside him, even though that was only a small part of it. "Have you ever let anyone down, Pastor Meadows?"

The pastor stared across the desk. "If I were to recount the times, we'd have to send out for lunch, possibly dinner."

Elliot managed a smile, though he suspected it was unconvincing. They'd found Gerald's body buried beneath the rubble of the old apartment house in Tulsa, just like Elliot said they would, but Gerald had not been alone. A veritable graveyard, Dombrowski had called it. The property outside of Stillwater, owned by Professor David Stephens, yielded similar results, including the remains of Corey Sherman, Jake Sherman's missing brother. No one had bothered to look for the Depression era victims, but Elliot suspected they were out there somewhere, if nothing more than scraps of bones, scattered by the coyotes across the hills of Eastern Oklahoma.

"An old friend of mine stirred up some trouble he couldn't handle," Elliot said. "With his back against the wall, he needed my help. But I let him down. He's dead because of it."

Pastor Meadows shook his head. "You know better than that, Detective. We can't go through life looking back and wondering if things might have turned out differently had we done this, or that. Not only is that kind of thinking counterproductive, it's potentially destructive as well."

Elliot glanced at the floor.

"However, I suspect you already know that," the pastor said. "In fact, I think something else is bothering you. Why don't you tell me what it is?"

Elliot sat forward. It was true. He'd been skirting the issue, but only because he wasn't sure of how to talk about such a thing. "I've been a cop for a long time," he said. "I've seen some pretty bad stuff."

Thoughts of the obsidian knife snaked through Elliot's head, how it had pulled him in, how he'd almost given in to it. "But something dark and vile on a level way beyond my understanding has walked across my soul."

Elliot felt tears building up, but he held them back. He'd known that expressing what was going on inside of him would be difficult. "I feel unclean," he continued, "unworthy of being here, in God's house, even of being in your presence."

Pastor Meadows sat forward, his eyes reflecting both interest and concern. "If I had to guess I'd say you got into your profession not only to bring a little light into the world in the form of justice, but to redeem yourself as well."

Elliot wondered how the pastor could know about that, motives behind a behavior even he had trouble admitting, but as he thought it through he realized the process was not fantastic. He often sized people up in a hurry, had, in fact, gotten pretty good at it. "You could say that."

"Well," the pastor said, "at least in that respect, we have something in common."

"I'm not sure I'm following you."

"What I'm saying is I'm not all that different from you, Kenny. Being a pastor does not shield one from the weaknesses, desires, and emotions anyone else might experience. It's all about the choices we make, whether we give in to sin or resist it."

Elliot nodded. The pastor was trying to demonstrate that he was, in fact, on Elliot's level. It was a strategy he'd often used himself. "I appreciate your honesty," he said, "but it seems I haven't effectively communicated the gravity of my situation."

The pastor shook his head. "I guess I'm going to have to break out the big guns, heavy artillery if you will." He leaned forward. "What I'm about to tell you is no secret, but few people know about it just the same."

"All right," Elliot said, acknowledging his understanding of the quasi-confidential nature of the matter. It was something he was used to, being a cop.

"There was a time," the pastor continued, "when I, too, considered myself unredeemable. Don't get me wrong. I come from a good family, had good parents who treated me well, made every effort to raise me up right. But I took to rebellion, determined, it seemed, to destroy myself. My young adult life was nothing but a downward spiral. One night, after finishing off my second fifth of vodka, I realized I'd sunk about as low as a person can and still be alive. It wasn't enough to stop me, though. Instead of dwelling on how to pull myself out, I started looking for something else to drink.

"I don't know how I ended up where I did, an old glass-fronted building with a light inside. Could be I thought the light was neon, thought the place was a bar, or a store where I could find more alcohol. I started pounding on the door, beat on it until someone let me in; an elderly black man who must have been pushing eighty opened the door to me. Had the tables been reversed, I'm not so sure I would have done the same.

"It was when he flipped on the lights that I realized where I was. The old guy had converted the place into a church, a house of worship. He gingerly guided me to one of the pews and pressed on my shoulders until I sat. After that, he walked out of the room."

Elliot rubbed his temples. Hearing Pastor Meadows revealing such personal matters put a knot in his stomach. "You don't have to do this, Pastor. Not on my account."

"Indulge me on this, Kenny. It's important to me. Anyway, something happened to me while I was sitting there alone in that makeshift church. When the old man finally came back into the room I started crying. It was like all those years had finally caught up with me. He handed me a hot cup of coffee and sat down beside me. When he put his arm around me, I just let it all out, told him things I hadn't even told my parents. I must have been there for hours. We talked about a lot of things, but the old guy told me one thing that I will never forget. You could say it changed my life. He was a good man. A few years later, I went to his funeral and cried like he was my own father. It drew quite a few stares from the predominately black audience."

Elliot noticed one of the other pastors waiting outside the door of the office, and when it became obvious Pastor Meadows wasn't going to say anymore, Elliot had to ask, "What was it the old man said to you?"

Pastor Meadows smiled. "I'm glad you asked. I'm always happy to share his wisdom. This is what he said: 'There ain't no sin bigger than God's grace, son. No, sir.' He was right about that, Kenny. And I can't think of any truer words to tell you."

Elliot thought for a moment then smiled. "Thank you, Pastor Meadows, for everything."

"Anytime you want to talk, feel free to call or stop by."

The pastor at the door cleared his throat.

Pastor Meadows stood and shook Elliot's hand. "Why don't you reflect on what I said, and we'll talk later."

Elliot rose to his feet and walked out of the office. He thought he held a straight face, but he wasn't sure. Pastor Meadows had spoken to him as if he were a long-time confidant, an old friend, sharing pastoral duties and the problems that went along with such a responsibility. He had done so out of concern for Elliot's wellbeing, of that he had no doubt, but Elliot didn't know if it had helped or if it had added to the confusion.

Elliot strolled down the hallway, his footsteps echoing in the large expanse.

Outside, he traversed the sidewalk past the fountain, but as he started across the parking lot, he paused.

A man with large shoulders and biceps leaned against the pickup. The look on his face said he wasn't in the mood for games.

Given his present condition, Elliot wasn't sure he could take the man, if it came to that. He slid his hand inside his jacket and wrapped his fingers around the handle of the Glock. At a distance of about six feet away, Elliot stopped. "Something I can do for you?"

"You Elliot?"

"Who wants to know?"

"Funny you should ask."

Elliot tightened his grip on the Glock. "Maybe so, but you didn't answer my question."

The man leaned forward, transferring his weight from the truck to his feet.

Elliot took a couple steps back. He pulled the Glock and leveled the barrel with the man's forehead.

If Elliot's actions frightened the big man, he did not show it. Instead, as if he was an old friend, hurt and confused at Elliot's pulling a gun on him, he held his arms out, palms up and said, "I was told you could help me."

"Help you with what?"

"My identity, Detective. Do you have any idea what it feels like to die in someone else's body?"

Keeping the Glock trained on the suspect, Elliot chanced a glance over his shoulder, looking for bystanders, should gunfire erupt. In nearly the same instant, he returned his attention to the suspect.

The man was gone.

Elliot reconsidered the suggestion earlier posed by Carmen that he had experienced too much as a cop. He made his way to the vehicle and checked the bed of the pickup.

Only a few tools and items occupied the truck bed.

He moved around the truck and threw open the passenger door.

The man was gone.

As Elliot holstered the Glock, he thought of Carmen and Wayne. He wanted to be more of a part of their lives. Carmen had shown him she and Wayne wanted that too. He was going to make that happen. However, as he climbed into the truck, the unnerving question posed by the strange man he'd seen earlier wandered through the recesses of his mind—*Do you have any idea what it feels like to die in someone else's body?*

By Bob Avey

Detective Elliot Mysteries

Twisted Perception *
Beneath a Buried House *
Footprints of a Dancer *

* Published by Deadly Niche Press

CPSIA information can be obtained at www.ICGtesting.com
Printed in the USA
BVOW08s0018251113

337196BV00001B/37/P